My Dear Emma

My Dear Emma

Happy reading!

JoAnn Meaker

JoAnn Meaker

ISBN-10:148014195x
ISBN-13:978-1480141957

ACKNOWLEDGMENTS

This book would not have been possible without the assistance of some wonderful people. First and foremost, I am eternally grateful for the love and unwavering support given to me by my husband, Norman. During the research phase, he drove me all over Virginia and New York as I learned about the Civil War period involved with the story. He was my sounding board as I developed the characters, and he did a final edit for me as well.

Others have helped along the way, too. Thank you so much to my good friend, Liz Albright and my sister-in-law, Rene Meaker for reading the first drafts of the book and giving me some wonderfully vital suggestions on making improvements. Thank you to my fellow Walkerton Writers who also help critique the work in progress, especially James and Emma's storyline.

Thanks go to the various people I met and interviewed as I gathered information for James; to my fellow researchers on ancestry.com; and to the new family members we discovered and met while working on the Beardsley family tree.

Say, Must Our Country Perish?

By Mrs. Cordelia Beardsley Wilder

Say, must our country perish?
With all that's true and brave
The arm of right and freedom
Be powerless to save?
Must we fling down our banner,
To worthless traitor's yield?
Our heroes lie unhonored
Upon the battlefield?
Hark! Hark! There comes an answer,
We go to join our brothers
Three hundred thousand strong.
We yet will save our country,
We know we can, we must;
We'll take the traitor's banner,
And trail it in the dust.
"Twill be a tearful parting
To bid loved ones adieu
But they will bravely cheer us
And tell us to be true.
Our country shall not perish
Our hopes shall not be crushed,
For God will surely bless us,
And aid the cause that's just.
Oh, 'tis a fearful struggle,
A nation's blood to spill,
But the Union, now, forever!-
Oh, yes! We'll surely conquer
The traitors; they must yield
And we will bear in triumph
Our banner from the field.

Chapter One
Early April

Thunder boomed, announcing the arrival of an early spring storm. Rachel watched the wind whip the fallen leaves around the mourners as they emerged from the small chapel and made their way in solemn procession to the gravesite. The sky was grey, with dark angry clouds racing nearer.

She drew her daughter, Julia, closer, protecting the five-year-old from the cold wind. She gathered the child's long hair, tucked it under the knit cap and tightened the strings. *Goodness, it feels cold enough to snow.*

"Ashes to ashes … dust to dust," the minister intoned, his words lost in the increasing booms of thunder, robes fluttering in a sudden gust of wind.

The words had little meaning for Rachel. She wanted this funeral to be done, wanted the minister to finish speaking the words that made no sense, wanted to leave before the threatening storm hit. The only protection from the approaching storm was the faded canvas canopy over the small group and that wouldn't do much if the coming rain was whipped sideways by the wind.

She stood shivering, restlessly standing and trying to concentrate on the minister's words, but her thoughts kept drifting away. In her mind she heard another clergy's voice, saw a larger crowd of people surrounding the open grave of their comrade-in-arms, her husband. That day had been misty, too, as she stood, wracked with sobs, holding tightly to her young daughter's hand. She had almost collapsed during the full military ceremony – especially during taps and then the folding of the flag, done with precision by the honor guard. Now a scant four weeks later she was burying another family member.

Rachel's grandmother was in the casket on the pedestal in front of them. All around the open grave, the marble stones, carved with names and dates, seemed so cold, so meaningless. After the last months, her heart felt as cold as the marble. Try as she would she couldn't seem to feel the emotion expected of her today. Too much sadness had already occurred in her life lately – this one more trauma was almost too much for her to bear.

The funeral director approached, handed a rose to each of the mourners, and asked them to place it on the casket. Julia looked up at her mother. With a slight nudge from Rachel, the two walked forward and placed their roses on the casket. Rachel placed her hand on the polished wood surface and said a silent thank you. That was all she could manage.

She stepped back and watched as each of the small group of mourners stepped forward. She didn't know most of them. They were older friends of her grandmother, townspeople whom she hadn't met in the short time she'd been in this town. She vaguely heard the words of sympathy they expressed and then felt the hand of MariBeth reach out and touch hers.

She grabbed the outstretched hand and clung, needing the anchor. They had met in the local diner not long after Rachel and Julia arrived in town. Even though Rachel had only known her for a short time, MariBeth had become close, helping Rachel take care of her daughter and, in the last few days, with the funeral arrangements for Nonna, her grandmother. *I don't know what I would have done without her.*

The mourners hurried to their cars as the rain began to fall. Rachel paused again to look at the casket, then turned, grasped Julia's hand and hurried to follow MariBeth to her car parked not too far away. Just in time. They reached it and hustled inside, the rain coming harder as the storm front approached. Julia got in the back and buckled herself into the booster seat. Rachel got into the passenger side, thankful that MariBeth had driven this morning.

Starting the car, MariBeth turned slightly to Rachel and said, "Do you want to come to my house for lunch?"

Rachel didn't answer at first, didn't seem to hear, and then responded in a quiet voice, "No, thanks, we just need to get back to Nonna's house."

"Okay, Rachel, but please, give me a call if you want to talk. You've been through a lot lately. Don't close people out."

"Yeah, right." Rachel slumped into her seat, turned to look out toward the gravesite and saw the grave diggers already beginning to lower the casket into the hole. "Why couldn't they have waited a bit?"

"I don't know – maybe with the storm they needed to hurry their job along." MariBeth started the car moving. Thunder rumbled overhead. The windshield wiper slapped as they rode in silence along the winding, narrow roadway of the cemetery.

"Yeah, I guess." Rachel closed her eyes and leaned her head against the rain-stroked window.

Reaching the main highway, MariBeth turned right and picked up speed, still cautious of the rain-slicked roads. Fifteen minutes later MariBeth pulled into the long winding driveway of the house on the hill. Nonna's house was a white three-story Italianate-style home. Architecturally it was a beautiful house. Along the roofline were the decorative corbels that appeared to hold up the roof overhang. Decorative caps gave each window an eyebrow. Shutters lined the windows, their maroon color matching the main door. The front porch wrapped half-way around the side of the house. Looking closer, though, it was evident that age and years of neglect had taken its toll. Paint was peeling in several places, the porch railing was missing spindles, and two of the shutters were hanging loose, nails missing.

Although the front door was street-side, the entry used most often was by the driveway, near the detached garage set back behind the house. Today, though, MariBeth stopped by the stepping stones that curved to the front door. She turned off the engine and they sat in silence, listening to the rain pelting the

4

windows. The storm was passing quickly and Rachel could feel the even colder temperatures as the front moved by. She shivered again, sighed and said, "Do you want to come inside? Some of the ladies from Nonna's church stopped by yesterday and dropped off some casseroles, or I can make some soup and I think I have the makings for a salad."

Maribeth hesitated, then said, "Sure, but I should be making lunch for you, please let me help."

Rachel nodded, and then turned to look at her daughter, sitting in the back seat of the car.

"Honey, we're going to have lunch. Would you like a toasted cheese sandwich?"

"Can I have applesauce too?" Julia looked at Rachel with sadness in her big brown eyes.

Rachel was concerned. Julia had been through so much during the past three months. "No problem, Sweetie. And if you eat it all, there might be a treat for you," Rachel tried to put some enthusiasm in her voice. It was hard to do.

The three dashed, through the still-pouring rain, from the car to the front steps of the house. Rachel cringed with the knowledge of what lay beyond the door. She turned to MariBeth. "I apologize for the mess inside." She inserted the key, shoved open the creaky door and took a deep breath before entering the house.

MariBeth walked in behind Rachel and stopped, her eyes widened at the site before her. "Wow, I had no idea."

The house still smelled of Rachel's grandmother in the last stages of the illness that had taken her life. Medications and that distinctive old-age smell permeated every room. So much of the house was in need of repair and the rooms were cluttered with all sorts of "junk" Nonna had collected over the years – things she couldn't take care of as she'd gotten older and frail.

Standing in the front hallway, MariBeth saw the living room to the left, straight ahead the kitchen, and the stairway to the second floor bedrooms.

Collectibles hung on the walls, on shelves along the ceiling, on the bookshelves, and even on the floor. Papers and clothing littered the room. Piles of books, magazines, and newspapers were tucked into corners. Dust bunnies competed for space amidst the clutter.

Rachel looked around, saw the place through the eyes of her new friend and was embarrassed to admit, "Yep, we've been here for four weeks now and this is still what it looks like."

"What happened?"

"Let's have lunch and then we can talk." Rachel glanced at her daughter and MariBeth nodded. Little ones with big ears – no need to have Julia hear what she couldn't understand. Rachel often had a hard time remembering that Julia was only five. Most of the time, she could hold an almost adult conversation with her young daughter. She had to remind herself to be careful what she said around her.

"Julia, go wash up for lunch," Rachel said and watched as Julia dashed down the hall to the bathroom.

Rachel turned to her friend, "Want to do the salad?"

MariBeth shrugged out of her coat, "Where shall I put this?"

Rachel glanced at MariBeth. Today, she was dressed stylishly in a blue suit and cream silk blouse. Her extra pounds were carefully disguised in the well-fitting outfit. She wore her long coat belted at the waist, her long hair neatly coifed, was tucked under the brim of her hat. Rachel felt rumpled and frumpy in comparison.

"Toss it wherever, there's no room in the closet." They tossed their coats, hats, scarves and purses on the nearest chair and walked down the hallway into the kitchen. What was once a large, bright room was now cramped with all the clutter.

Rachel opened the fridge and frowned. Pretty empty. She'd had little time to go to the grocery, and felt a sense of relief and gratitude to Nonna's friends. After working together, making lunch in silence, Rachel stacked papers together to make room for the dishes on the kitchen table and the three sat down to eat.

MariBeth watched the little girl eating her sandwich. She was such a sweet girl with so much sadness in her young life. The five-year-old had long brown hair that hung straight down her back almost to her waist. She was thin, with brown eyes and freckles sprinkled across her nose. MariBeth thought she was handling things much better than her Mom at this point.

When she finished her lunch, Julia asked, "Mama? Can I play on the computer?"

"Sure thing. Let me put in the password for you." Julia could keep herself busy all day on the computer if Rachel let her. Knowing that computer time was rare, Julia's eyes lit up as they walked into the den in the back of the house. The laptop was sitting on a small table. Once Julia got started, Rachel went back into the kitchen.

"Want another cup of coffee?" she asked MariBeth.

MariBeth held out her cup and Rachel filled it. "Okay, Rachel, now talk to me. Since we've met, you've hardly had the time to tell me anything about you, about your past."

Rachel stared down at her cup of coffee, sitting there untouched. She sighed deeply before speaking. "Nonna agreed to take us in when we had nowhere else to go. I told you my husband died. Well, that's not the whole story." She leaned back in her chair and spoke softly, glancing down the hallway making sure her daughter was still occupied.

"Jon was a wonderful husband and father. We were married for fourteen years. With him in the army we spent the first seven years traveling. He was in training classes, each lasting only a few months, and then we were on to the next one, often in another state. When the training ended, Jon was assigned to go overseas – to Iraq. Then Julia came along, while he was there."

Rachel glanced down the hallway again before continuing, "Money was always tight, but I didn't feel right trying to get a teaching position since we moved so much. When Julia was born, I knew she needed some stability in the craziness of military life, so I stayed home with her. Jon was able to come home once, but got reassigned for another tour, this time to Afghanistan."

"That's when things began to go bad. I knew

something was wrong. His letters and phone calls sounded odd, his voice a monotone, like he'd lost all interest in me, in his daughter, in life. I suggested he see someone to get some help, but he kept brushing me off. Then his tour finally ended and he came home."

She paused and took a sip of her coffee. "We welcomed him with open arms. Julia was so happy to see her Daddy again. At first, it was great to have him home, but he just wasn't the same. He couldn't sleep, was restless and drank too much. Then he couldn't stand to have us in the same room. He'd get startled by the slightest noise and Julia made him nervous.

Again, I tried to get him to see someone, to talk about what he was feeling. He still brushed me off, pushed me away. That's not the way the men in his family dealt with things, he said. So we continued tip-toeing around him. He'd sit most days in his chair, with the TV on, but I don't think he was really watching it. Just sort of sat and stared. He shut me out and, even worse, he shut out Julia.

This went on for months, and I couldn't take it anymore. I'd even considered contacting a divorce attorney. Then, one day I came home…" she paused, dropped her head down, and covered her eyes.

Tears spilled out from between her fingers. MariBeth reached out and touched Rachel's arm. "I'm so sorry Rachel. You don't need to tell me anymore."

"Yes, I do," Rachel choked. "I've held it in long enough. What I told Jon to do - talk to someone - he never did. Not even to me. I couldn't help him. Things went from bad to worse. He couldn't get a job and neither could I. Then the bank notified us they were going to foreclose on our house. The day after we got the notice, I was out looking for a job, like I did most days when Julia was in school. I pulled into our driveway, and heard the sound of a gunshot from inside our house. I ran inside calling his name. I found him in our bedroom, slumped in a chair. I just fell apart and ran to one of my neighbors, who called the police. When they came, they questioned me for hours. They were suspicious of me, I know."

"In the afternoon, as Julia's bus pulled to a stop in front of our house, I ran out to her. I couldn't risk her seeing all the blood inside the house. We had to spend the next few nights at a neighbor's down the block. Then, because of the suicide, Jon's life insurance wouldn't pay. We were evicted with nowhere else to go."

MariBeth reached for the nearby tissue box and handed it to her friend. "What about other family, couldn't they help?"

Rachel looked up, eyes red. "I have no other family. No brothers or sisters. My Mom and Dad died a while back. All I had was my grandmother, and I hadn't seen her in years. We were living on the west coast, and she was here. The last time I saw her was when she flew out for our wedding."

"I was desperate and called her. She welcomed us, let us stay here. I could help her, she said. I could do things for her, she said. But, just after we arrived here, she got sick and wasn't strong enough to do much. I took care of her the best I could. Then, as you know, three days ago she just slipped away and died peacefully in her sleep."

Rachel groaned, "And now I'm back to square one. I don't know what to do."

MariBeth looked puzzled, "What about staying here? Can't you do that?"

"I'm not sure." Worry creased Rachel's brow as she imagined getting kicked out of this house too.

"Didn't your grandmother have a will? Maybe you are mentioned in it somehow."

"I don't know." She gestured to the piles around her. "If she did, I can't even begin to know where to look in this mess. I've called Neil Walker, one of the attorneys in town, to see if he can help me figure this out. I have an appointment to see him tomorrow."

"That's a good plan," MariBeth said, looking around the room. "Do you need some help?"

"Probably, but let me talk with the lawyer first. I may not even have any legal right to stay here, much less sort through all this stuff."

"When you find out let me know. MariBeth checked her watch. "Sorry, to leave you now, but I need to go." She stood and headed for the front door, reached for her raincoat and slipped it on. She turned to Rachel, who had followed behind, "Give me a call, okay?"

Rachel opened the door. "Sure," she said. "And thanks for being there with me today. I don't know if I could have handled that funeral alone. You've been such a help to me and to Julia."

"No problem." MariBeth gave Rachel a quick hug and left.

Rachel shut the door behind her friend, leaned against it, and closed her eyes. She was so tired both physically and emotionally. There was so much to do.

In all the time she'd been here, it had been so difficult not to make sense of the disorder in the house. She itched to get the place cleaned and organized, a trait she'd inherited from her mother. Apparently the gene didn't come from her grandmother though. Rachel had spotted an issue of *Better Homes and Gardens* with the main topic "How to Organize". Evidently Nonna never read it. Right now, Rachel wanted to be like Samantha on that seventies TV show, *Bewitched*. She would wiggle her nose and make it all go away.

Bang! The sound startled Rachel and her eyes flew open. She heard Julia cry out, "Mama!" Running down the hall, her heart racing, Rachel fully expected to see an injured Julia. But when she got to the den she saw the girl on the floor, banging her hands and feet in a full-fledged tantrum.

Lord, give me strength. I can't deal with much more today. Rachel knelt down, scooped the child into her arms, and said in a calm voice that mocked her internal turmoil, "Julia, what's the matter?"

Through loud sobs Julia managed, "I hate that game. It's stupid. I can't do it!"

"Are you upset with the game, or something else, Sweetie?" Rachel knew that the game was only the catalyst to this latest breakdown. Julia had been vacillating emotionally since Jon's death. She really didn't understand. She wanted her Daddy and, in her five year old mind, she expected him to return. Today's funeral didn't help at all.

Julia sniffled, "Mama. I want to go home."

"But we are home, Julia."

"No, no, I want to go back to our old house. I want to see Daddy."

Rachel sighed, tears springing to her eyes, "We can't go back. Remember? Daddy died, just like Nonna. He is not at our old house anymore." Rachel hugged and rocked her daughter until the sobs quieted then reached for the nearby box, handed a tissue to Julia and used one herself.

"I'm sorry, Mama. Don't cry."

Rachel gave her a gentle hug, "I'm sad, too, Sweetie. I miss Daddy and I miss Nonna."

"I miss them too, Mama." They sat together until their tears stopped.

"Are you hungry? Do you want something to eat? There's some chicken casserole left from lunch."

"I don't want casserole. I want chicken nuggets."

"Julia, I don't have nuggets. Let's see what's in the fridge and you can choose from what's there, okay?"

"But…"

"No, Julia. I know you're upset. It's been a hard time for both of us. Let's get you something and then it'll be an early bedtime for you." Taking her daughter's hand they slowly made their way to the kitchen.

* * *

With dinner completed, Rachel locked up and turned off the lights before heading up the stairs with Julia in tow. She helped Julia change into her nightgown and slip under the covers. Sitting on the bed, Rachel smoothed Julia's hair and leaned to kiss her forehead.

"Good night, Sweetie. I'll be just down the hall, if you need me."

Rachel turned out the light, leaving a nightlight to spread a soft glow in the room. She made her way to her own room, got into bed, curled up into a fetal position, and cried herself to sleep.

Chapter Two
The next day

The alarm rang and Rachel blindly reached out, turning it off with a groan. She'd had trouble sleeping last night and morning had come much too soon. Some days she just wanted to stay under the covers and never come out. It was only her daughter that helped her carry on. Day by day, step by step, she'd begun to make strides forward, but mornings like this were hard. She didn't feel rested and the job ahead of her seemed insurmountable.

She tossed aside the blankets and padded barefooted down the hallway to the bathroom, where she turned on the shower. It took time for the hot water to make its way up from the basement and through the house's old pipes. Rachel needed those minutes to wake up. She stepped into the shower and quickly washed and shampooed her long hair. After a quick towel dry, she wrapped the towel around

herself, and walked back down the hall to the room
her grandmother assigned her.

She had tried to make some sense of the room,
piling some of the accumulated things in one corner
of the room, but it still felt cramped. *I hope that
lawyer has some good news today. I can't live like
this much longer.* Dressing quickly, she slipped on
black slacks and a white cotton sweater. She pulled
her hair into the usual ponytail and slipped on black,
comfortable flats. She worked on her makeup,
applying it quickly and efficiently and then stepped
back to gaze in the mirror. The months of working to
hold her family together, then Jon's suicide and
Nonna's illness and death, had taken their toll. Her
slacks were threatening to fall off her shrinking
waistline. She tightened the belt another notch. This
would have to do, she told herself. At least I'm clean
and presentable, not at all beautiful. Her hazel eyes
gazed back, with the deep sadness that still lingered
there.

She walked down the hall. "Julia? Time to get
up, Sweetie!" She spotted the girl in the small room,
still tucked in bed. The canopied twin bed was
between the room's two windows with nightstands on
each side. It had been used mainly as a storage room
before they came to live there. Rachel had to move
the piles into the corners and several boxes
overflowing with papers were stored under the bed.
Rachel leaned in the doorway and saw her daughter
hiding under her Disney princess blanket.

Julia had insisted that they needed to bring that
blanket – one of those things that couldn't be left

behind. They didn't bring much from their old house, just what could be carried in the car.

Rachel remembered the day clearly. Packing and repacking the car had been one of the hardest things she'd done in her life. Yeah, military life, with the ever-constant relocation from one station to another, had her familiar with packing light. There certainly wasn't an opportunity to gather much in the way of life's memorabilia. But this was much worse. Julia had stood beside the car, watching carefully as Rachel packed each item. Several times she'd wailed, and had even thrown a tantrum, when one of her prized possessions – at least to her young mind – made it to the discard pile instead of in the precious space in the trunk or the back seat of the car.

At one point, Rachel recalled, she'd had to call in a neighbor as she felt her body tensing and her anger at Jon and the circumstances he'd forced on them by his actions reach the near boiling point. She didn't want to take it out on Julia.

So many times Rachel had wanted to throw a tantrum herself. In her mind she could see herself throwing things, breaking dishes, stomping through the house tearing up the place – but on the outside she forced herself to present a calm presence for Julia's sake. Oh, but it was so hard.

The five day trip from California to Oxford was so long. Rachel was thankful there were still cheap places to stay along the way. With no income, the money she had from the sale of their furniture had to last. It seemed to be going too fast for her peace of mind.

Rachel stepped over a pile of discarded clothes and nudged her daughter, "Come on, now!"

"Aw, Mama." Julia's voice was muffled under the blanket.

"None of that – you need to hustle this morning. I've got an important meeting after I drop you off at school." She pulled the blanket down and saw her daughter's smile. Tension in her shoulders eased. She sat on the side of the bed, gave Julia a hug and tickled her. Julia giggled.

Rachel continued to be amazed by Julia's spirit. One minute she was in tears, mourning her Daddy, and the next she's giggly and happy. Rachel had started to read the book given to her at the funeral home about how children deal with death. According to the book, Julia's reactions were all natural.

"What do you want for breakfast?"

"How about a breakfast cookie? That way you don't need to cook, I can eat it in the car and I can stay in bed some more."

"Always the negotiator, aren't you?" Rachel's smile didn't reach her tired eyes. She stood and went to the doorway, "Get going. I'll see you downstairs."

Julia sighed and got out of bed. She dressed quickly, ran downstairs, and greeted her mom in the kitchen. "I'm ready, see." She twirled around.

Rachel glanced at her daughter, dressed in her usual pink. Today she'd chosen a pink corduroy skirt, white top with pink trim. White tights and pink sneakers completed the little girl's outfit. Nicely done, Rachel thought.

"Good job, Julia. I like your outfit." Rachel handed her a breakfast cookie, her lunch sack and backpack. "Okay, here we go." The two left out the back door.

* * *

Rachel started the old white Chevy Impala, and groaned in despair when she heard the sound of the engine roaring. The hole in the muffler had gotten worse during the drive across the country. She needed the car to last, knew she needed to do the repairs, but without money, she was stuck. *Sure hope the police don't hear the obnoxious sound. I certainly can't afford a ticket!*

Rachel drove the ten miles deep in thought, oblivious to the signs of early spring around her and of her daughter's endless chatter in the back seat. She pulled into the drop-off lane at Julia's school, St. Johns Academy, on Front Street. The line of cars moved quickly as children exited the cars and hurried into the front door of the school. Teachers lined the walkway, watching their students, encouraging the dawdlers to move.

When her turn came, she turned to Julia, helped her release the booster seat belt, and blew her a kiss. "Have a great day, Sweetie. See you later."

"Bye, Mama!" Julia slammed the car door and raced into the building, hair flying behind her.

Smiling, Rachel exited the school's driveway and drove another two miles to the center of the small town of Oxford. Metal plaques on either end of the town square boasted the town's history. Surrounding the square were streets lined with two-story buildings housing a variety of businesses, a pharmacy, two restaurants, and on the corner, a large bank. The bank was an impressive building, three stories with windows along three sides. Glancing up, Rachel noticed the engraved stone indicating the structure was built in 1894. On one corner of the stone structure was a three-story round turret giving the bank the appearance of a medieval castle. On the second floor of the bank, a sign in the window indicated the office of Mr. Neil Walker, Attorney at Law.

Rachel parked the car in the slot across from the bank, grabbed her purse, shut, and, out of habit, locked her car door. *I wonder if anyone locks their door here. Can't imagine crime in this tiny town.* Shivering, she pulled her coat tightly around her. The calendar may say spring, but the air was still cold. The warmth of the California sun seemed so far away. She wondered if she'd survive in this cold air. She pulled open the door and was greeted by a blast of heated air. *Ah, much better.*

The stairs to the second floor were just inside the door to the right. The arrow on a sign nearby indicated the direction to the lawyer's office. Following the sign, her steps dragged as she climbed the stairs, dreading the encounter with the attorney and the information he might have for her. Her situation was grim. She was hoping that he would have a glimmer of good news. The only door at the top of the stairs had the lawyer's name on it.

She pushed it open and saw a twenty-something standing in the small reception room. She had short, curly, brown hair with a stripe of pink, lip piercings and a heavy layer of makeup. A colorful tattoo of a large rose peeked out from her short-sleeved shocking-pink top. *That outfit looks out of place in this rural town. She should be in Oakland.* No one else was in the room and Rachel saw the name plate on the small oak desk – Patsy Lee. Where's the receptionist, she wondered. Miss Pink Top moved behind the desk and Rachel's eyes widened in surprise. What was that rule about judging a book by its cover? Patsy looked up, smiled brightly and asked, "Hello. What can I do for you?"

Rachel thought she hardly seemed old enough to be in charge of a lawyer's office and all that it entailed. It couldn't have been more than a year ago she'd crossed the stage to get her high school diploma. *Funny, seems the older I get, the younger the workers look!*

Rachel shook off those thoughts, made an effort to smile in return and said, "I have a nine o'clock appointment with Mr. Walker."

Patsy looked down at the desk appointment book, "Ah, yes, Ms. Benton. Please have a seat. He'll be with you in a minute."

"Thank you." The waiting room had only two chairs available. The walls were dark walnut paneling with one small window shedding a small amount of natural light into the room. Rachel sat and picked up a magazine trying to calm her nerves. She had hardly gotten a glance at the first page before the inner door opened and Neil Walker came out, hand extended. "Mrs. Benton. Neil Walker. Please come in."

Walker looked to be in his late thirties. His brown eyes were hidden behind wire-framed glasses and his long hair, dusted with a hint of gray, was tied back in a ponytail. His brown suit was slightly rumpled giving him a carefree, rakish look. He didn't look at all like the stodgy lawyer Rachel was expecting.

He turned and held the door for her to enter his office. It was another small room, located in the turret corner of the building. Behind him was the usual display, a law license, diplomas and awards, all neatly framed.

Across the room, however, was something unusual for a lawyer's office, she thought. On the round walls, she saw hanging some hand-drawn certificates, lettering done in Old English calligraphy, embellished with gold leaf letters. The framed pieces looked like something a monk would have spent hours creating. They were beautiful works of art.

Two long windows, free of window treatments, gave a panoramic view of most of the "downtown" area of Oxford including the town square. Rachel saw a young couple walking in the Square, dressed in shorts and short sleeves. She was amazed. *Here I am freezing and they think its summer.* She noticed an ornate sword propped against the end of his desk, but pushed her curiosity aside.

He motioned to a straight-backed, padded chair and she sat down, loosening the ties of her coat. He took a seat behind his desk.

"First of all, Mrs. Benton…"

"Rachel, please."

"Rachel, then. I'm so very sorry for your loss. I realize this is a difficult time for you, and I'm here to help in whatever way I can."

If he only knew, thought Rachel. She sat with her hands clasped tightly together and twirled her wedding ring. "I'm not sure where to begin," she said.

"Ah. Let's see." He referred to a manila file opened on the desk before him. "You're living in your deceased grandmother's house and her will has yet to be found, is that correct?"

"Yes, to both questions. I don't even know if she had a will. My daughter and I have only been here a short time, and my grandmother took ill so quickly after we arrived, that I haven't had time to do much of anything. I was hoping that you can tell me what I need to do."

"Well, legally, there are several things we need to consider. If your grandmother has a will, and in it you are named executor, then we proceed with filing the paperwork needed to begin the probate process. That's pretty straightforward. But if you're not listed as executor, we'll need to see who is, and find that person. Most wills name multiple executors or name an attorney or other professional as one. Let's say your mother was named as executor. She can then proceed…"

"But my mother died years ago."

"Well, in that case, were you named as executor in your mother's will?"

"No. She didn't have one."

"Okay, then, if none of the executors listed are alive or can be found, the court will choose someone to administer the estate. The courts prefer to name a family member. So that would mean you, if there's no one else who will step forward."

"I have no one else left, Mr. Walker."

"Neil, please."

Rachel smiled weakly, "Neil. As far as I know, there's no one left in my family except me and my daughter."

Neil nodded. "On the other hand, if there isn't a will? Well, we'll deal with that later."

"It sounds complicated. How long will all this take?"

"In either case, this part should go quickly, but the rest – it will take months to resolve completely."

Rachel felt her stomach lurch. *That can't be.* She leaned forward, "You don't understand. I don't have months. I need to have this resolved as soon as possible. We don't have any place to go. I have a daughter..." She was babbling, she knew, but so flustered, so upset the words kept tumbling out. "I was hoping we would be able to stay in the house."

He raised his hand to stop her. "As for that, whether the will is found or not, you can still live in the house during the process, since, as you say, you are the only living relative."

Rachel let out the breath she didn't realize she'd been holding. She leaned back in the chair. *She and Julia would not become homeless again.*

"Oh, thank you! That's such a relief," she said, smiling. "I've really been itching to get that place cleaned and organized. There's stuff everywhere – and I won't be able to tell if there's anything important until I weed through the mess. I wasn't able to do anything while Nonna was alive. She wouldn't let me touch a thing." She stopped and took a deep breath. She was babbling again.

He stood, moved from behind his desk and held out his arm to shake her hand. "That sounds good. You go ahead and get started. I'll check around to see if any of the other lawyers in town has your grandmother's will. Once the paperwork is processed and you are named executor or administrator, you'll need to do an inventory of the contents inside it, pay bills, complete legal paperwork, and then you can begin selling the things you don't want and even the house if you prefer. It's a long and tedious process, I know, but, as I said before, I'm here to help."

Rachel rose from her chair and took his extended hand in hers. His hand was warm and shake firm. They walked toward the door. "I'll get back to you if I find the will. Hopefully one of us will find the thing quickly. Thanks so much for your help." She left him standing there, watching her.

Rachel walked through the outer office, noticing the receptionist busy at her computer. With a quick wave, Rachel left the office with a spring in her step, pleased with the good news.

Chapter 3
Later that day

Leaving the building, Rachel was hit with a blast of colder air and tightened her coat's belt again. She heard a sound overhead and saw a flock of Canada Geese winging their way north, honking in the familiar V-formation. *I can't believe they think it's spring.* The temperatures were so much colder than the familiar warmth in California.

Rachel's stomach grumbled. Realizing she hadn't eaten since the night before, Rachel walked across the street to Margo's Diner. The sign in the window boasted free, unlimited Wi-Fi. It made for a great meeting place for business people in three-piece suits, with their laptops and files spread around them, heads together, deep in corporate discussions. Others, like her, were unemployed, struggling to find work. Having lost their home Internet, they took advantage of the diner's service. It was cheaper to order a cup of coffee and slowly drink it while scanning the Internet for a job than paying for monthly Internet service at home. She was grateful for Nonna's church friends, who periodically stopped by to visit, relieving Rachel for an hour or two. She would come here, bringing her own laptop, get her emails and check *Facebook*.

A bell jingled when she opened the door, and several heads turned to watch her enter. Rachel smiled in response, but didn't recognize anyone this morning. A mother, sitting in the corner with two preschoolers, smiled in return. Everyone else quickly returned to looking at their screens, fingers flying over keyboards.

The place was small with only a dozen wooden tables, most were filled. The walls were trimmed in floral wallpaper, and decorated with black and white photographs showing homes and businesses from the history of the town. Oldies music played in the background.

Rachel found a table by the window and glanced outside to the "downtown" of Oxford. The town was a far cry from the bustling city of Oakland. This rural town in the Southern Tier of upstate New York was so tiny in comparison. According to the Internet search she'd done, it boasted a population of forty thousand. She saw the cars traveling down the main road and remembered reading that it was once a canal connecting Binghamton to Utica. Canal boats, also known as packet boats, had carried goods and people to towns all up and down the waterway before the coming of the railroad.

She looked out at the town park. Called the Square, it was really much more rectangular in shape.

The trees there were beginning to leaf out. The blooms of crocus and yellow daffodils lent a splash of color near the gazebo at one end of the Square. A grey haired couple sat sipping coffee and watching several robins darting in the grass looking for their wormy breakfast. She glanced across the street, up at the lawyer's office, and saw Neil Walker standing in the window. He waved and she nodded then quickly looked down, embarrassed.

Thelma, the sole waitress, wandered over to Rachel. "Do you know what you want?" she grumbled. Rachel looked up and saw tired eyes, and drooping shoulders. Apparently it had been a long morning for her, she thought. She looked as if she couldn't wait for her shift to end.

The smell of greasy burgers permeated the air, even at this early hour, making most of the menu items seem unappetizing. Rachel ordered a cup of coffee with a blueberry muffin and the waitress wandered off. The morning paper, left behind by a departed patron, was rumpled. Rachel reached for it and glanced at the headlines. So much of the news was bad. She didn't have the energy to read the details in the stories. Instead, she turned to the employment ads. She was not very hopeful of getting a teaching position in this small town. When she got here a month ago, she'd read that many districts were on austerity budgets, cutting positions rather than hiring. Still, it made sense to check for nearby towns. A short drive would not be out of the question if the position was a good one. Glancing through the ads, she didn't see anything at all. She knew she needed to also keep checking the websites of the districts in the area. Many of them no longer used the newspaper for advertisement. She'd have to keep taking advantage of the Wi-Fi here, or go to the library since Nonna didn't have any use for the Internet. *Living in that house sometimes feels like I've gone back in time.*

She was so relieved she could stay in the house as the estate was being processed that she felt the weight of the world lift off her shoulders. Things had been so hard for so long, it was amazing to feel even a small sense of relief instead of constant dread. After Jon died, she hadn't known what she and Julia would do, where they would go... and now here they were, in this little town. At least they had a roof over their heads, but money was still a problem. Without a job, Rachel had no source of income. Thankfully, after the bank had repossessed their house back in California, she was able to sell some of the household furniture. That money would only last a short time longer. She mentally took inventory of her remaining funds.

After traveling across the country and spending a month here, she only had a few hundred dollars left. The refrigerator needed filling, the car needed gas and repairs, and Julia needed new shoes and, with summer coming, some new clothes. She sighed. What she really needed was a job.

How could he have done this to us? It wasn't fair. She didn't do anything to get in this fix. If Jon had been more of a man, had gone for help as she had suggested, perhaps all this wouldn't have happened. She pushed her anger aside. *It won't get me anywhere.*

Looking out the window to the town square, she tried to decide how to start in the house. Two floors, attic, basement and garage all filled with what Rachel considered to be mostly garbage. How her grandmother could live in such a mess, she couldn't fathom. She was used to keeping a neater house. Rachel caught episodes of *Hoarders* on TV and couldn't imagine a person living in such a condition. Well, Nonna was almost a hoarder. She shuddered to think of what might be found under all the piles in the house.

Her cell rang. Glancing at the screen, she smiled and flipped it open.

"Hi, MariBeth."

"Hey. How'd it go with the lawyer this morning?"

"Not bad. We still need to find the will, but my biggest worry is resolved. He said I can stay in the house until the estate is finalized."

"That's fantastic."

"I'm going to start cleaning it out today – want to help?"

"Let's see." She paused. "I can't doing anything this morning, there's a meeting at work, but I can come over this afternoon, say about two. Is that okay?"

"That's fine. I need to stop at the store and make sure I have plenty of garbage bags on hand. It's going to be quite a job."

"Okay, I'll see you later."

Snapping her phone shut, Rachel tossed some money on the table, left the diner, and, after a quick stop at the grocery, drove slowly back to Nonna's house. The old Chevy grumbled the whole way.

Fifteen minutes later she pulled into the driveway and parked. Rachel noticed the early spring apparent in the garden beds surrounding the house. They were badly in need of raking. Leaves from last fall were piled around the house almost smothering the emerging flowers. She could see the tops of daffodils trying to find the sunshine. More work to do! But this will need to wait until I take care of the inside, Rachel thought. I need to find that will.

Opening the front door, she wrinkled her nose with the impact of the putrid odor. *Ugh – first things first. I don't care how chilly it is – this place needs a good airing.*

She went from room to room on the ground floor, opening as many windows as she could. She struggled with the ones that had been painted shut, finally deciding to leave those for now. In the living room, access to the windows was blocked by the stacks of the local newspaper, *National Geographic* magazines, and other unidentified papers that had been piled in front of them. She moved each pile to the center of the room in order to get to the windows to open them.

The refreshing spring breeze began to spread through the five rooms on the ground floor. Rachel climbed to the second floor and, after opening the windows in her room and Julia's, stopped at the doorway of Nonna's room. She hesitated, and leaned on the doorframe, remembering her grandmother lying in her bed under her quilt, so sick at the end. She had faded so quickly.

Had it been only a month? It sure seemed like much longer. She remembered Nonna had greeted them at the door giving them both a brief hug. Her gnarled, arthritic hand grasped the cane, tapping it on the hardwood floor. She had shuffled slowly, hunched over, making her way into the living room. Rachel and Julia had followed slowly behind. Nonna put the cane aside, held onto the arms of her favorite overstuffed chair in the bay window, and slowly sat. She pulled a small afghan over her legs and settled back. On the tables nearby were the things she had needed most – tissues, glass of water, her glasses, something to read, a box of crackers. Rachel had been too tired to really notice more than her grandmother at that moment.

Nonna was an eighty-eight year old, small and frail woman. Her skin was translucent with veins clearly visible. She wore a pink flowered dress and blue cardigan, her white hair neatly combed, blue eyes behind glasses perched on her sharp nose. She'd lived all alone in the four-bedroom house and, until just recently, had still driven her Ford Escort.

"I'm so pleased you could come, Rachel." She spoke in a whispery voice. "You can stay as long as you need, and perhaps help me a bit. I'll need help getting groceries and going to the doctor. I've been having trouble getting around lately. Haven't felt well and I've been so tired."

Rachel had looked around the rooms. The house was so messy, almost filthy in places. She could tell Nonna hadn't been feeling well in quite a while. She found it hard to believe that her grandmother would willingly live like that if she could do something about it.

"Julia and I are really grateful, Nonna. I don't

know what we would have done if you hadn't agreed to take us in. I had nowhere else to go, once we lost our house. We will both help you as much as you'd like.

"I'm so sorry about Jon. I'm just glad to be able to help, Rachel. It's been so long since I've seen you. After your mother died, I'd been meaning to come out to California to visit, but I couldn't seem to find the time. I haven't met your daughter. This is Julia, right?" She leaned forward. "Come here, child, where I can see you."

Rachel brought Julia out from behind her, "Julia, say hello to your great-grandma."

"Hi," Julia said quietly, standing close to her mother.

"Ah, Rachel, she looks just like your mother when she was little," said Nonna, smiling as she remembered the past.

"Yes, I know. I wish Mom had lived longer so she could have known her granddaughter," Rachel said. "I miss her so."

"As do I, my dear. A parent should not outlive her child." She sat back. "Well, let's get you settled. You must be tired from traveling across the country."

"It has been a long trip," Rachel agreed.

"You can take the blue room upstairs and Julia can have the pink one. I left some sheets and towels out on the beds."

"Thanks, Nonna." She looked around once more, noticing the disorganized mess. "Once we're settled, Julia and I can help clean up some of these piles of stuff. I can get started cleaning tomorrow."

"Oh, no! I don't want anything touched." Her

voice rose and she became agitated, gripping the arms of her chair. "I can't even think of going through them. Please, just leave things the way they are."

Rachel shuddered. She much preferred neatness, not the overwhelming disorder she saw all around her. But she needed to stay. She was reminded again how much she owed her grandmother. "All right, then. I'll just clean some of the dust around the piles."

Nonna had relaxed in her chair and closed her eyes. Rachel had every intention of starting the cleaning, but Nonna became seriously ill the next day. Taking care of her needs became a 24/7 job, and Nonna wouldn't allow anyone else to help her. No nursing home, no nurse's aide. Just Rachel. Four days ago, Nonna had quietly breathed her last during the night.

Chapter 4
The same day

Rachel shook her head, returning to the present. Nonna's room was large and showed the same signs of disrepair as the rest of the house. The faded pink floral wallpaper was peeling in several places. In front of the two windows were piles of books and more newspapers and magazines, partially blocking the view to the yard below. Around the room, the walls were hidden behind pictures, paintings, and other hanging collectibles. A four-poster bed sat along one wall, with a nightstand tucked next to it and the nearby window. A five-drawer dresser, a mahogany secretary's desk and a closet completed the room. *I would think if she had a will, it should be in this room.*

She hesitated again, and then purposefully walked to the bed. Grabbing all the bedding, she tossed them out of the room into the hallway. She flicked open a garbage bag, moved to the night stand, swept all the medications into it, and then emptied the wastebaskets. Recent issues of *USA News* and *Smithsonian* magazines that were piled on the floor next to the bed were added to another bag for recycling. Going from pile to pile, after a quick review of each of them, Rachel was able to quickly eliminate much of the clutter. Several trash bags joined the bedding in the hallway. She opened one window and breathed in deeply the clean, fresh spring air. *It's chilly, but at least it's getting the smell out of the house.*

She paused and glanced around. Now I can get a sense of what might be more important in the room and finally look for that will, she thought. Rachel wiped her hand across her sweating brow and sat at the oak secretary desk. It was a beautiful piece of furniture with drawers below the writing surface. Rachel slowly went through each cubbyhole and the tiny drawers below them. She found a stack of recent mail rubber banded together, much of it unopened. Releasing the band, she riffled through the envelopes, noting the return addresses. Most of it looked to be utility and medical bills, some of it junk mail. She put these aside to add to the pile of mail she had collected downstairs during the time she had been taking care of her grandmother. She had hoped Nonna would recover enough to look through them and take care of the bills that were accumulating.

Rachel knew that Nonna had been confused with today's modern technology. She didn't own a computer or cell phone. Based on the mail, until recently, Nonna had continued to write and receive letters. The names on some of the return addresses had no meaning for Rachel.

She was going to have to ask the lawyer what she should do with the unpaid bills. Was she responsible for paying them? She had so little money left and could hardly pay for her own bills, much less Nonna's. Setting aside the bills to show the lawyer at their next meeting, she tossed the junk mail into the trash. Unfortunately, so far, no will. If finding the darn thing meant she could begin the process to finalize Nonna's estate and know what her future would be, she needed to find it as quickly as possible. Not knowing was so stressful and she had Julia to think about. She certainly didn't want to end up on the street, homeless.

Rachel worked her way through each drawer of the desk, then the nightstand. She started piles of her own. What to keep, what to trash, what to donate? The room looked much better now, cleaned of the more obvious garbage. Next would come the dusting and vacuuming – something that hadn't been done in a long while in this room, she could tell. The dust bunnies under the bed and around the room had created another generation of baby dust bunnies.

Her stomach rumbled and Rachel realized it was well past lunch and a long time since that muffin at the diner. After closing the bedroom window, she went down into the kitchen and on the way, closed all the other windows she had opened. The chilly, spring air had whipped through the house, dispersing the old musty and sickly smells. Taking a deep breath, she felt refreshed, and after a cup of coffee and sandwich, felt able to continue her search for the will. She started for the staircase when the doorbell rang.

"Coming! Just a minute!" She hurried through the living room to the back door in the kitchen and peeked through the curtained window in the door to see MariBeth standing there. She opened the door with a flourish. "Oh, I'm so glad you're here."

Smiling, MariBeth walked in and closed the door behind her. "Ummm, smells so much better in here!"

"Yes, it took most of the morning to air out the place. It really should have been done long ago."

Maribeth took off her spring jacket, and Rachel saw that she was elegantly dressed in designer jeans and a light blue silk blouse. Her shoulder length hair was expertly coifed. Mindful of her own grays beginning to sprinkle through her hair, Rachel couldn't tell if her friend's hair color was natural or came from a bottle. Again Rachel felt she came up short in comparison.

MariBeth eyed her friend closely, "So, how are you doing, Rachel, really?"

"Oh, as good as can be expected, I suppose. The lawyer's news was very helpful and I'm much relieved. But still…"

"You've been through a great deal, Rachel." She hesitated, then took a pamphlet out of her pocket and held it out. "Here."

"What's this?" Rachel read the cover, *Dealing with Death.*

"It's a brochure for a grief support group in town. It meets at the local church. I heard about it the other day, and thought of you. I remember what you told me yesterday about your suggesting to Jon about getting some help. Well... maybe you need some, too." Maribeth stopped, and bit her lip. "But it's up to you."

Rachel glanced down and then met Maribeth's eyes. "Thank you. I'll think about it."

"That's all I ask." MariBeth, looked around and asked, "So, what can I do to help?"

"Well, right now I'm looking for the will, and trying to get rid of piles of junk. But, as I started working I realized that maybe there might be something important or valuable in the piles. I'm no expert on historical stuff, antiques and such. That's where you can help. Didn't you say that you worked at a history museum?"

"Mm-hmm," she mumbled. Her eyes darted around the room, taking in all the details. "You know going through this house will be like a treasure hunt. You never know what you might find. Where were you working?"

"I just started upstairs in Nonna's room. I started making three piles – discard, keep and donate. Now I realize that I might have to have a valuables pile. My lawyer indicated I'll need to make a list of everything if I'm the executor for the estate."

Rachel led the way up the stairs, and stopped at the top. Spotting the pile of trash bags and laundry, she muttered a groan and said, "Goodness, I forgot to take care of these."

"Let's start here, then." MariBeth bent and grabbed a handful of laundry.

Mindful of what her friend was wearing, Rachel said, "You don't need to do that. You'll get your clothes dirty." Rachel knew the silk blouse was expensive, and so were those designer jeans that MariBeth was wearing. She thought of her own wardrobe. In all the years of their marriage, she'd never been able to buy clothes unless they came from a discount store. She did a lot of her shopping for herself and Julia at Goodwill. Sometimes she would find designer jeans or a top there, but although no one else could tell, she was always aware that they were second hand clothes. She glanced down at her dust covered slacks and sweater and wondered what MariBeth thought of her.

"It's all right – I'm here to help." MariBeth started down the stairs. Rachel followed with a bag of trash in each hand. They made two more trips before the hallway was clear of laundry and trash. When they returned to Nonna's room, Rachel stopped and leaned on the doorframe. MariBeth moved into the room and saw several photos in standing frames on the dresser. She picked up an eight-by-ten framed photo. "Who's this?"

"That's my Mom and Dad on their wedding day." She pointed to the next photo. "And that's me and Jon taken a few years ago. I think Julia is ten months old there."

"You all look so happy." MariBeth noted, then seeing the sadness in Rachel's eyes again said, "I'm sorry, Rachel." Changing the topic, she asked, "So what's next?"

"I finished going through the desk and stopped just before tackling the closet. Nonna might have stored her will in there."

She crossed the room, opened the closet door and saw Nonna's clothing hanging in jumbles. More dust bunnies were making their home in the many pairs of shoes and worn slippers strewn on the floor. Rachel winced as she pushed aside her grandmother's clothes, feeling Nonna's presence in them. She was going to have to take care of discarding the old clothes later. Pushing aside some dresses, on the right side of the closet, she saw shelves from floor to the ceiling filled with shoe boxes. Were they filled with shoes, or something else, she wondered. Taking a stack from the top shelf, she turned and handed them to her friend.

"Here, take this and I'll get another." MariBeth took them and moved to sit on the bed. Grabbing another stack Rachel joined MariBeth.

Opening the first box, instead of shoes, she found it stuffed with old postcards – old, old, old postcards. The second box contained more of the same. "Yikes! If all these boxes are like this – it's going to take forever to go through!" Rachel frowned, knowing her time was short. She needed to find Nonna's will fast.

MariBeth reached in to look at some of them. They were not the plain white cards, or cards you might find in a gift shop of a hotel. She noticed a Valentine on one, an Easter Bunny on another. "You'll have to be careful when you go through these boxes. These postcards can be valuable to collectors. I've even seen scrapbooks of postcards like these in museums." She turned it over and tried to read the faded writing on the back. "You don't know. There could be something valuable in all this. I know you're worried about the will, but don't just discard these things."

"It's going to slow me down, that's all," Rachel

said frustration clearly evident in her voice.

Rachel reached for the next stack of shoeboxes, opened the top one, and found a bundle of letters neatly tied in a faded purple ribbon. The envelopes were post dated 1910. MariBeth took the next box which contained letters dated 1911. In another box – 1917. Boxes and boxes of letters!

"Oh, my – she saved everything didn't she?" MariBeth voiced in excitement.

"I guess so," said Rachel not feeling as enthused. She sat back and looked at all the opened boxes surrounding them on the bed. "What should I do with these?" There was a tower of six more unopened boxes before them and more still in the closet. She wondered what the other bedroom closets contained.

"I'm not sure, Rach. I think you are going to have to read them. They might contain something important, maybe about someone in your family. You won't know unless you go through them. That way you can decide if it's important to you and if you'll want to keep them. But, aside from that, they are also important historically and a museum might be interested in them. So don't toss them in the trash."

"I'd never thought of that." Rachel looked around and thought of what was here on the bed and what was in the other rooms of the house and sighed. The job ahead just got bigger than she originally was expecting. It was going to take a lot of time to plow through all of these letters, as well as clean and inventory the rest of the house.

MariBeth saw the tired look and said, "While I can't help read the letters, I can help with the inventory – looking at the furniture and such. I've been going to antique shows for years now. I have some sense of the value of antiques."

Rachel nodded. "I've watched *Antiques Roadshow*, a time or two. I'm always amazed at how much some of the items they bring are worth. But before we can get to the furniture, I have to clear some more of the garbage in each room. And I still have to find that darn will, if there is one. So it will be a few days."

MariBeth eyes swept the room seeking hidden treasures. "No problem. Just give me another call when you want me to take a look."

The two walked down the stairs to the front door. Rachel saw MariBeth out and started back up the stairs when the phone rang. She quickly picked it up, "Hello?"

"Mrs. Benton? This is Julia's teacher, Miss Campbell. Can you come by the school? She's had a huge meltdown and I had to send her to the nurse's office. She's sitting there waiting for you."

"I'll be right there." Rachel's stomach twisted in knots, thinking about her little girl. She drove to school as quickly as she could, given the condition of her crumbling car, parked and hurried into the school. At the nurse's office, she spotted Julia, eyes red with recently fallen tears. She rushed and knelt in front of her and wrapped her arms around the little girl. Julia started to cry again.

"What happened?" Rachel turned to ask the nurse.

"Well, near as I could tell, one of the other kids in the class mentioned something about her father, and then your grandmother and she just exploded.

She started shouting, and throwing books, and then she just collapsed on the floor of the classroom, sobbing. I was called to go down to get her and I brought her back here. She's been crying off and on since, asking for you. I think it best if you take her home since it's almost the end of the school day."

"Thank you, I'll do that."

"Mrs. Benton. You might want to consider taking her to a counselor."

"I'll think about it, thanks." Rachel mumbled. She took Julia's hand and they slowly walked out of the school. What a pair we are, she thought.

When they got home, Rachel washed Julia's face and then sat her down on the sofa.

"Want to talk about it? What happened in class today?" Rachel quietly asked.

Julia looked into Rachel's eyes. "Mama, I don't want you to die," Julia whispered.

Rachel drew her daughter onto her lap. "Oh, Sweetie. We can never tell when anyone will die, but most people live a long, long time. I plan on being here until you are all grown up and have babies of your own."

"Like Nonna?"

"Like Nonna." Rachel nodded. "Julia, it's okay to feel sad, it's okay to cry, and it's even okay to get mad. But it's not okay to throw things at school, or here either. Will you remember that?"

"Yes, Mama," she said softly, wrapping her arms around Rachel's neck.

"Good, now, want to help me fix dinner?"

Julia nodded again and smiled, tears forgotten.

Chapter 5
The next day

Early the next morning, after Julia left for school without complaint, Rachel gathered all the bills and assorted mail she'd seen in her grandmother's desk, and scattered elsewhere in the house, and brought them down to the kitchen. After fetching a cup of coffee, she brought it to the table, sat and started through the stack. She needed to decide what needed to be paid and what could wait. *How much money will I need to get by? What will I have to sell?*

After an hour she had finally finished opening all the envelopes and discovered two months of unpaid bills, water, gas and electric, phone and cable. Adding to that was an unpaid tax bill, and several bills from various doctors in town. Some of them included letters with angry language, threatening to send the bills to a collector if Nonna didn't send the money due them. Rachel groaned and placed all those in one pile.

Next, she sorted through the bills from the funeral home. The cost seemed so outrageously expensive, but Nonna had told her what she wanted before she died, and Rachel had felt obligated to follow through with her directives.

Rachel took a calculator and added up the past due bills, and sat back. She felt tears starting, her stomach churning. The total was almost twenty thousand dollars. She realized she was going to have to work quicker to make sense of the contents of the house, so she could sell some of the things to pay the bills. *I can't seem to catch a break.* When she had decided to come east and stay with her grandmother, she figured she'd have time to figure out what to do next with her life. Since arriving she'd been met with one crisis after another. *How's that saying go? Something about weight of the world?* She felt like it was all piled on top of her shoulders.

She spotted the brochure about the grief support group that MariBeth had handed her and decided it would be good for her to give it a try. Perhaps she'd learn how to help Julia, as well as herself, get through all this. She reached for the phone and gave the number a call. Twenty minutes later, she'd learned that the group met that night at a church in town, and she'd be welcome to attend. There was a child sitter available right at the church, so bringing Julia would not be a problem.

* * *

Rachel had no idea what to expect as she entered the church that night. She left Julia with the other three young children, tended by two teenage girls. When she opened the door to a small meeting room she saw chairs set up in a circle, with one chair left open for her. The others in the room turned as she entered. A woman stood and walked to Rachel, holding out her hand in greeting.

"Hello, Rachel. Welcome." Her smile was warm, her voice soothing. "I'm Sara. Come, join us."

Rachel sat and listened as Sara introduced the group. There were four men and three women and, as Sara mentioned each name, Rachel nodded, but she didn't remember anyone's name except the woman who sat across from her. Maggie was a late twenty-something dressed simply in Levi jeans and a knit top that looked straight off the rack at Target. Her blonde curly hair was cut short. If she wore makeup, it wasn't noticeable. She had a warm smile and a relaxed way about her.

Rachel bit her lips and sat twiddling her ring. She didn't know what she had gotten herself into as she listened to the stories the others told. Such sad, sad stories. One couple told of the stillbirth of their child, another told of the accidental death of a good friend. The stories brought tears to Rachel's eyes. This is not working for me, she thought. It's making me feel worse, compounding grief instead of making me feel better. I certainly don't feel like telling my story to any of these people.

Except maybe Maggie. When the younger woman spoke, Rachel felt a kindred spirit. "My cousin was depressed but everyone thought he was getting better. He had been seeing a therapist and was on medication. Then, out of the blue – he took an overdose and was gone before we knew it." Maggie's voice was wavering as she spoke. Rachel wanted to reach out and give her a hug.

The group went on for another hour, each person speaking as they felt the need to share their stories. When it was Rachel's turn, she just told the basics, mentioning Jon's suicide and Nonna's recent death, and left it at that. As the group wrapped up, Sara reminded them of the next meeting in two weeks. Not for me, Rachel thought.

She gathered Julia from the child's play room and the two left. In the parking lot, Rachel saw Maggie just about to get into her car, parked next to hers. Maggie turned when she approached.

"Hi, Rachel."

"Hi."

"Listen, I could tell you didn't like the group. Don't feel bad, it's not for everyone. If you want to talk sometime, give me a call, okay?" Maggie handed Rachel a slip of paper with her phone number on it. "I'm available any time."

"Thanks. I'm glad you were here tonight." Rachel watched as Maggie got in her car and drove off. She pocketed the slip of paper and drove home, thinking. *Well, that was a waste of time - except for meeting Maggie.*

* * *

Days later, after working long hours each day, piles of junk were outside, in and around the trash barrel – dozens of bags, waiting for the garbage truck to collect them. Now, in each room, there were smaller piles that still needed to be reviewed, but it all was much more manageable. She had all Nonna's paperwork organized into color-coordinated folders, neatly labeled. Rachel was tired, but a good tired. She woke each morning with a goal – a room to clean, a pile to sort. For the first time in a long while she didn't obsess on Jon's or Nonna's deaths. She was too busy sorting, organizing and cleaning.

Unfortunately, the will was still undiscovered. She couldn't understand where it might be, if it was here at all. She hadn't heard from Neil Walker, yet. Maybe it wasn't here in the house at all. She couldn't give up looking, though, until she heard from him.

Rachel remembered Nonna's closet. She felt drawn to the boxes she'd been finding. *Maybe it's tucked in one of the boxes I haven't opened.* Climbing the stairs to Nonna's room, she went back to the closet and reached for another cardboard carton. She dragged the box out and set it on the bed. This one felt heavier than the others. Inside the carton was a small, hinged, wooden box, engraved with the initials EB. She reached in and removed the box.

Cautiously lifting the lid, Rachel found two little books and another stack of letters, again tied with a ribbon, much more tattered than any other she'd found. Forgetting all about looking for Nonna's will, she brought the box downstairs, made herself another cup of tea and moved to the living room.

Sitting in Nonna's overstuffed chair in the living room, and resting her feet on the worn needlepoint footstool, Rachel carefully took the top book into her hands. It was small, only about two inches by four inches, maroon with a brass clasp on the side and gilded edges. A thin white ribbon sewn into the binding was used as a bookmark. Embossed in gold lettering on the cover was the date 1862. Looking at the other book she saw that it was dated 1863. She gently riffled through the pages and saw daily entries neatly written in ink. *Wow, diaries! This is amazing. I'm actually holding a piece of history from the time of the Civil War.* She certainly was no history buff, but she knew that this was an astonishing find. It was the oldest thing she'd found so far in everything she'd gone through in the house. Her tea forgotten, she settled back in her chair, and gently opening the first diary, began to read.

Chapter 6
March – August 1862

March 3, 1862

James gave me this diary today. I was so surprised to receive such a wonderful gift. How could he know it was my birthday? I have been here for such a short time. I didn't know he even took notice of me, a lowly domestic in this household. I do forget sometimes to call him Sir as I must his father. He is so near to my own age.

He stopped me in the hallway and handed me a simply-wrapped package. Oh, he looked so handsome in his Sunday go-to-meetin' clothes. His dark hair and sun tanned skin stood out against the light tan shirt he was wearing. He smiled at me with a twinkle in his hazel eyes and wished me a happy day. I smiled back at him, and when our hands touched I thought I would swoon for sure. Did he notice? Might he feel the same?

I will have to write here as often as I am able, but I know days will probably go by without entries because of my many duties in the household. Oh, some days it is so hard to rise early and get out of my warm bed, especially on cold mornings, to tend to the kitchen fire. I must get the porridge started then wake the girls to assist them in preparations for school. Even though Miss Ella is nine years old and Miss Ida is seven they still require help. They like to dawdle and chatter and it takes much encouragement on my part to get them out the door on time. Goodness, they are so unlike their brother. James is quiet, studious and serious. As I work around the house sometimes I come upon him reading or studying his lessons. I know he will be done with schooling soon because I have overheard discussions between him and his father about what he will do once he graduates the Academy. They turn into heated words at times. It sounds as if James does not wish to follow the plans his father has set for him.

James said I must be sure to keep this diary hidden carefully. He said his father would not approve of the gift and would be furious. I would be scolded or even let go. I agreed with him, but for a different reason. If I am to write the words and feelings as I should in this book, then I would not want anyone to see it.

My box room, tucked here in the attic, is small and I wasn't sure where I could hide this book until I found a good spot, under a loose floorboard, near my bed. Now that it can be safely hidden, I must get to sleep – dawn comes early and so do my morning duties.

Oh, be still my heart – it flutters so, as I lie here, just thinking about James in his own bed.

March 7, 1862

I think back to when Pa told me he'd found a position for me. I was so happy to be leaving our little house. Since Ma died six months ago, Pa just sat at the house in a drunken stupor most of the time after work. Although he never hit me, he would rant and rave over the slightest thing I did. When he needed to have more income, for his drinking mostly, he decided to send me to this household to work as a domestic. My friend, Sara, told me that most domestics move a great distance from their homes so they cannot tell tales of the household where they are placed. If Ma were still alive, the thought of going so far would have saddened me, but not now. So I left my home and traveled here to Oxford – almost two days distance. Pa expects me to send him money, but I won't be visiting him any time soon, I am thinking.

The thing I miss the most, besides Ma, is my schooling. I only had two years to go, but, unfortunately, had to put it all aside for this. I miss my friends there, too, Charlene and Margaret. Oh, I have found a new friend here, Becka Wells. It is good to be able to talk with someone else who is a domestic maid. But she lives on the other side of town and we only meet on our infrequent days off, or when we cross paths when running errands in town.

Since I have been in Mister B's household, things are so much better. Even though my room is small, and my duties are never ending it seems, at least there is peace and quiet. I find I can even smile a bit for the first time since Ma died. I get along fine with the housekeeper, Mrs. Roberts. She is a kindly woman whose husband is off fighting in the war. She gives me encouraging words as I work around the house. And with James here...things are good.

March 15, 1862

Mrs. Roberts has been so good to me, teaching me all that I need to learn. Mostly I am responsible for taking care of the girls before and after their school day, and helping with other household duties while they are in school. I have been cooking and serving the food, washing dishes for the noon meal, taking care of cleaning, making beds, laundry and ironing, and mending. My days are very long – eleven to twelve hours a day and with only one afternoon a week off, I do not have much time for leisure. I find that, as I am working around the house, I keep a watchful eye for James when he is home from his schooling. Does he notice how red my face gets when we cross paths?

March 20, 1862

This afternoon was a free one, so I went into town and met with Becka Wells at the park. It was so good to sit and do nothing for a time. We have been comparing households lately. Hers seems much like mine except that there is a missus as well as a mister. I told her how pleasantly surprised I was to find such a grand house.

Mrs. Roberts has a room off the kitchen and my box room is in the attic. Aside from these two servant rooms, there are four bedrooms, one for each of the girls, one for James and one for Mister B. I must take care of them all, except for Mrs. Robert's room, of course.

Becka tells me that in her household there are two young boys and their parents. The house is a bit smaller and thus her tasks easier.

March 25, 1862

I was talking with Miss Ella this morning and discovered that their mother died early last year. Poor James. I am sure he feels as I do – I miss Ma so much. I wish I could have more days free of household duties. If we had more time we might go down to the river to sit and talk. But not here - not in this house.

March 29, 1862

I cannot seem to find the energy to write in this book as often as I would like. My days are full, and, by the time I am permitted to return to my room, I barely have the energy to slip out of my clothes and get into bed. The days have gone by quickly and I have noticed James more and more. Sometimes when I come upon him, he looks up at me and a wisp of a smile appears on his face. I have noticed him watching me as I am working around the house, and I can feel the flush of embarrassment rise to redden my face. I wonder what he is thinking. He still has his head in his books most of the time. The end of his schooling is but three months away.

This afternoon I came upon James and two of his friends, Charles and Harris. They were talking about the war. News comes to town and they must talk about it at his school. I admit I have not concerned myself with the news since I do not have anyone I know involved. The war seems so far off when I hear the names of the distant towns, like Manassas or Antietam. Oh, I try to do my share but my duties here are so many, I do not have free time to spend knitting or sewing for the men fighting.

April 10, 1862

I felt like a spy today. Miss Ella and Miss Ida were in the living room with James this morning. He was teaching them how to play checkers. The little girls were giggling as they worked to learn the game and James, dressed in his overalls and faded shirt, sat there with them. I am not used to seeing him in such casual clothing. His dark brown hair was tousled as he ran his hand repeatedly through it. He was so patient with them and laughed often, his hazel eyes twinkling.

I wish I could have joined them, but I cannot intrude on family gatherings when not invited. Did James know I was there? I wonder if he heard the sound of my heart beating so loudly.

April 25, 1862

Today was a beautiful warm day and I had the afternoon free of duties. The cloudless sky was so blue and the early spring flowers along the banks of the river were blooming. James took me down to the river to watch the spring freshet. When he explained to me what it was about this morning, I couldn't imagine such a sight. He said that when all the rain and melting winter snow makes the river run high, we'll be able to see the lumber rafts, logs and other winter debris flowing swiftly down river. Today it happened.

We sat on the blanket under a willow tree apart from everyone, but close together. James held my hand until it was time for us to go back to the house. I found it so easy to talk with him and he shared with me his thoughts about the war raging to the south. He tells me that he has been talking with his friends considering what to do after schooling ends.

Am I falling in love with him? Does he feel the same about me? I worry that his father will notice. Surely there would be words. I may even be dismissed. I must be very careful for I know of nowhere else to go. Would Pa take me back or find me another post?

April 28 1962

Today I met James in town as he was walking home from school. I was picking up the household mail, something I do every day. As we walked we talked about the news of the war, about his sisters, about his father, and made an agreement that we would do this daily. Oh, I am so excited to know that his feelings grow for me as mine do for him.

May 5, 1862

James was ill today and did not attend school. In the afternoon, as he lay on the sofa in the living room under quilts, I brought him tea and toast. He asked me to stay. I sat in a nearby chair and we chatted for a while. Today we got to talking about our mothers. He told me his took sick of a respiratory illness last Christmas time and within a week had died. His sisters took it hard and it was up to him to help them. His father grew more distant and angry, it seemed. I told him of my own father and about my mother's *death just six months earlier. I told him she died birthing a stillborn infant. We have much in common and I feel we are growing closer.*

With James coughing so, I do pray that he gets better quickly and does not succumb as his mother did.

May 17, 1862

I was cleaning Miss Ida's room and overheard James and his father arguing again today. The arguments seem to happen with regular frequency lately. James was in his room with his father. I could hear James telling his father what he planned when he finished schooling next month. Apparently his father disagreed with James' desire to become a doctor and wants him to follow in his footsteps in the quarry. James was having none of it and told his father – who exploded with angry words. I would have thought Mister B would want James to be happy, but I guess his own plans for his son seem best to him. I slipped past the door and down the stairs without them knowing I had overheard them. I really wanted to go into the room and stand beside James to support his decision. What would he have thought about that, I wonder?

May 25, 1862

Mister B is still trying to control James. Today was awful. Early in the day, Mister B came to me and told me I was to serve tea and sandwiches at noontime as he was bringing a guest for James to meet. I thought it was a friend of Mister B's, but no – it was a young lady. Her name is Martha Simms. Oh, she looked so dainty and fine in her beautiful silk gown. Her long blond curls were tucked neatly under the matching poke bonnet. Her skin, so creamy white, tells me she probably spends most of her time indoors. As I served the food, I noticed her smooth hands – not like my rough work-worn ones. I could tell James did not know what awaited him. His expression when he entered the dining room was priceless. He couldn't hide his surprise. At first I figured he was enamored with the delightful young lady, but as the luncheon progressed I kept seeing his eyes move to mine and he would wink at me. I felt much better after that and I hope no one noticed. I do not think that James will accept any more surprises from his father.

June 1, 1862

James finished his schooling and the family went to the graduation ceremony today. I caught a glimpse of him as they left for the Academy. James looked so handsome. When they returned, he waved his rolled-up diploma, broad smile lighting up his face. I served the family at their celebration dinner and when I passed near James, he touched my arm and smiled at me. Making sure no one was watching, I smiled back.

at him then hurried from the room. Later I handed him the small gift package I had for him. He thanked me, gave me a quick hug, and kissed my hand before moving quickly away when he heard the approaching footsteps of Mister B. It was a happy day for James and I am so very proud of him.

June 28, 1862

What an amazing day – another warm and sunny one. James and I were in the town square along with many other townspeople. What a sight we saw. Professor Squire's air balloon was spread on the ground in the square. We watched as he filled it with the hot air from the flame pointed right into the middle of the opening of the balloon. Once it was filled, he jumped into the basket and it rose up in the air. It floated up and up, and then over the treetops, moving along the river about a mile before gently settling back down to the ground. It was so beautiful.

We did not touch, or look at each other. We still cannot risk being noticed he said. But, I so ached to be able to hold James and share with him my excitement. Even though he has told me he loves me, as I love him, I want to be able to tell the world how we feel, but we must wait, he said. How much longer can we wait? How much longer can we keep our love a secret from his father and sisters? Ella and Ida, those little imps, nearly caught us today. I almost fainted in fright when they came upon us in the

*drawing room holding hands. James made a quick
excuse and they didn't pursue it any further. They are
still young girls and may not notice what we have
tried so hard to hide. But what about his father – if he
has noticed he hasn't said anything to either of us. I
pray that continues.*

June 30, 1862

*Mrs. Roberts told me the news today and I have
been feeling ill since. My father, may he rest in peace,
has died. She told me that she received word that he
passed after an injury at work. Now I have no one –
except perhaps, James. Mrs. Roberts told me to take
the rest of the day to myself so I retired to my room.
Even though I was not close to Pa lately, he is ... was
... still kin and I will miss him. Later in the day,
James came to my room with some tea and toast. He
remembered the day he was sick, he said, and wanted
to repay the kindness. I am afraid I looked dreadful,
my eyes red from crying most of the day. I so wanted
him to take me in his arms. I think he wanted the
same, but we need to be so cautious.*

July 15, 1862

*James told me he saw a broadside hanging on
the wall outside the tavern. "Volunteers Wanted for
Company K – 10th NY Cavalry... pay and rations
begin when enrolled," it said. He wanted to be able to
enlist right then. But instead, he went to talk with his*

father about it. Mister B was not pleased. I heard their shouting from my attic room. I covered my ears but could still hear the angry words.

"You will not do this!" shouted Mister B.

"I will, Father. I must - for the Union" said James.

"Will you give up all this, for your stubbornness?"

"I will give all this up for my country," said James.

I can hardly see my writing for the tears. James is so brave. I shudder to think what might become of me if James decides to go off to war.

July 20, 1862

James walked with me today as I fetched the daily mail. I missed our walks since he finished school and was glad to have the opportunity to talk with him about his decision to enlist in the Cavalry. He told me he feels it his duty to do his part. He did not want to be one to stay behind leaving the fighting to others when he is able to go. While I am so proud of him for his sense of duty to our country, I am sad to know that he will be leaving. His being here has made all the difference in how I feel. I do love him so, and I know he loves me too. I will surely worry the whole time he will be gone.

July 30, 1862

News of the war is all around us. The 114th Infantry Regiment was recruited in the neighboring town of Norwich and many men from Oxford have signed to volunteer for that unit. It fills my heart with pride to think that my James has been thinking about joining too, but so far he has not signed papers.

August 30, 1862

James saw the recruiting doctor today – along with everyone else who intended to enlist. He told me about it. I had to laugh. He said he had to take off all his clothes. Then he had to jump, bend over, and kick. The doc checked his chest and back by pounding on it. They even looked in his mouth, checked his teeth and tested his eyesight. I guess he passed because he showed me the certificate he got from the doctor. I almost wished he hadn't passed. Then he would stay here with me. But I am being selfish. I know our country needs all the men that are willing and able to go. Still...

August 31, 1862

James enlisted with the 10th Cavalry today and he is no longer speaking with his father. Now they avoid meeting each other in the house and meals are eaten in uneasy silence. This morning I watched him, from afar, when he signed his name to the list. I am so proud of him and wish that his father was too. We are all still under the same roof, but the tension is now tight as a violin string. I almost wish he would not go. I don't quite know what I will do when he does. But I am being selfish. Our country needs him.

I saw Becka Wells today. She is still in the Fisher household on the other side of town and is my only other friend besides James. She told me her brother is considering enlisting but has not yet signed papers. We so seldom get the same day free from our duties but we will have to try to get together more often now. It will be so lonely without James to talk with and I will surely miss his comforting and loving arms around me. Along with the sweat from the heat in my little third floor room, there are now tears staining my pillow tonight.

September 5, 1862

The town is filled with sadness and with pride. The men of the newly formed 114th Regiment gathered together in Norwich to muster in. Yesterday they left for Binghamton on the canal. James told me that he slipped away last night at midnight to watch the ten boats as they passed through Oxford filled with the regiment. It was so quiet, he said, the men all asleep, the boats making no noise as they passed under the bridge. I pray that they all return safely. James was filled with excitement as he told me. He longs for the time when his regiment gathers to leave. The day will come too soon for me.

September 10, 1862

On our walk today, James and I talked about marriage. We feel it is the right thing to do, but he wants to know how I feel about his leaving for the war. I told him of my misgivings, of missing him, of longing to be in his arms. But I also told him I understand his willingness to serve and won't stand in his way. We promised to write to each other as often as we are able.

He asked if we were to marry, where I would want to live. He does not have any money of his own, and since his estrangement with his father, sees no way of having any until he is paid for his service. I told him I would stay in the house and keep our marriage quiet so that I would not be dismissed. No telling what Mister B would say to our being married given our differences in station and his anger with James.

September 15, 1862

What a glorious day. Mrs. Roberts had the day off and went to spend it with her sister, Mister B was at work and had a late meeting, and the girls were at school. That meant that James and I were in the house alone.

We sat in the parlor, sipping tea and felt as if we were already married. And, wonder of wonders, as our time alone drew to a close he leaned to me and kissed me so tenderly it brought tears to my eyes. I am such a lucky girl. To think that not too long ago, I was miserable, living with my father and now…

September 23, 1862

We did it! We are married. When the Justice of the Peace said those words – and I said "I do" my heart nearly took flight like a freed bird. After our vows we went off together down to the river. I can't believe I have his ring now and wish I could wear it on my finger, but we still must hide our love from his father so I must wear it on a string under my bodice. We still can't risk his father's anger.

Oh happy day, but sad at the same time. We have only a month left together until he must leave with the others to muster in and travel off south to war. I am making James a quilt with material from my old blue day dress so that when he sees it and wraps it around him at night he will think of me.

October 15, 1862

What a gloriously beautiful fall day. We attended a husking bee today at the Fisher Farm on the other side of town. What fun to join with the others to husk the corn – together we were able to fill four hundred bushel baskets. Later in the day, lanterns were hung and food was aplenty. We even played a fun game. Whenever a red corn was found, the finder was entitled to give a kiss. And I was one of the lucky ones. So I went to James and kissed him. He was so surprised. It was our first public kiss. It sure felt good to me.

October 27, 1862

One of my duties today was helping James pack his bags as he gets ready to depart on the canal boat tomorrow. He was issued his clothing two days ago. I was able to slip the finished quilt into one of his bags. I made him a housewife too. He said that's what all the soldiers call the sewing kit. Hopefully it will help him when he needs to do mending of his uniform while he is away. My heart is breaking. I am very proud of him, yes. This is something he is truly committed to doing. I must be as brave as he is when seeing him off tomorrow, but for now, I am afraid tears are spilling onto these pages.

I'm not sure I will sleep tonight. I am praying James will be able to find his way to my room again, so we can be together one last time before he leaves. I'm sure his father is suspicious of us, but I do so want to be in James' arms and have his kiss one last time.

October 28, 1862

Ah, the joys and sadness of this day are almost too much to bear. James came to me last night and we slept wrapped in each other's arms. It was heaven. He slipped away early in the morning and then the whole family - and much of the town - turned out in the town square for the breakfast celebration. The park was filled with people, tables set up all around with food for all to partake and enjoy. So many of our town's young men, and some older ones, too, are leaving today. Boys came from the nearby towns of Coventry, Sherburne, Greene, and McDonough, too.

It will be good for James to be traveling with his school friends - Harris, Charles, and William. James' Uncle Brunson was with them too. As they all climbed aboard the canal boat, the band played "Yankee Doodle" and the "Star Spangled Banner". The ladies all stood alongside the road, waving their hankies, as the men marched by. I called to James and he turned and waved, then joined the others. That's the last I saw of him. My steps are weary now. I can't seem to stop the tears from falling. Thank goodness there are many tears today, so mine didn't seem so out of place. Oh, but how much longer will I be able to hide?

I told James that I would write to him as often as I am able. I am so pleased that one of my duties is to fetch the mail from the post office each day. Mister B would probably want to know why James is writing to me.

Chapter 7
Later that day

The back door slammed. "Mama? Mama, where are you?" Rachel dropped the fragile book in her lap. She had been so engrossed in her reading she'd lost all track of time. Julia was home from school.

"I'm in the living room, Sweetie." Rachel heard her daughter's running footsteps and then the young girl bounded into the room, filled with that energy she always seemed to have at the end of the school day. The girl's long hair had come free from the barrette and fell across her face. Her blue jeans and pink shirt had traces of lunch splattered on them. Hugging her daughter, Rachel shook her head, "Look at you! You're a mess."

"No problem, Mama. It'll come out in the wash, right?" *Ah, yes,* thought Rachel, *never ending laundry in this household.*

"Yes, and you'll help with the wash too," Rachel

said smiling, giving the little girl another squeeze.

Julia reached out to grab the tiny diary from Rachel's lap. "What's that, Mama?" Rachel snatched it up out of reach.

"It's a diary, a very important and fragile book, Julia. Not for you to touch. I was just reading it."

"What's it about?"

"It's about a girl, older than you, who lived a long, long time ago."

"Is it about a Princess?"

"No, it's not about a princess, like most of your other books. This girl wrote about the things she did, so it's a story of her life."

"Can you read it to me, please?" Julia climbed up onto Rachel's lap.

"I need to read it myself first. Remember our rule." Rachel was careful about the books Julia read. Julia had started reading when she was four and could read just about anything, but Rachel worried about the content of the reading material. She didn't let Julia read the newspaper or magazines and monitored the books that Julia took from the library. "But, I promise, as soon as I finish reading it, if it's okay for you to know the story, I'll read it to you."

"Oh, all right. Can I have my snack now?" Julia hopped down. Putting the small diary back inside the wooden box with the letters, Rachel followed her daughter to the kitchen where Julia climbed onto the stool at the counter. Rummaging in the cupboard, Rachel found crackers and spread strawberry jam on them. Cutting an apple she placed all these on a plate and put it in front of Julia. A cup of juice completed the afternoon snack that was a ritual after-school event. Rachel was rummaging through Julia's backpack for notices from school when her cell phone's jingle rang out.

After a quick glance at the phone number, she answered. "Hi, MariBeth, how's things?"

"Great, but I haven't seen you for days. How's it going with you?"

"Ah, coming along. Most of the trash has been taken out and I'm now working on going through some of those new piles I've made – things I need to sort more carefully. Still haven't seen signs of the will, though."

Rachel thought about the diary. For some reason she didn't want to share the diary find with MariBeth yet. Something was holding her back. She felt a certain connection to the diary's author, whoever she was. It was too soon to share the discovery. Rachel guessed that MariBeth would want to take it for the museum, or ask questions she was not ready to answer.

In her usual optimistic way, MariBeth replied, "You still have a lot of places to look – and lots to organize. Want some help poking around?"

"Sure, come on over for dinner and after I get Julia to bed we can look together. Maybe you'll have some ideas."

"Can't wait – see you at six. I'll bring dessert." Rachel closed her phone and slipped it into her pocket. She looked forward to Maribeth's visit.

* * *

Dinner was nothing special, hamburgers and French fries with corn and applesauce. Rachel had long ago decided that making elaborate dinners for her daughter was a waste of precious time. Julia had a limited palette and the risk of a tantrum over dinner forced Rachel to create only those dinners that she knew her daughter would actually eat. Thankfully, MariBeth didn't seem to mind. They sat at the table, munching on their meals, making casual conversation mindful of the five-year-old's presence.

Searching for a safe topic, Rachel asked, "So, what's going on at the museum?"

MariBeth hesitated, and then said, "Well, I usually spend a lot of time working on cataloging and taking care of things that have been donated to the museum. But lately I've begun to work on some new exhibits for an event we have coming up. It's going to take me a few weeks to gather everything from the collection storage room and place it properly to display. Then I have to make the information cards that go with the items. It all takes time."

She turned to Julia, "One of the displays will be about children's toys from long ago. You might like to see some of the old dolls and doll strollers we'll have on display."

"Oh, Mama, can we go? Can we, please?" Julia begged, turning to look at Rachel working on a pot of coffee.

MariBeth laughed. "It's not ready yet, Julia. I'll let your Mama know when it's done. Okay?"

"But I want to go now," she frowned.

"Sorry, honey. There's nothing there to see yet."

"Oh, but when will it be ready?"

Rachel glanced at the time. "Julia, it's time for bed. Go get your jammies on and brush your teeth. You can read in bed for a few minutes until I come up and read to you for a bit."

Distracted from her train of thought, Julia slipped from her seat and took her plate to the sink. Giving MariBeth and Rachel quick hugs, she ran down the hall and upstairs.

Rachel smiled as the little girl scampered away. She was mindful of the tantrums that have taken place lately and was pleased that Julia didn't seem to dwell on them. Jon had been away so much of her young life that having him gone wasn't much different. After attending the group talk the other night, Rachel realized Julia seemed to be handling things quite well. Better than I am, she thought.

* * *

"Nighty-night, Sweetie. Sleep tight." Rachel leaned over, gave Julie a big hug and kissed the end of her nose. She turned on the nightlight and left the door slightly ajar. Downstairs she found MariBeth loading the dishwasher.

"You didn't need to do that... but thanks." Rachel passed her the last of the dishes.

"No problem. Great dinner, by the way, thank you!"

Rachel was grateful her friend didn't expect a gourmet meal. Wiping her hands, Rachel walked down the hall to the living room followed by MariBeth.

"You've done a wonderful job so far with this place, Rach. It seems so much larger since you've removed all the trash and piles that were stashed all over the place."

Rachel nodded. The living room did look bigger. Nonna's overstuffed chair sat in the bay window with her table and lamp nearby. The chair was worn from years of use, the antimacassar on the back hiding the stain from years of Nonna's hair products rubbing against it. The chair had become Rachel's favorite place. From the chair, she could see into the dining room, to the front door, and, through the windows, outside into the front yard. Across from the chair was the television and in the corner the fireplace.

MariBeth pointed, "Have you checked those bookshelves?" Recessed shelves framed the central window on the street side of the room. "From here I see books, folders and just loose papers stored there. The will could be tucked in between."

"No, I haven't checked there yet. I can't imagine Nonna storing such an important paper on those shelves. She paused. "But, I guess it's as good a place as any — let's do it."

* * *

Rachel sighed and wiped a hand across her brow leaving a dirt smudge. "This is so frustrating. Where could Nonna have stashed such an important paper?"

They had worked for a couple of hours. Stuffed between the books were several pages, paper clipped together, that looked promising, but no will was found. She looked at MariBeth and saw her open another book she had taken from the shelf and mumble to herself before carefully replacing it. Rachel had seen her pause and open several, looking at the first page before placing them carefully back on the shelf. *What could be so interesting in those books?*

She was just about to ask when MariBeth stood, wiped her hands on her black slacks leaving a dust trail, and looked at her watch. "Wow, look at the time. I've got to go."

Rachel glanced at the mantel clock and saw that it was nine-thirty. "I didn't realize it had gotten so late. Sorry."

"No problem," MariBeth walked past the bookshelf and turned to eye the books again. "I have a couple of books on antiques that I can bring next time. They might be helpful when you're doing the inventory."

"Sounds great."

"Rachel, you're doing a great job here. Don't be too hard on yourself. I'll talk to you soon."

The two walked to the back door and, with a quick hug, MariBeth left.

Bookshelves forgotten, Rachel's mind returned to the diary. She turned off the lights, locked the doors and carried the wooden box up to her bedroom. She quickly got ready for bed, slipped under the blankets, and brought the diaries and the ribbon-bound letters to her lap.

She decided to set the diary aside for a bit. The girl's entries - the story of James leaving for the war - reminded her of the pain of Jon's departure to Afghanistan. *I need to put those aside for now – and see what's in the letters.*

She untied the faded ribbon and the letters fell free. Each of the light brown envelopes was about three-by-five inches and had a canceled ten-cent stamp on them. They were all addressed to Madam Emma Beardsley, Oxford, New York. Carefully reaching into the opening, she removed the first letter and unfolded the thin pages. It was difficult to read, the pencil writings had faded, but she was able to make out the words. Rachel settled back again and began to read the first letter.

* * *

November 1862
My Dear Emma,

    It has been two weeks since I left you standing on the sidewalk in Oxford and not a day has gone by that I don't think of you. I confess I tried to conceal from you that my heart was breaking. Thinking of leaving you for such a long time, especially with our vows so recently exchanged, has been painful.

    After that amazing send off from the folks in town, we boarded the boat. I could see you waving to me as we left the dock. Could you see me sitting near my friends? After the boat got underway, we got to talkin'. Harris told me of his new girlfriend, Margaret. He told me he had a hard time saying goodbye to her. I told him about you, Emma, but had him promise to keep it a secret for now. Charles mentioned his sister, Adeline, who is newly married, had traveled to our town to see us depart. He saw her in the crowd, waving us goodbye, then turning to her husband and crying on his shoulder. William kept his hat pulled down low on his head and didn't say much. I could tell he was having a hard time leaving his home and family but did not feel like sharing.

    We traveled quietly along the canal all day stopping briefly in Greene after seven long hours.

While some got to sleep, it was a tiring trip for me. I am not used to being in such close quarters with noisy sleepers. The chorus of snoring, snuffling, moaning and groaning kept me from falling asleep. I know I shall have to get used to this as I left behind my comfortable bed and quiet room. I must have slept some because I was startled awake after the seemingly endless journey ended in Binghamton some ten hours later and we bumped into the dock. We were told to stay aboard the boats until morning when we were ordered to march to the barracks for breakfast. There we were met by some townsfolk and they cheered for us, waving flags and singing songs just like the folks in Oxford. After eating, we marched again to the depot to await the arrival of the train. We took the cars to Elmira. The train ride was not a long one, thankfully, because it was very dirty and a tight fit in the boxcars. When we arrived we disembarked, gathered our belongings, and made our way to muster in.

So we are now officially Company K of the 10th New York Cavalry. Do you remember me telling you of Wheaton Loomis? Before joining up he ran the packet boat on the Canal for a time, and before that he was a farmer. He is now our Captain. I think he will be a kindly officer. He is always ready with a greeting for me and the other boys from Oxford. He is the same age as Uncle Brunson, who is our Sergeant. It is comforting to have a relative nearby, but I must remember not to call him Uncle. I know Uncle Brunson will be as good an officer as he was a teacher. He often helped me with my studies. Even though he lived in the next town, we would travel there often to visit and he would ask how my schooling was going. I was grateful for his kind words and assistance then and I am grateful he is here now.

We got our clothes pretty quickly and, so far, have had good food, and comfortable quarters here in Elmira. We were also given a weapon, a haversack of food, a canteen and a rubber sheet. They told us the sheet is used to keep the damp earth away from us when we sleep or as a raincoat in a storm. Since I have not done any sleeping outdoors I must take their word for it.

After getting our gear, we boarded the cars again for Washington, where we stopped for a bit before the train continued on to Alexandria. We finally arrived there on the 2nd of November. The weather is warmer here than at home, which is quite welcome since we were only given some Virginia dirt upon which to set up our beds. I was grateful for your quilt. Adding it to the one blanket we were given kept me warm all night.

Unfortunately, the food is not as good as what we left behind. The meat we were given today was crawling with all sorts of critters and we complained mightily. Someone said that the pork was so animated that it could walk off in the middle of the night. After the camp commander heard, he had it replaced with fresh meat, thank goodness. The other food we have is a thin flour-and-water biscuit called hardtack. Some of these I found so hard it can almost break my teeth. I learned to soak the hardtack in water and then fry it in pork fat. Some found theirs to be moldy. But the worst of the hardtack has weevils in them. When we soak it in coffee, the weevils float and can be skimmed off. I know what you are thinking. You find it difficult to know I left the good cooking of Mrs. Roberts for this. I agree. I surely do miss home cookin'. I am hoping you will send me a box with some jam, milk, maybe chocolates, and anything else you think would pack well.

Yes, I have been very busy, but you are still in my thoughts each day. I do so miss you Emma, and pray that you are faring well. Please do write often. I long to hear the news from home and you must tell me how you spend your days.

Your loving husband,
James

* * *

Rachel took a deep breath and carefully inserted the letter back in its envelope. She felt chills run up and down her spine. Now she knew the names of the two people. The diary belongs to Emma Beardsley and the letters were written by her husband, James. *But how did these come to be here in this house? Why would Nonna have them? Can these people actually have lived here? Are they distant relatives? Oh why did there have to be so many unanswered questions? I wish I knew about these before Nonna died. I could have asked her about them.*

She realized by keeping an eye on the dates and alternating the reading of the letters and diary entries, it would give her a more complete story. She couldn't wait to read more. Glancing at her bedside clock she realized it was not too late. Excited to continue, she reached for the next letter in the bundle and read.

Chapter 8
December – January 1862

December 15, 1862
My Dear Emma,

I have not received a letter from you for days. I know that it is not unusual, but I look forward to getting your letters so much - I watch for each delivery. We are on the move south and perhaps the mail has yet to catch up with us. I pray these words find you in good health and you are in good spirits.

Is my father worrying you? I know the situation in the house must not be a pleasant one, but you must make the best of it. Father will surely be even more upset than he was when I enlisted if he finds out about our marriage. I have not yet received a letter from him, and even if he does write, I have no desire to correspond with him. I still have not forgiven him for the ugly words he spoke. I don't know if I ever will.

Since my last writing, we went across the Potomac to get our horses in Washington. They were a fine lot of animals. I was assigned a dark chestnut Morgan just fourteen hands tall with strong muscles. He has an easy temperament and so far we get along famously. I have named him Buckley.

Unfortunately, the eight-mile ride back to Alexandria was without a saddle and I ended up with blisters on my rear parts. I was not alone though. You should have seen the men hobbling about. What a sight!

On the 2nd we left to join the rest of the regiment at Brook's Station, in Virginia. When we got there three days later and were greeted with a snowstorm. We had little protection from the elements - just that rubber sheet, remember? I was so cold and miserable. I even saw some of the men dismount and walk to prevent their feet from freezing. We had little sleep and by the time we returned on the 9th we had spent three days in the saddle. I am so sore .

The very next morning our Company detached from the Regiment and was ordered to General Vanderbilt, an infantry unit. Now I hear comments all the time from the infantrymen. They seem to think that we, who are in the cavalry, have a much easier time of it because we ride all day. Well, I tell you, the only difference to me is the part that gets sore - instead of their feet, it's our bottoms. Oh, I suppose it is easier for us a bit. We do get to hang our gear on the saddle instead of carrying it all on our backs.

Emma, you would have found it humorous to see the boys try to gather their things and find places on the horses for all their belongings. When the order came to move out, some of them, in their enthusiasm, put spurs to their horses' sides and then found themselves galloping along, losing their belongings left and right. My friend, Oscar, forgot to tighten the cinches of his saddles properly, so as the horse ran, the saddles slipped, and so did he. I couldn't help but laugh. Men and horses were all over, not in the neat and tidy marching order of four across that was expected. The officers were not amused.

I am anxious to know the news of home. How are Ella and Ida doing? What do you hear of my little cousin, Merritt? In your last letter, you mentioned he was sickly. I pray that he is well and as feisty as always.

I need to finish now and get this in the next post. Write back as soon as you are able.

Your loving husband,
James

* * *

December 20, 1862

Some days I have trouble deciding how much to write in my letters to James. In his last letter, he wanted to know about his little cousin. I'm afraid the news I tell will not be good for him to hear. The poor little boy, only eight years old, took his last breath last week. James told me he was always such a healthy and happy lad. Seems the sickness came quickly and his Pa and Doc Farland could do nothing to keep him from death. Now he rests in a grave his Pa made for him in the cemetery on the hill. Story I hear is that Merritt was afraid of the dark and on his death bed requested of his Pa that a window be put in his grave so he would not be in the dark. Those who attended the funeral tell that the stone slabs of the grave are arranged so there's a small window facing east which allows the morning sun to shine in. Even though I did not know Merritt, I am saddened by his passing. Such a sad tale to tell James.

* * *

December 20, 1862
My Dear Emma,

Since writing my last letter we have been very busy moving around. Mile after mile we ride and just when I think I cannot go another step, we hear the bugle call for us to halt and dismount. Sometimes we are in the saddle so long that when I get down from my horse I can barely stand. In recent days we traveled south to Fredericksburg. On December 11th, after we halted, I watched as men worked to lay five pontoon bridges across the Rappahannock River. I never saw the like before. They took flat boats and placed them side by side across the river, and then laid planks on top of them so the rest of the units could cross the river. It was a dangerous affair because all the while the men were working they were under fire from the Rebels from their side of the city of Fredericksburg. On the 12th, the army crossed over the bridges and into the city. Although the rest of the regiment went, our Company and Company L were not involved so we did not cross.

The morning of the 13th started foggy, but when it cleared the battle in Fredericksburg raged. All day, from our side of the river, we listened to the sounds of the guns and cannons and saw the clouds of smoke rise above the battlefield.

Later that night, Jonas and I were talking. He overheard some of the infantrymen telling of the great battle in the city. So many on our side lost their lives in that battle as line after line of them tried to take Prospect Hill and Marye's Heights and were met by a barrage of bullets from the entrenched Rebels behind the wall. It is times like these that I feel grateful that I am a part of the cavalry rather than the infantrymen who were engaged in the battle across the river. Our unit was kept in reserve and did not participate in the battle.

That night we also heard that our commander, Brigadier General Bayard, was severely injured in his leg. Word going around is that he declared to the doctor he did not want to live without a leg, and so he declined amputation, and subsequently died. I was saddened to learn that he had been preparing for his wedding and had leave papers ready in his pocket. How sad is that!

Colonel David McMurtrie Gregg was promoted to take his place. We can only pray that he will be as good a leader as General Bayard. After the battle the men around here have become very despondent. Morale has been very low of late. Many of the men had endured battles before I arrived and most of the battles so far have been with Generals that seem to lead into defeat instead of an uplifting victory. Amos told me he heard deserters are many.

Today I also heard a tale about a new communication devise being used here. Seems a gentleman with the same last name as me invented a telegraph of sorts. I don't understand how it works. I heard that the wires were extended over the river into Fredericksburg. General Burnside was able to send messages, through the fog and smoke of the burning town during the battle, to his commanders and supply base over seven miles away. I do not know if this person, George Beardslee, is a relative but it would be an odd thing if it was so. His son, Frederick, is said to be in the Signal Corps that is using the Beardslee telegraph machine. I would surely like to see it in action, but I know that will never happen.

Our camp is very uneasy tonight and I have no idea what is to happen tomorrow. I shall finish *this letter and get it in the post so that I might try to get some sleep.*

Your loving husband,
James

* * *

December 25, 1862

Christmas Day morning has arrived and I find I have some time to myself after working extra long yesterday for Mister B and the girls in preparation for the festivities today. The town is celebrating the day, even though there is a war going on. The Fire Company held a festival and all the donations they collected today will go to the sick and wounded soldiers.

I hear that some of the celebrations will be muted to respect those killed. Some in town will be sad knowing a husband or a father or a brother would not be coming home. I am not celebrating today at all. I live in fear that I may hear similar news of James and I dread the day. I have no cheer today, so I will spend it here in my lonely room.

I do so wish that James were with me on this holiday sharing the warmth of my bed instead of miles away sleeping in a tent. I pray that the box I sent has reached him all in one piece and that he enjoys the chocolates I was able to pack inside. I have written him another letter which must be posted tomorrow.

I have not been feeling well lately. My usual bowl of porridge has not set well for several mornings now. And I can hardly sip my tea. I fear that I am taken ill as little Merritt was and hope this will pass soon.

* * *

December 25, 1862
Fredericksburg, VA
My Dear Emma,

Merry Christmas, my dearest wife. I pray that you are well and that these few lines will find you in good spirits on this holiday. I would have liked to be there with you but it is not to be. I did get your box for which I thank you. When I opened it, the food and supplies that you packed filled me with such joy. What a delicious treat it is, especially the chocolates. Tonight I am going to share some of the jam with Amos. Do you remember me telling you of him? He's the farmer from Unadilla three years older than me who shares my tent. He is a likable chap and we often spend time discussing our families. Yesterday we had our likenesses taken by one of the traveling photographers. We had one taken together. When you get them, you'll be able to tell he's two inches taller than me. He has blue eyes, brown hair and fair complexion, just like his two brothers, he tells me.

I am so pleased you sent the tintype you had taken. I shall keep it with me always. You look so pretty, I can see the twinkle in your eyes even though you did not smile for the photographer. How I long to run my fingers through your long brown hair after removing the pins to let it fall free.

Remember me telling you about the battle in Fredericksburg? This war is so strange at times. Two days after battle was done, after the fierce battle in which hundreds of men were maimed or killed, a flag of truce went up. Both sides, us and the Rebs, went out into the field with the task of getting wounded removed. What a sight to see. The same men, who had just been in battle together, were now in the same field shaking hands and talking. To celebrate Christmas some of our men even traded coffee, tobacco, and sugar with the Rebs. What an amazing sight to see.

Since then the nights have been dark and it has been raining off and on for a couple of days. I have been soaked to the skin most of the time. During the week after the Fredericksburg battle, we had picket duty in and around Stafford County here in Virginia. While we were on picket duty, we were able to obtain fresh meat and vegetables from the nearby farmers and even slept indoors in deserted homes on occasion. I can hear you are asking what picket duty might be? It is when we go out ahead of our camp, form a line, and watch for any signs of the Rebs. It is tiring duty, sometimes wet and miserable, and always dangerous. We are not permitted to remove our weapons, nor sleep. We never know when a Reb might come creeping up, or a sharpshooter aim in our direction.

On the 23rd, we moved to camp near Belle Plain Landing on the Potomac Creek near Falmouth in Virginia. We are told this is where we will be staying through the winter. To honor the General, we are calling it Camp Bayard. We commenced chopping down trees and built small log huts. The sides are chinked with mud, and we hang tents over a ridgepole for a roof. It has a stone fireplace at one end, and a short doorway opening at the other. On either side of the doorway, Amos and I place blankets for our beds. My little hut is quite comfortable, though a far cry from my spacious room back home. If I close my eyes and ignore the snores coming from Amos and the clatter of sounds coming from beyond the hut walls, I can almost imagine I am in my own bed in Oxford.

Emma, I wish you would write to me as soon as you get this letter. I cannot wait to hear from you and know how you are faring. What is the news of Oxford? Can you tell me anything of my sisters? I miss them almost as much as I miss you, dear wife.

Your loving husband,
James

* * *

December 30, 1862

Mrs. Roberts left in tears today. Before she went she took me aside and gave me a warning about

Mister B. She told me he had been inappropriately forward with her and wanted me to be careful that he might do the same with me. I am sad to see Mrs. Roberts leave. She has been almost like a mother to me. I can only hope that whoever replaces her is as kind.

I shall certainly be wary of Mister B. We have not had much interaction since James left, and to my mind that is all for the best. He has not said anything to me about a new housekeeper, but I am sure one will be hired quickly. I cannot do it all.

I cannot imagine James sleeping in such a small hut. This house has so much space that we are fairly lost in it at times.

* * *

Rachel ran a hand across her aching head, glanced at her clock and saw two hours had passed. It was now midnight. She'd become so engrossed in the lives of Emma and James and wanted desperately to continue reading, but forced herself to turn off the light. She rolled over and closed her eyes.

She stood with Jon at airport security. She knew she couldn't go past those screening machines, much as she wanted. Tears streamed down her cheeks, her arms wrapped tightly around him hoping to postpone the separation as long as she could. She felt the strength of his arms through the coarseness of his uniform.

"It will be the last tour – I promise." He kissed her gently, aware of his surroundings and of the wide-eyed daughter looking up at them. Two year old Julia had her thumb securely in her mouth. He gently released Rachel, stepped back, bent down and hugged his daughter.

"I will see you soon too, Pumpkin. You be a good girl for Mama!" He stood, turned, and with Rachel watching, he mounted the horse standing there, and with a touch of his spurs to the horse, he galloped off through security.

"Papa, wait!" Julia dashed down the dirt road after her father.

"Julia, don't!" Rachel screamed, racing after her.

Chapter 9
The next morning

She woke with a start, breathing hard, her hands clutching the blankets. Looking around she realized where she was and shook her head – the mixed-up dream already fading. She moaned. The feelings and memory of Jon in his uniform leaving for war was so close to Emma's story, she felt a certain connection to the girl from the past.

The clock on the nightstand read eight-thirty. She'd forgotten to set the alarm. Good thing it was a school vacation day, she thought. Morning had come much too quickly, another rainy, cold day that fit perfectly with how she felt inside. Rolling over and tucking the quilt under her chin, she mentally ran through the list of chores that needed to be done – continue the house inventory, clean the house. *Oh, and find that darn will.* Not necessarily in that order.

But all she really wanted to do was cuddle under the quilt with a cup of tea and read the letters and diary. She still wondered if she had some sort of connection to these people. *How can I learn about them? Maybe MariBeth will have an idea.* Again she realized how much she has been depending on her new friend. She made a mental note to come up with a way to repay her.

She heard the rain and looked at the window. With a groan, she swung her legs off the bed and glanced out the rain spattered window. The view of the backyard reminded her of all the work that needed to be done outside as well as inside. Dressing quickly in a faded sweat suit, she slipped on a ratty pair of sneakers ready to tackle another area of the house.

Hearing her daughter quietly playing in her room, she called, "Julia, are you dressed yet?" She walked down the hallway and stopped at the doorway to her daughter's room and found the answer to her question. She was still in her nightgown.

"Julia, what are you doing?" Rachel looked with dismay at the stacks of old books strewn around on the floor. Aside from a twin bed, and a dresser, Julia's room had an oak shelf that held a collection of old books. Since Nonna's death, Rachel had cleaned the room of the usual clutter that had been found all throughout the house. While she'd cleaned the room, she had ignored the four shelves of books.

Julia was seated in front of the bookshelf with a book in her hands. She turned to look at her mother. "I'm sorting the books, Mama. I heard you looking at books downstairs last night with MariBeth. I thought I could help." She turned back to the bookshelf and pointed to the top shelf. The books there were all the same size. "I'm putting them back in order, see." Julia smiled and watched as her mother's face broke out into a wide grin.

"Ah, that's my girl! You like order just like me!" Rachel reached into the pile of books. "What goes next, do you think."

"Let's do the extra big ones." Julia found three books that were the same size and Rachel helped add them to the pile.

There was a bulge in the back of one of the books. Rachel could see several folded pages. Mindful that the papers could damage the book, she opened it and removed the pages. Her eyes widened with surprise. The outside fold of the page said, "Last will and testament." *Nonna's will, at last.*

Rachel stood, grasped the will to her chest, then knelt and gave Julia a big squeeze. "Julia, you did it!"

"What did I do, Mama?" Julia squeezed back, and then squirmed out of Rachel's arms.

"You found Nonna's will – a very important piece of paper. I have been looking for this for days – and here it was all along."

"Did I help?"

"Oh, you sure did help! Thank you." Rachel gave the girl another hug.

Julia wriggled free, stood and grabbed her favorite teddy bear. "Bear and I are hungry. Can we have some breakfast?"

Rachel said, "You sure can. You both deserve it." She turned and followed Julia and Bear down the stairs and into the kitchen. "After breakfast we can finish putting the books on the shelf."

Rachel scrambled eggs, made the toast, and poured juice, while Julia poured an imaginary cup for

Bear.

With Julia settled at the kitchen table, Rachel walked into the living room. Armed with a cup of coffee, Rachel reached for her cell and dialed the lawyer's office. She didn't want to read the will until Neil Walker agreed.

"Law office, Patsy speaking, how may I help you?"

"Hello, Patsy, this is Rachel Benton. Can I make an appointment to speak with Mr. Walker today?"

There was a hesitation, and then Patsy said, "It's his short day. He usually leaves early for practice, but he has an opening this afternoon at two, will that do?"

"That's just fine. I'll need to bring my daughter – it's a school vacation day today. Will that be all right?"

"No problem. She can stay in the outer office with me while you're meeting with Mr. Walker."

"Thanks so much. We'll see you at two."

Rachel snapped the phone shut and set it into her pocket. Things were looking up today, she thought. Now what shall we do with the rest of the morning? Ah, perhaps the basement. I haven't touched that so far. It's a good choice for today.

She walked back to the kitchen and said to Julia, "How would you like to help me with an adventure this morning? Bear can come along, too."

"Where are we going, Mama?"

"To the basement!" She tried to sound excited about the plan to entice her daughter into cooperating. "We can do all sorts of exploring there and see what we can find."

Julia frowned, "Umm… will there be bugs? I

don't like bugs."

Rachel nodded. "I don't like bugs either or spider webs. You can swat at them with the broom. And I'll bring some bug spray and a flashlight too. Let's finish breakfast first, do those books in your room, and then we can go downstairs."

Chapter 10
Same Day

Armed with garbage bags, cleaning cloths and a broom Rachel opened the door to the basement. She really hated basements and avoided them as much as possible. Dirty, dank and damp, they almost always were covered with webs. This first foray down the stairs was everything she expected. She could see old dust covered spider webs festooning the ceiling rafters. *Ugh!* Using the broom to swat them away, Rachel led the way down the stairs. Julia followed with Bear in a pail.

The single, bare bulb didn't give much light to the large space. The two small windows were partially blocked by the well outside and didn't add much more light. The room was partially finished, with the old furnace and hot water heater behind an incomplete partition in one corner along the near wall. Pipes and ductwork were everywhere, and the ceiling joists were held up by old railroad ties. *Was that typical of architecture in the late 1800s?* Rachel thankfully noticed that in some places additional metal supports had been added.

Rounding another partition in the middle of the room, toward the back, there was a ladder which went through the ceiling to the floor above. *Now that's curious. I haven't seen a sign of that ladder on the upper floors.* She wanted to climb that ladder to see where it led, but set aside her curiosity for now – there was too much to be done today before she could take on another task or satisfy her curiosity.

The cement floor was covered with dirt and debris and more piles of stuff. While Julia swatted with the broom at bugs, seen and unseen, Rachel began to sort and discard. Bags full of trash began to accumulate at the foot of the stairs. Along one wall, old worn shelves held a jumble of old bottles, crockery and jugs. She had no idea if they had any value, so with a quick dusting, she decided to leave them be for now.

Rachel paused and looked around again with a sense of accomplishment. It felt so good to get the place in order. And she found that she was actually enjoying the de-cluttering. She felt such a rush of exhilaration as she tossed the first few bags into the trash. Just as with the rooms upstairs, she felt as if a physical weight was coming off her shoulders as she cleaned each room. Much of the house was clear of the clutter now. Gone were the old medicines, junk mail, old newspapers, flyers, pamphlets, bottles, and containers that could never be reused.

"Mama! Come here. Look what I found." Julia's muffled voice came from behind an open door at the far end of the room. Rachel crossed the expanse of the basement and walked into the small room to find Julia kneeling on the floor – face smudged with dirt, her shirt and pants filthy. Under her hands was a small ten-inch square slab of white marble.

Rachel knelt beside her daughter. "Be careful with that. Let me see." Taking a damp cloth, Rachel cleaned the dirty, chipped stone, and reached out to gently touch the letters that appeared. She sat back in wonder, "Wow!"

"What is it Mama?"

"It looks like a little gravestone." Her forehead was furrowed with curiosity. *Okay, now why would this be here in the house? Nonna, what is going on here?*

Julia read, "CORNELIA JANE, daughter of." She paused and looked at Rachel. "It looks like Papa and Nonna's stones. Is somebody buried here?" She looked at the dirt under her hands and rubbed them on her shirt. "I don't like this."

"Let's not touch anything else here. I can't tell for sure, but you're right, it does look like the top part of a headstone. The rest seems to be missing." She looked around but didn't see any more of the stone. "It looks like it's been here a long, long time."

"Can I have it, Mama? I wanna bring it to my room."

"No, let's just leave it here for now. We'll have to ask MariBeth to help us find out more about it. In the meantime, come out of there. There's nothing else down here for us to work on today. Let's get those trash bags up the stairs."

Julia stood and grabbed Bear, who seemed to

have collected as much dirt and grime as the little girl.

"I'm hungry. Is it time for lunch?"

Glancing at her watch, Julia realizing that the morning had flown and it was already noon. "It sure is, Sweetie. We'll need to clean up, and then we can go to Margo's Diner for lunch. I have an appointment this afternoon, and maybe afterward we'll go to the library."

"Yay, can I get some more books?"

"Sure can. And you can pick a video, too."

Rachel gently set the stone back onto the dirt, turned and followed her daughter up the stairs, a trash bag in each hand. *Now there's another mystery in Nonna's life. I wonder what else I'll find in this house.*

Chapter 11
That afternoon

An hour later, mother and daughter entered Margo's Diner looking much more presentable. Rachel was dressed in khaki slacks and a navy blouse. She'd spent more time than usual standing in her closet trying to select an outfit. She didn't want to think why that might be. The upcoming meeting with Neil Walker couldn't be the reason, she told herself. Julia didn't have such troubles. She'd chosen her purple tights and pink dress, her favorite colors.

The diner was busy, filled with moms and their school-age children. Rachel found a table in the corner and, when the busy waitress arrived, ordered lunch. As they waited for it, Julia worked on coloring the child's place mat. Rachel's mind wandered, then settled on a nearby conversation she had been overhearing for a minute. Two older women were seated at the next table. Rachel recognized them as acquaintances of her grandmother. Sarah O'Neil and Lilly Robeson. The ladies' blue-gray hairstyles made it look like the two had just come from the beauty salon next door. Although they spoke quietly, their voices could be readily heard.

"Didn't you hear the news on the radio this morning, Sarah?" She leaned forward, arms resting on the table.

"No, I haven't had time to listen. What did you hear?" Lilly moved her chair closer to the table.

"Two more houses were broken into yesterday. They said it happened along the Woodham Road. Isn't that near you?"

"Oh, goodness. Yes, that is close to me. I hope the police find whoever is doing it quickly. I'm not going to be able to sleep."

"What's happening to our town?" Sarah shook her head. "We've never had to worry about locking our doors before. Now I lock everything."

"I've never been fearful of living alone before… but now? I'll certainly be locking my doors from now on."

The waitress stopped at Sarah and Lilly's table interrupting the conversation. Rachel wondered how close Woodham Road was to her grandmother's house. *Should I be concerned? I'm going to have to listen to the local news more often.* Rachel felt comfortable in this new town, so different from the loud bustle of the much bigger, impersonal city of Oakland. She was enjoying the quiet, calmness, the beauty of the small town. And Julia had settled into the school quite easily, even though she'd had trouble, the kids were kind. She hoped this news wouldn't change her mind about Oxford.

* * *

After lunch, Rachel, with Julia in tow, crossed the Square and entered the lawyer's office promptly at two. The outer office was empty again. Today the perky Miss Lee was wearing a lime green top with mesh stockings under a too-short black skirt. Stiletto boots completed the outfit, such as it was. Rachel forced herself not to stare at Patsy in this new wild outfit. This one could use the intervention from the reality show, *What Not to Wear*. Although Rachel didn't go in for the designer's styles, at least she would suggest Patsy wear more conservative clothes befitting a law office.

Patsy looked up at Rachel and said with a smile, "You're right on time, Mrs. Benton. Mr. Walker is waiting for you." Patsy came from behind her desk and knelt before Julia. "And who are you?"

Julia hid herself behind Rachel's leg. Reaching behind, Rachel gently maneuvered her in front. "This is my daughter, Julia."

"Hello, Julia," said Patsy. "Would you like to help me with some papers out here while your Mama talks inside with Mr. Walker?

Julia looked for encouragement from her mother, and then silently nodded.

Patsy said to Rachel, "I've got a four-year-old nephew. Julia will be fine with me."

Rachel nodded, and to Julia said, "It'll be okay. I'll be right inside that door." Rachel crouched down and said to her daughter, "You be good." She reached into her ever-present tote bag. "Here's your sticker book."

"Okay, Mama." Julia took the book and sat in one of the office chairs.

Patsy gestured to the inner door, "You can go right in, Mrs. Benton."

"Thanks."

Rachel opened the door and stopped short. Neil Walker was standing, back to the door, sword in hand, poised in *en guard* position attacking an unseen opponent. He was dressed in loosely fitting pants, and an overlarge white shirt with billowing sleeves. A vest and fringed boots completed the outfit. A matching hat covered his long hair flowing down his back almost to his shoulders. Both he and his secretary needed an intervention in appropriate clothing, Rachel thought. She stifled a laugh, "Oh, dear. Is it safe?"

He whirled around, face turning red. Then, with a flourish he bowed and said, "Ah yes, milady, you are quite safe." He propped the sword at the end of his desk, pointed to a chair and said, "Sit. Please."

Rachel sat in the same chair she'd occupied the last visit. "I hope you'll have good news for me?"

"Not at all curious about that sword or my outfit are you?" He raised his brow, pointing to the sword, a grin on his face.

She smiled in return, feeling her own face reddening. "Oh, I'm curious all right. I'm just not one to question people. If you want to tell me what you were doing, you'd tell me, right?" Though, she admitted, he made quite a dashing figure in his clothes. Her fingers itched to run through his long, flowing hair. *What am I thinking? Jon hasn't been gone long, and here I am, with a body aching for this man.* She realized he'd been talking.

"… so I joined a re-enactment group called the Society of Creative Anachronism. We're like Civil War re-enactors, except we immerse ourselves in the Middle Ages and Renaissance era researching and then recreating that time period in history." He pointed to the illuminated documents hanging on the wall. "I did those."

She stood and walked over to get a closer look. "I noticed them last time I was here. They're beautiful."

"It took me months to learn the calligraphy, and then to use the gold leaf to embellish it. Now I'm responsible for creating those reward documents for others in our group." He paused. "I have sword practice later this afternoon. Thus the outfit. I'm also getting ready for the Renaissance Faire that begins next month. It runs on weekends during the summer." He paused again, looking at her. "You should go, and take Julia. She'd love it."

She shrugged, "Maybe I will, once I get the house and estate more in order."

"Ah, yes. You certainly are focused!" He moved to take his seat behind his desk.

"I have to be, right now. My daughter and I have nowhere else to go and no money, so resolving this issue as quickly as possible is important to me." Rachel reached into her tote bag once again, removed the will and handed it to the attorney.

"I understand. Let's see…" Neil took the papers, opened them carefully and began to read. "Ah, this is pretty straight forward. Your grandmother named your mother as the executor. Since your mother has died, and there is no one else in your family, we will have to apply to the probate court for you to be appointed as administrator *cum testament annexo*."

"What was that?"

Neil smiled. "Oh, I know – legalese. All it means is administrator with the will changed. The change being made means someone other than the named executor will act as such. The court gives preference to family members, so this should be pretty straight forward."

"How long will that take?" Rachel frowned; worry beginning to settle in her stomach again.

"We'll begin the process right now. You sign some papers and an affidavit that attests to your being her granddaughter. Then I'll send the paperwork and the will to the probate office. Once they receive the papers, it should take only about a couple of weeks or so."

Rachel groaned. What will she do for money in the meantime? She was hoping to begin to sell some smaller things to have money to live on. "Can I borrow money from the estate?"

"Unfortunately, no, that's not possible, not yet. You will need to be named as the estate's personal representative first. If you need something in the meantime, you might consider going to the bank to get a loan to hold you over."

Rachel felt sick to her stomach and hung her head down looking at her hands and the ring on her finger. Once more she felt angry with Jon. *Why? Why would you leave us like this?* She didn't think the bank would consider her for a loan. She was new to town and didn't have any collateral. *What do I do now? What about all those bills stacked up? Will the bank foreclose on Nonna's house too?*

Tears threatened. She fought hard to contain them.

"Rachel? Are you okay?" His voice was filled with concern, eyes worried.

The sound of his voice, filled with sympathy, was her undoing. Tears spilled down her cheeks. He pushed a box of tissues across his desk to her, and came around from behind. He reached his arm to her, concern evident on his face. She held her hand up, shook her head and he stopped in his tracks.

"I'm sorry."

"Rachel, it's okay. You've been through a great deal. All this is a lot to handle." He paused, his voice quieted. "I heard about your husband."

Rachel looked into his eyes and saw only caring.

"Yes, he died just before we came here." She told him about Jon's death, about going to a divorce attorney, about losing her house, the trip across the country, everything. He listened quietly, without interrupting. She sat back in her chair when she finished, exhausted.

"If only I had forced him to get some help. If only I had stayed home that day. If only…"

"Rachel…" he reached for her and again she stopped him.

"No… I need to think of Julia right now, and what I need to do to keep her safe." She looked up and, with a quivering voice, asked, "I found a pile of unopened mail around my grandmother's house. When I opened it all, I gathered all the bills and added them up. The amount is staggering. What do I do with those?"

He returned to his seat behind his desk. "They can wait. Once named administrator, you'll have the authority to pay any outstanding bills your grandmother might have from the estate's assets."

"What else will I need to do after I'm named administrator?"

"You've already taken care of the first step by handling the funeral arrangements. You'll be able to pay for it from the estate. You'll place a notice in the local paper, telling one and all that if they have a claim on your grandmother, for outstanding loans, for example, then they can come forward. You'll need to organize your grandmother's important documents. That includes her social security information, tax returns and bank statements. You'll need to find her birth and marriage certificates. You should check with the bank to make sure she doesn't have a safety deposit box. Check into life insurance, pensions and other potential sources of income. Oh, and you'll need to make an inventory of all her assets so it can be filed with the probate court. Once a period of time passes, you'll file the final tax return and be done."

Rachel sat back in her chair, overwhelmed by the news, "Whew, I had no idea it was so involved."

He turned to the file cabinet behind his desk, reached into his files and took out a brochure. Handing it to her, he said, "It's all laid out here."

She took the booklet. "Thanks, I guess."

"Rachel," he started, leaning forward, "do you have enough money to get by for now? I could lend you some, if you need it."

She was surprised, and dismayed. "Oh, I think I have enough to last for a couple more weeks. But, thank you. I'll keep it in mind should I need it." She looked into his eyes again, saw concern, and more. Her heart fluttered, but she didn't want to think what it all might mean. Not now.

He nodded, reached for a business card from the holder on his desk, wrote on the back, and handed it to her, "Here's my cell phone number. Give me a call, anytime, Rachel."

She took the card, "Thanks, Neil."

He smiled and cleared his throat, "Well, let's get those papers signed."

* * *

Ten minutes later, hand in hand, Julia and Rachel left the lawyer's office. As they walked to the library, she couldn't help but notice the material of the sidewalk. Not the usual concrete, the sidewalks were made of some sort of slate stone material with a bluish tinge. Rachel remembered the blue and gold sign at the end of the town Square. It mentioned the bluestone quarries that were vital to the history of the town. *Is that what these sidewalks are made of? They certainly have character. I'm going to have to find out more.*

They reached the library. According to the sign in front, it was built in 1809, was once the home of Theodore Burr and was donated to the town in memory of his wife. A modified Italianate home trimmed in white Victorian gingerbread, it was three stories, with white railings outlining the porches on the first and second floors. Two tall windows balanced each side of the main, ground floor entrance.

The cupola at the top was also framed with railings and two chimneys rose from the roof on each end. Pushing open the front door, Rachel could feel herself walking back in time. Even though it was now filled with books and modern equipment, she could imagine what it was like as a single family home.

Inside, the first floor had a main central room with rows of shelves stacked with books. At one end, a smaller room held the children's books. Brightly decorated with primary colors, the shelves were appropriately smaller, books within reach of even the smallest child. The other end of the main room held the computer and research area. Shelf signs there indicated the books were not to be removed from the library. The computer stations were neatly arranged on individual tables, with wooden sides offering privacy for patrons. Most of the times Rachel had come here, the library was not busy, but today, a school holiday, the place was bustling with parents and children.

Ahead at the circulation desk, Jen Frasier, the librarian, sat absorbed with her work. She looked to be about sixty, had short, silver wavy hair and wore her reading glasses halfway down her nose. Nearby two young teen pages were moving carts loaded with books ready to be re-shelved.

Rachel turned to Julia, "Go ahead and find some books and a video, then come back to me. I'll be at the computers."

"Okay, Mama." She skipped off, her library tote bag hanging from her shoulder.

Rachel stood in front of the circulation desk. "Excuse me."

Ms. Frasier glanced up, "Yes, how may I help you?"

"I'm trying to do some research on the house I'm living in. Is there anything here that can help me?"

"There are a couple of ways to research information about the homes and people who lived in town in the past. The local history section is over there," she pointed to the shelves along the east wall. "You can start there. And you might also want to check with the town historian or the local historical society." She rummaged through a nearby stack of papers, found one and slid it across the desk to Rachel. "Here's the information about the Society's meeting times and contact information."

"Thank you." Rachel walked to the shelf indicated by the librarian, browsed the shelf and took a couple books that looked promising to a nearby table. Opening *Architecture in Oxford* she found photos of many of the houses in town. There was the federal style house down the street built in 1836 and a classic revival built in 1855. Then, turning the page, she found Nonna's house. The caption said, "The Applebee house is set away from the road, and backs to the Chenango Canal. It was said to have been a station on the Underground Railroad. It has a ladder extending through an upstairs closet from the cellar to the attic, where the slaves were hidden."

That's Nonna's house, thought Rachel. She'd found the ladder in the basement. She was going to have to follow it up and see where it led. This is getting so exciting, she thought. So many connections to the past. No mention of a gravestone, though.

That's still a mystery. How she wished Nonna was still alive. She would know the answers.

Rachel went to the nearest computer station, started a search on Oxford history, and found a website with information about the quarries she was curious about. She read that in the 1800s the town's quarries, some of the most productive in the United States, shipped stones all over the northeast. The stones were used for sidewalks and curbs, not only here in town, but in Boston, New York City and Philadelphia. The steps of the capital building in Albany, Grant's Tomb, Times Square and Rockefeller Center all were made with stone quarried here. Even the bank building, where Neil Walker's office was located, had bluestone carvings on top.

Not only does my house have a curious history, this town's history is interesting as well. And, surprise, surprise, I'm having fun learning about it too. She continued reading until she felt her daughter tap her arm. Julia sat down with an armful of books and one video.

"Mama?" Her eyes were bright and happy. She so enjoyed reading, and the library had a wonderful children's section.

"Hi, Sweetie. Did you find some good books?" Rachel sorted through the little girl's choices making sure they were appropriate. She set one book to the side. "You're not ready for this one, Julia," she told the girl.

"Aww." Julia glanced at Rachel's face and saw the look. "Oh, okay." Rachel smiled at her daughter, gathered up her things and checked out the books. On the ride home, Julia begged her to read all her books that night.

"I'll read one tonight at bedtime. But you can look at them while I make dinner."

Later, with the bedtime routine completed, Julia was safely tucked under her Princess blanket and Bear snuggled next to her. Rachel turned off the light, the Disney nightlight providing a soft glow to the room.

"Night, Mama,"

From the doorway, Rachel blew a kiss. "Sleep tight, Sweetie."

Julia giggled and rolled over.

Rachel walked down the hall and into her room. She was pleased with the changes she'd made to the room. No longer were there piles in every corner, and those determined dust bunnies were banished. Anything further, though, would need to wait until the paperwork from the lawyer was finalized and she could use the estate's funds. The money she had remaining from her travels across the state was dwindling rapidly. She still wracked her brains trying to come up with a plan. She didn't want to go begging for money from MariBeth, or anyone else for that matter!

She took the diary and the next set of letters with her down to the living room. She was anxious to learn more about Emma and James. Fetching a cup of tea, she got comfortable in Nonna's overstuffed chair. Sitting there Rachel could almost feel her grandmother's arms wrapping around her. She sipped her tea, opened Emma's 1863 diary to the first entry, and started to read.

Chapter 12
January – April 1863

January 1, 1863

The New Year is here and although many people celebrated, I could do no such thing. Since Mrs. Roberts left, the situation in this house has gotten much worse. Mrs. Flynn, the new housekeeper, has arrived. She is much older, and not as pretty, as Mrs. Roberts. She is definitely not as kindly either. She watches me so carefully and seems to find fault in the least little thing I do. I keep the pantry organized as I am told, and yet if she finds just one thing out of place, I am severely scolded or sent to my room without dinner. I don't know how much more of this I can take. It is a good thing I spend most of my day caring for Miss Ella and Miss Ida. If it weren't for them I'm not sure how long I will last here. And yet, even they have been miserable lately and have begun taking it out on me. I know they miss their brother as I do. You would think it would bring us closer, but because I cannot share my true feelings for James with them for fear they may slip and tell their father, that opportunity is lost.

* * *

January 5, 1863
My Dear Emma,

A new year is upon us. I am sitting here in my hut with one of the candles you sent me stuck at the end of my bayonet so that I might write these few lines. I want to thank you so much again for sending me the box and all that was inside. The first thing I saw were the pairs of socks you made. I am wearing one pair. Even though I really did not need new ones yet, I put a pair on to remind me of you. I am glad you included the fried cakes, the dried beef and applesauce. It made for a most delicious dinner I shared with Amos. Oscar and Harris and some of the others have gotten boxes too. It seems you ladies have been very busy, which is a good thing. I would not wish to hear you are lamenting our separation.

Most of our time lately has been spent drilling with long hours in the saddle. Do you remember me telling you of Buckley, my horse? He is such a beautiful creature and I am doing my best to keep him that way. I tend to him as often as I am able, but when we are out on picket duty or marching in the mud he tends to get pretty grimy. I have to be mindful of his health as well as mine so I watch to be sure his mouth does not bleed and that he does not get a sore back from the sack I use as a saddle blanket. I check his hooves to be sure he does not have a stone, otherwise he might go lame. All this mud makes it all the more likely it might happen. If he gets a scratch on his leg, I make sure to bandage it with strips of fabric from an old blanket.

When we have free time Amos and I have been trying to improve our little huts to make them more comfortable. We chink ours with mud, but unfortunately this only lasts so long. Once it rains, the mud washes away and we need to do it all over again.

We do get to relax and have some fun, too. Whenever there is snow, the boys have a bit of a snowball fight. I suppose that is better than sitting in a small hut all day. Seems odd, though, to be here, preparing for battles, training on our horses, and yet have time to run around throwing snow at each other.

I am in receipt of your letter with the news of little Merritt. He was such a dear little boy. It saddens me to know that I was not there to be of comfort to my family at their time of grief. I received a letter from Father today. I am not interested in hearing from him and so have left the letter unopened. Perhaps one day I will feel differently, but not yet. I much prefer receiving letters from you. I worry about you and hope these few words find you well.

Your loving husband,
James

* * *

January 5, 1863

I have discovered why I have been feeling so ill of late. I am in the family way. As near as I can tell, it happened just before James left, so the baby will probably be born in July. So far Mister B has not noticed, but I cannot tell how much longer that will last. Will he dismiss me from his household employ when he discovers? I don't know what to do if that happens. Where can I go? Mother and Father are both gone. Perhaps there's another relative that might take me in. I must begin to make inquiries to prepare. What little money I have saved from the cash gift I received for Christmas will not go far and James has not yet gotten paid.

Even with all these worries, I am thrilled to have a little part of James growing inside me. I feel that he is here with me, so I am not contemplating any action to rid myself of this child.

* * *

January 12, 1863
My Dear Emma,
I am so very overjoyed to hear the news of our child. Oh, that I am here and you are there! Such

distances should not be at times like these. I knew that night we lay close together, embracing and kissing all night would perhaps lead to this. We must begin to consider what you will do. My father will surly react negatively to the news and would not want you to be near my sisters during this time for fear of influencing them.

I have heard that we will soon be getting paid for the time since we enlisted. I will keep a small sum, but send the bulk of my pay to you so you can look for suitable lodging. You mentioned that you will be searching for someone who might take you in - do you have someone in mind?

Take care, my love, and write to me as often as you are able for I look forward to reading your lines - even more so now.

There is not much happening in camp - we drill and spend hours riding around, practicing formations and shooting in preparation for upcoming battles. It has been cold and snowy and I wish I could be there with you sharing a warm bed, instead of here in this cold hut with Amos.

Your loving husband,
James

* * *

January 15, 1863

What a week this has been. It happened again this evening. Mister B confronted me in the living room and placed his hands on me, touching me so that I felt dirty inside. I have done nothing to encourage this and yet he has approached me several times now. Just another reason for me to leave and go quickly. I have asked my cousin if she would mind taking me in. I should hear from her soon.

January 17, 1863

Mister B approached me again today. I stood firm, pushed him away, and told him about me and James. He does not believe me and will not acknowledge that I am married to his son. I never thought that it would come to this. I thought he might be angry with me because he is angry with James, but not this, this touching. Now there is certainly no love lost between us. I would have preferred that my child know his grandfather but now it is not to be. I must leave early tomorrow. Little Ella and Ida have no idea what is to become of me – and they will surely be upset when they hear the news that I am gone, but I cannot think of them. I must think of my baby – and me.

I am so thankful that Cousin Louisa has agreed to take me in. Her husband, Orrin, is off fighting in the infantry and because of that we have a lot in common. She says I will be able to help with the chores around the farm until my time comes. Tomorrow I will travel by stage to Union Center. She says she will meet me there. I do not have much to bring with me, just some small tokens of courtship with James. I will have to pack them carefully. I will not miss this room, or this house. Since James left there is little here for me. Oh, I will miss Ella and Ida as I have grown fond of the girls, but Mister B? Never...

January 18, 1863

What a day this has been - my first stagecoach ride. I never could have imagined such a trip from Oxford would be filled with such new sights and sounds. I hardly slept last night for fear of not waking in time to catch the stage. I arose while it was still dark and quietly left the house without a backward glance, so glad to be leaving. I took my carpetbags with me to the tavern and waited a short time before the coach arrived, pulled by four elegant horses. The morning sun was just beginning to brighten the sky when I boarded and sat on the leather seats near the window so that I might see the sights as we traveled. My bags at my feet, I kept my hand free to hold onto the strap as the driver suggested. The ride would be bumpy, he said, and if I didn't want to hit my head on the roof, I should be careful to hold the strap tight. We set out and crossed the canal filled with the boats carrying supplies down to Binghamton; the same canal that took James away from me.

The driver was right. The trip was terribly bumpy as we traveled over the plank roads, but otherwise uneventful. Even though I was tired, I couldn't sleep and watched the landscape go by until we arrived at

Union Center late in the afternoon as the sun was setting. From what I could see of the town, it is even smaller than Oxford. I could see a small church, post office, a general store and the tavern where the stage stopped.

Louisa met me at the stage with her buckboard. I had not seen her in such a long time, but she has changed hardly at all. She is not much older than I, a tiny woman with dark hair and even darker eyes. She welcomed me warmly giving me a tight hug. It felt so good to have her loving arms wrapped around me, instead of the curt words and evil glances I have gotten from Mister B lately.

The ride to her farm was a cold one, with the wind blowing. Thankfully it did not snow today. We arrived at her farm an hour later. All I could see was a lantern in the window, it was so dark. Considering the late hour and knowing how long I had traveled, she showed me to a room just down the hall from hers and told me we'd talk in the morning. I was appreciative of that and settled into my new room. Oh, goodness. It is so much larger than my old box room; I am fairly lost in it. When I lifted my lantern high, I could see there is a four poster rope bed, a chest and even a desk that I might write more easily. I will have to be sure to do all that I can to help Louisa in her chores and make my being here as comfortable for her as I can.

January 20, 1863

When I woke this morning it was to the warmth of my new room, and the smells of breakfast cooking. What must Louisa think of me, still abed? I was so tired last night; I barely got into my bedclothes and my head on the pillow when I was fast asleep.

I made my way down the stairs to find Louisa in the kitchen. She greeted me again with a hug. After we had eaten, she gave me a quick tour of her house and farm outbuildings, chatting all the while. I think she is genuinely pleased to have me here.

The house is delightful, larger than the one I grew up in, but smaller than James' large home. She had three bedrooms upstairs, and a sitting room and kitchen downstairs. The furniture was simple, yet in its way, elegant. Outside the house was painted a cheerful yellow with green shutters framing the two front windows on either side of the front door. The porch spanned the front of the house, its railing painted white. Quite warm and homey I must say. We didn't spend too much time outdoors, except for her to show me the barn and the chicken coop. Chores needed to be done early and as she showed me around, she gave me directions, so I could be of help to her. Oh, I think I am going to like being here.

Later in the day I packed another box for James. It is his birthday next week, and I want to surprise him. Perhaps I will send a lock of my hair for him to keep in his pocket, close to his heart, that he might think of me.

* * *

January 25, 1863
My Dear Emma,

I am so pleased to know that you have found suitable lodging with Louisa. I would very much like to meet your cousin. She sounds like a caring person. I do not know her husband, Orrin. We are in different regiments and so our paths do not cross very often. I must make an effort to see him soon that I might come to know him better. Perhaps we can share news.

Oh, Emma. How I wish I were there with you. I am so sorry to know that you had such difficulty with my father. Words cannot describe how I feel toward him right now. He was such a stubborn mule before I left, treating me like a young boy, making decisions for me instead of treating me like a man. If I can join this war, I can certainly make my own choice in the path I would take for my future. And that includes you. If he had been proper instead of acting as he has, he might enjoy having his grandson (or granddaughter) on his knee. But that is wishful thinking and will not be. I know he has been melancholy since the death of Mother last year, but that is no reason for carrying on as he has done. It will be his loss now.

Have you given thought as to what name we shall give the baby? I have no strong feelings about names, except that we don't name him for my father.

I have not heard anything further about our pay. Be assured I will send money to you as soon as I am able.

Your loving husband,
James

* * *

February 5, 1863

I have found that duties are many on a farm, even though it is midwinter. The cows must be fed and milked, the chickens fed and eggs gathered. We need to chop the wood for the fireplace and stove, and fetch water from the well. We have begun to take in wash for other families in order to supplement the meager earnings we make from selling butter and eggs.

Louisa and I have joined the Ladies Guild today. We earn eleven cents for each shirt that we sew. Between us we have been able to make eight a day. In the evening, with chores done, we sit comfortably by the fireside chatting and knitting for the baby and for the soldiers. The socks I am knitting for James are almost finished. Louisa is thankful for someone other than her young son to talk with and so it pleases me to know that I am helpful. The time passes very quickly but I still long for James. Letters from him are so infrequent, even though I write to him often.

I have begun to consider names for the baby. If it is a boy I shall call him James after his father, but if it is a girl, well, I will have to think on it.

* * *

February 10, 1863
My Dear Emma,

I am writing these few lines hoping that they find you in good health. I want to thank you for the box you sent to me for my birthday. It was certainly greeted with much enthusiasm on my part. I shared some of the sweets with Amos so he sends his thanks as well.

It is a very cold day today but some good has occurred. This morning we were given our pay - going back to the end of October. Three months pay, about forty dollars. I am keeping a little to pay the sutlers for some paper and stamps. I also purchased an ID tag. It is a small metal disk that has my name and regiment stamped on it. Many of the boys are getting them to wear under their shirts - just in case. I am sending the remaining pay for you and for the baby.

I have not had much of an opportunity to sit and write. Most of the time so far we have been on picket duty - first at King George Courthouse and then Mathias Point, about a thirty mile ride from Camp Bayard. The weather has been very bad lately, with rain and wind for days. Last month, on the 28th, we had a foot of snow, but then the weather warmed up a bit and turned it all to slush. That made for muddy fields and muddy marches.

While we spend much of the time on our horses doing picket duty, General Burnside took the rest of the army on one such march. When I got back to my hut, I heard the story. At the onset of Burnside's march, the weather was fine, but it got progressively worse with snow, at first, turning to rain. The hardened ground softened so that the wagon wheels got stuck in the muckiness. Men slipped and fell losing their shoes to the thick mud. Some of the horses were in mud up to their bellies. New roads had to be built to help get them out of the mud. Trees were chopped; fence rails taken down and laid in the mud, then covered with brush to make it passable. What a mess! Later I saw a sign in the roadway the Rebs had posted. It said "Burnside Stuck in the Mud". Such a sorrowful thing.

I am thankful we were on picket duty. Although not as miserable as the Mud March, it still was not very pleasant. Our line was over fifteen miles long. We left again for picket duty and remained until January 24th.

When we returned to camp we found some changes had been made. Lincoln replaced General Burnside with General Hooker. Hooker is now the third leader of our Army since I have been here. On Sunday, which for most would be a day of rest, we had an inspection by this new General.

In the days since, he has been working to make our lives better, as much as he is able, I suppose. I have noticed a change in the sanitary conditions and our diet. We were even given some new clothing and new shoes. Sure makes a person feel better to have new, bug-free things to wear. Hooker assigned differently designed badges, to signify our different regimental groups, that we will wear pinned to our hats. Ours has two crossed sabers in scabbards, cutting edge up. Quite distinctive.

I hear he also wants to have more drills and that the regiments will be re-organized. He will put all the cavalry units in one corps under Brigadier General Stoneman. The 10th NY will be in the third division, first brigade and our company leaders will be Wheaton Loomis, Ben Lownsbury, and LD Burdick. We have rearranged our camp so that our huts are now in rows that looked more like streets and we have added decorations to make it more like home.

All this does not help much, in my mind. Our days are long, but the nights are longer. That is when I lie abed thinking of you, wishing you were here in my arms - or rather, I were there with you in your warm bed. I hope you never tire of me saying the words... I love you Emma.

Your loving husband,
James

* * *

February 20, 1863
    What a first rate day. I received a letter from

James, and he sent money. It should last a good while and for that I am thankful. It does me good to know that I can help pay for supplies when next Louisa and I go to town. Perhaps I can even get a length of material to make a new day dress. I must be careful, though, for I do not know when the next pay will come.

I cannot think how James is doing – out there in the elements. He says he is not engaged in fighting as yet. Again I am thankful. But it cannot last too much longer, I'm thinking. Even though we are still in the grip of winter and the snow is still flying, I know spring is on its way.

I have learned so much in my time here with Louisa. She is a grand teacher, so patient with me. Working in James' father's household, I mainly took care of the girls with much cleaning, washing, and sewing. Those things I knew. I know nothing of farming and even some of our household tasks are foreign to me.

Today, I helped make soap. Oh what a smelly task it was! The tallow had to be boiled and smelled like the animal it came from. Then we had to get the lye by passing water through ashes. The mixture of lye and tallow had to be stirred for hours. My arms felt like leaden weights they ached so. Yet we were not done. Salt was added and the soap skimmed off, placed in wooden frames to cool and then cut into bars. Having done this today, I now know why Louisa is so careful with her slivers of soap. Tomorrow we make candles, for our supply is growing small.

* * *

February 29, 1863
My Dear Emma,

What a cold and miserable time this has been. There is a foot of snow on the ground and it is very cold. Spring cannot come too soon for me. I am tired of sitting on my horse in the cold, watching for signs of the enemy.

Amos has taken ill. For the past three days he has not been able to keep any food down and has diarrhea as well. He went to the doctor yesterday, was given medicine, and put on the sick list. I am trying my best not to catch his illness.

Recently I spent four days on picket duty at our usual place along the Rappahannock River. Then, after two days rest, our unit was assigned picket duty at King George County, a new location for us. We did not find this too bad. We found abandoned buildings to sleep in at night, and the area had a lot of wild turkeys. We do keep a good watch because the Rebs are now beginning to move around. A little over a week ago Company M joined our Regiment and so we became a complete Battalion for the first time.

Emma, I fear I am not too cheerful in this writing and for that I am sorry. You are so far from me, and I am lonely. Even though there are many around me, the boys are just not as soft and as pretty as you. Oh, sometimes there are women hereabouts, as sutlers, or some of them come from the area, asking if they might assist us in some way. Yes, they are pretty, and it does me good to see them, but seeing you here instead would do my heart much better.

Perhaps you can send another box. I find I need more socks, some writing paper and new pencil, and some more needles and thread. It is amazing how much wear my uniform pants take. With the long hours we spend in the saddle, the material wears thin quickly. Can you also include one of your bars of soap? Laundry for me is just washing in a nearby creek, or sometimes boiling my clothes in a cook kettle. I am ever vigilant in trying to get rid of the ever-present lice that invade my clothes and take residence on my skin and in my hair. Some of the men around do not bathe or wash their clothes at all. You can imagine the smell.

I should close this writing of these lines. The post is ready and I must go to bed. Please write to me often. I long to read the words you write, telling me of your days, and the news of the town.

Your loving husband,
James

* * *

March 1, 1863
    The days are passing quickly. I am almost

halfway through my pregnancy and the baby is growing large inside. I cannot believe how big I have gotten. My clothing needs to be let out once again. Louisa seems to think that perhaps there is more than one baby inside. I cannot even think of having two babies at one time. We are only preparing for one.

Louisa is such a caring person and so full of energy. I know I should be doing more, but I cannot seem to last as long as she. We have been hearing news from the battlefield and know that things are beginning to stir where James is now. Louisa's Orrin has moved further to the south and is already engaged in battles. She is as anxious as I to hear word. Each time we go to town we meet with the other ladies and share news.

We have been busy today baking for tomorrow's sale. We are joining with the ladies of our Guild to raise as much money as we can to send to the U.S. Sanitation Commission. They do such good work sending food, clothing, and medical supplies to the battlefield for the soldiers.

My pies are not as perfect as Louisa's but I am learning and pray someone will buy one and think it is tasty.

* * *

March 17, 1863
My Dear Emma,

Happy Birthday, my dear wife. It is amazing what a year will bring. So much has happened to us since I first gave you that little diary. I would have liked to send you something but the sutlers here only sell things for us to use and I am afraid not much is there for me to send to you. I know the best present I could give you is for me to come home and take you in my arms, but that is not to be. So I must just send you my wishes that you have a wonderful day. Are you and Louisa planning to celebrate? I hope you are well and as happy as you can be given our circumstances.

I smile when I think of you standing in the kitchen with flour everywhere as you make your pies. In my mind's eye I can see a touch of white on the end of your nose, and I wish I were there to kiss it off. Just thinking of tasting an apple pie makes my mouth water and stomach rumble. There is no such thing hereabouts.

As I sit here taking pencil to paper to write these few lines, I am listening to the spring peepers and watching the robins searching for their dinner.

There is not much other news to tell. For the most part, the boys are not as pleased with General Hooker as they were with General McClellan and wish little Mac was back here again. We have continued to go on picket duty every few days and in between there is the drilling and fixing up of our quarters. The last time we went to Lamb Creek Church we saw some Rebels picketed on the opposite side of the river. We were told not to get friendly or to speak with them in any way. On the 11th, a group of them tried to cross the river on a boat, but our picket line repelled them and they hurried back to their own side.

Subsequently I found myself taken ill for three days - must be from being out in the cold and rain on picket duty. My throat was so sore, making it very difficult to swallow, and I had a bad cough.

Time seems to move slowly as we wait out the winter months, listening for the call to leave our huts to begin moving again. To pass the time sometimes I read the newspapers the men from Oxford share around. It is one way I can learn of the things going on back home, but mostly I hear news of other towns and other states. I heard about Captain Loomis. Do you remember me telling you of him? He's the packet boat captain that joined with our company? Well, on March 14, at Belle Plain, he resigned and left to go home to Oxford. I envy him his ability to do so.

Some of the men gather together and play cards. I much prefer the game of checkers. I have an ongoing challenge with Harris; he has beaten me less than half the games we play. The other day, the Irish Brigade celebrated St Patrick's Day in fine style. They held a horse race, and foot and sack races. I even watched a greased-pole climbing contest. There was food aplenty for the day.

I must admit - while all this makes the time go by, I do so look forward to getting your letters so I can read the lines you write. It is in that *way that I feel close to you. So please, write often.*

Your loving husband,
James

* * *

March 20, 1863

   Louisa is such a dear. She surprised me with a birthday present today, one that I will cherish forever. It is a locket, one of her own, she said, that she has given me to keep a likeness of James, close to my heart. Now I can keep him near, even though he is so far from me. I am so incredibly blessed to have Louisa. I am not sure how I would have survived if it were not for her kindness in taking me in. I do my best each and every day to make hers easier, though as my belly enlarges with the baby, I find I cannot do as much as I have before. Louisa has not complained and for that I am most thankful.

April 3, 1863

   Spring is beautiful and the warmth of the sun on my face does me so good after such a long winter. I walked down to the creek today and saw the flowers beginning to poke their way out of the cold ground. I waddled around and had a difficult time bending to pick them. Now that spring is here, there are more chores to be done around the farm, yet I find I cannot do as much to help as I would like. I spend my time doing as much as this baby, or babies as Louisa thinks, will allow. I can still feed the cows and chickens and fetch the eggs. I can still do some of the wash and certainly do not find the sewing and knitting any trouble so I must not think I am a total failure. Louisa does not complain. She is in fact, most grateful, because any chore I can do lessens those she must.

James doesn't seem to be in too much trouble right now, but I know that will soon change now that spring is truly here.

* * *

Rachel heard the clock on the mantle ring the hour. *Ah good, I have time to read more. This is so interesting – I really don't want to stop.* She went to the kitchen for a refill on her tea and hurried back to the letters and diary to continue reading.

Chapter 13
April – July 1863

April 10, 1863
My Dear Emma,

    The days are getting warmer, but we still have some snow on the ground from when it snowed four days ago. The result is the ground has turned to mud again.

    We have begun making preparations to move from our winter camp. I cannot believe that we have been here for only four months - seems like so much longer.

    A few days ago, a detail went to Falmouth and came back with seventy five new horses. It was very timely because we had a visitor to camp this week. Our own President Lincoln came by train to view the cavalry. We were roused very early and by seven o'clock we were on the move toward Falmouth. We all lined up, thousands of us stretching for miles. I was far down the line but still heard the twenty-one gun salute and then I heard the trumpets and drums. When the President got near, the colors were lowered and while still on our horses, we drew our swords and saluted. After he passed by, some of the boys said they thought he looked tired and worn out. He was wearing a plain black suit and his stove-pipe hat as usual. His horse didn't look big enough for him - his feet nearly touched the ground! Mrs. Lincoln rode in a carriage and his son, a boy about ten or twelve years old, rode a little black pony. It was a grand event for sure.

On a less cheerful note, today we were made to witness a new discipline - the sentencing of a court-martial. Two deserters from another Cavalry regiment were found guilty. As punishment they were led into the center of the square we made around them. They were branded with a letter D on their hips, and their hair cut short. The men were made to march around so we could get a good look at them and remember. It certainly made a vivid reminder that we are all in the army and cannot leave.

Do you remember the day we went to see the balloon rise with Professor Squire? What a sight that was. The army here is using such balloons to spy upon the actions of the Rebs across the river. One is sent up almost every day. It is such a beautiful thing to see floating in the sky, *reminding me of you.*

Emma, be sure to write of springtime in New York. I will miss seeing the freshet this time. Will you go? Perhaps you are too far from the river. But, if you are able, perhaps it would be a way to keep us together, if only in our thoughts.

Your loving husband,
James

* * *

April 25, 1863

I cannot imagine being a deserter as James said in his letter. I know this war is nothing to be taken lightly, but if we all do our part, then it will be done with and won much sooner. And then James will return to me.

I have seen men in town who have come home from battle, on leave to see their families. Some do not return. Louisa told me she knew one man who came home from the war to visit his family. While home his wife took ill and died. He had to stay to care for his children. There was another man who came home, took sick and could not return. If these men are caught here they would be returned to their units for court martial. Louisa says she heard the punishment varies a great deal for these deserters. For a small crime, some men are put to death – for a larger transgression, it seems they are fined some money. It makes no sense.

Our days are truly busy now. The fields are ready for planting. Louisa has hired some help to put in the corn. I am working on the kitchen garden. It is small enough that the baby does not get in the way too much. The days are warming up nicely. It feels so good to be outdoors in the sunshine instead of cooped up as we were in the winter.

I know that James is outdoors most of the time and wishes he could be here so he could enjoy the warmth of a fire indoors. I pray that this war will be over soon so that he can come home.

* * *

April 29, 1863
My Dear Emma,

I received your latest letter and must tell you that you should not worry overmuch. It is not good for the baby. I am sure that Louisa does not expect more from you than you can do.

Much has happened since I last wrote you. Just after Lincoln's visit, we left our comfortable Camp Bayard. Even though this place is not as good as the houses we left behind in New York, it has been home to us for almost four months. As I packed to leave, I looked around at our little log hut, and remembered the day we put it together - seemed like so long ago. We don't know what is ahead, but I am sure that we are in for some fighting.

When we left Camp, we rode along in our usual formation of rows of four across, and the first day traveled about twenty miles before stopping to make camp. We reached Bealeton and continued to ride around that area looking for the Rebs. For the next several cold and rainy days we would get on our horses, ride a little, camp and ride again.

Onward we rode ending up at Warrenton Junction. All this riding was in the cold and rain, rain, rain. There are dangers everywhere, not only from the Rebs. I heard that during one of the storms a man was struck by lightning and another killed by a hailstorm. Many have become sick from the constant marching in the cold wet weather.

This morning we commenced crossing the Rappahannock at Kelly's Ford on the same kind of pontoon bridges we used in Fredericksburg, remember? They are made of canvas boats strung side by side with wooden planks atop them. Some of the horses were skittish and their riders had trouble getting them to cross. Not so with my Buckley. He did a fine job. I am so pleased with my horse. He has served me well so far.

Now we are camped about two miles from the river. We were told not to build campfires. So I am sure something is afoot. Sometimes not knowing what the generals have in mind for us is nerve-racking. I do not know what tomorrow will bring. I must stop now, Em. The daylight is gone and I cannot see any longer to write.

Your loving husband,
James

* * *

May 8, 1863
My Dear Emma,

I sit down tonight to write these few lines to let you know that I am still in the land of the living and pray that this will find you in fine spirits. In the past two days I have been feeling poorly with another sore and scratchy throat and achy body. It has not stopped me from doing my duty as yet, but if it continues I shall go to the doctor to see if he can help me.

It is good that the crops are in the field, the days are warm enough, and the rains have held off so the planting could be done in time. What are you planting in your garden? I hope to be home in time to partake of the bounty of that garden, but if I am not, could you please pack me a box with some of the vegetables? I long for some fresh carrots. You can also add some more paper and a few stamps. I seem to go through them quickly as I am writing as often as I am able.

Wait, Emma... I just heard my name called for mail and will pause to go fetch it. Hopefully it is a letter from you....

No, not one from you, but another one from Father. I almost tossed it into the flames of our campfire, but at the last minute decided to add it to the others I have received. I really do not understand why I am keeping them. My feelings for Father have not changed. Do you hear from him? He does not know where you are I imagine.

What a time we have had in the last ten days. Under the direction of General Stoneman we have been raiding, traveling from town to town, crossing and re-crossing the Rappahannock and Rapidan Rivers. So much time spent in the saddle and in the rain - I ache all over. I do not mind gentle sprinkles, but the downpours we have been having of late soak me to the skin. It causes chills even in this warmer weather.

Anyway, when we charged through Louisa Courthouse we encountered some Rebs and, in the skirmish, three men were wounded and three were taken prisoner. Just before dinnertime, we left town and arrived at Thompson's Crossroads at ten that night, a pretty worn out bunch. We didn't even get to rest the whole night. At three in the morning, we continued on, this time moving east. When we got to Hanover we tore up a railroad. We were supposed to destroy a bridge but it was so heavily guarded, we just did the track and burned a warehouse. We rested briefly that night.

The next day, we were on the move again - this time we camped at Thompson's Crossing in the afternoon. On the 5th, we left camp at two in the afternoon and crossed the South Anna River about two hours later and the Pamunky River late that night. We continued these marches often stopping for no more than an hour or two. We were all so very tired. As we plodded on, it got so quiet you would have thought we were in a church meeting. The only noise we heard was when someone fell asleep in the saddle and slipped off.

It seemed to me that this raid has been more a test of our endurance than doing any significant damage. We did work together well as a unit and did do some damage to their rails. Perhaps that is all that we needed to do. We covered over six hundred miles in recent days and many of the horses didn't make it. It is good that a reserve herd is kept for replacements.

I am sore and wet and so very tired. I need to stop writing to get this posted before I go to sleep. Keep me in your thoughts, my dearest, as you are in mine.

Your loving husband,
James

* * *

May 9, 1863
My Dear Emma,

My letter of yesterday was filled with tiresome thoughts. I wish to let you know that not all is so glum. We do have some humorous moments - although it may not have seemed so at the time. Such a story I heard earlier today and I must tell it to you. On one of the marches in recent days, there came upon the regiment a soldier who called out that the woods were full of Rebels. The officers had the men draw their swords and gallop through the woods. The men hadn't had a chance to secure their belongings on their horses, so as they raced along, they commenced dropping their cooking utensils, supplies and even clothing. What a sight it was along that two mile stretch - discarded items everywhere. When the group reached the rest of the unit, they found the man was drunk. He was promptly arrested.

Another time, one of the Sergeants, thinking to find a better horse for himself, came upon a farmer with a very fine horse indeed. Wishing to make a trade the Sergeant put spurs to his horse and began to chase the farmer to the corner of a fenced area. Thinking he had gotten the farmer, the Sergeant went to make the exchange, but the farmer had other ideas. He pulled out a pistol and fired - the ball coming very close to the Sergeant's head. The Sergeant, thinking better of making the exchange, whirled about and took off. The farmer kept his good horse!

This war has dragged on and on it seems. When I first considered enlisting, word was that this would be a quick war, that the north would bring the southern states into quick submission. But considering all that has taken place since I have joined, it may be months before it is over. I find myself wondering what I would have done if I had known last year. Would I have joined? I am thinking probably yes. I still consider this battle for the union of our country a just one. I do, however, look forward to the day when I can return home and share your bed and sleep in quiet instead of hearing the sounds of shells exploding in my ears and men moaning in pain.

Your loving husband,
James

* * *

May 10, 1863

Such sad and tragic news from town today. Margaret Collins was killed as she made to disembark from her carriage. I heard her horse had been skittish and she was violently thrown against a wall hitting her head so hard she had a concussion. I remember James mentioned she was the beau of his friend, Harris. I wonder if he knows of the tragedy yet. Poor thing was only two years older than me. I should be more careful around horses from now on. I hope that James is careful around his horse, even though it seems to be a gentle one.

Later in the day I heard that another woman was killed by a freakish accident at her home. Her son was getting ready to go hunting and had taken down a gun that he didn't realize was already loaded. The gun discharged and the ball passed through the side of the house, and struck his mother in the right arm traveling through her body to rest in her left arm. She died instantly. Her son must be beside himself with grief. I did not know either woman, but am sympathetic. It reminds me that deaths occur everywhere, not only on the battlefield.

Should I be telling James these dreadful tales?

Will that cause him to fret and worry overmuch? Surely he has enough to be concerned about. And yet, what else do I have to say, except that I miss him so terribly.

* * *

May 14, 1863
My Dear Emma,

Today we were paid again, and I am including thirty dollars for you. I have kept just a little to help keep me in paper and stamps and maybe some fresh fruit now and then. Hopefully the money will last until I next get paid, and will help Louisa with the farm.

Since learning of the death of Margaret, Harris has been very despondent. Nothing I can say consoles him. He has been talking of leaving, of deserting this army, and asks if I would join him in going back home. Much as I want to go home and be in your arms again, watch my baby grow big inside you, watch him grow after he is born, I will remain here. I cannot imagine how I would feel knowing the townsfolk knew I had deserted my fellow soldiers. How would I be able to hold my head up before my son? No, I will stay. Harris will have to decide what is best for him.

I spent some time at the Potomac today doing some bathing and laundry. It is wonderful to feel clean and have something that is not full of vermin and dust to wear.

So many tragic events have been happening at home. I am praying that nothing happens to you. Please take care, that I may return to you and find you happy and in good health. I have been *writing as often as I can but some days find it difficult to have something of interest to say. This is one of those days. I hear that tomorrow we will again be on the move, so I will close so that I may post this tonight.*

Your loving husband,
James

* * *

May 15, 1863

More disturbing news from town today. Louisa says I should not be listening to these things as my days of confinement draw nearer. But I told her the story and she listened carefully. All along the canal towns a series of burglaries have taken place. Townspeople have been alerted to the fact and a watch has been posted near the canal to be on the alert for this person. I pray they find him quickly. I do so worry about our safety – two women alone on this farm, away from town.

May 20, 1863

We thought we heard someone in the farmyard last night and remembered about the robber from town. We clung together listening carefully. Then, brave Louisa took a lantern and went into the yard. I was glad she took the shotgun with her. It turned out to be just a red fox. Louisa shot at it and frightened *it away. The baby must have felt I was nervous – it was fluttering so.*

I made up another box to send to James today. I finished making socks and packed them with some preserves we had left. That will have to do until the summer crops come in and the garden is ready.

Oh, it will be good to have fresh vegetables again. The supplies in the root cellar are dwindling rapidly.

May 28, 1863

I was so surprised when I opened James' letter today and out spilled money. The thirty dollars came at such a good time. Tomorrow I can go into town and purchase a cradle for the baby. Louisa said she still thinks there are two and wonders if we should get two cradles. I cannot imagine two babies, and must be frugal in spending, so I shall only get one. As the days grow longer, I find myself with more time in the evening when I can sit outdoors on the porch, knitting and sewing for the baby. It thrills me to know that soon I will hold him, or her, in my arms. Wouldn't it be wonderful if James is here with me when the time comes?

* * *

June 8, 1863
My Dear Emma,

I can only write a few lines as we have been very busy. General Stoneman has been replaced by General Pleasanton. I believe it is because of the disastrous raid Stoneman led in the rain last month, but I cannot be sure. In the past weeks, we have been on picket duty, off and on, near Liberty, Fayetteville and Sulphur Springs. After being relieved from one duty we were assigned again, this time at Warrenton Junction.

Picket duty has gotten much more dangerous now since the enemy is near and we are in constant threat of attack. In addition to keeping our eyes and ears open watching the roads and forests, we have become watchful of the animals. The horses' ears twitch, or a flock of birds suddenly taking to the air gives us an alert so we can spot the enemy.

Yesterday we broke camp in the afternoon and began to ride. The day was very warm and marching along the roadway was terribly dusty, making it hard to breathe.

Today we reached Kelly's Ford and camped but we are not permitted fires. It means we have no coffee or hot food for our supper. We have heard Hooker has ordered us to cross the Rappahannock River tomorrow and attack at Brandy Station. As I sit here I can hear William and Charles talking about the preparations for tomorrow. Charles reminded him to pin his ID tags to his uniform. I shall do the same. As we prepare for the battle, I am both anxious and enthusiastic. I can only pray that one of these battles will force Lee to *retire and it will be the end of this long war.*

Emma, it has grown dark and I can no longer see. With no fires, I must end of this letter.

Your loving husband,
James

* * *

June 11, 1863

This morning Louisa went into town and heard the sad tale about her dear friend. When she returned this afternoon, she was in tears as she told me the story. Seems her friend, Charlotte, had been preparing some milk pails by scalding them on a fire. She got too close. The flames caught on her hem and quickly spread up her dress. She ran toward the house, screaming. Her father rushed out to her, tried to put out the flames, but was not successful. She perished in his arms.

This chore is something we do here all the time and so we really must be vigilant when doing it. Tragedy is everywhere it seems. We need some good news. Louisa took to her room until afternoon chores when she emerged with reddened eyes. Even though I didn't know Charlotte, I still feel sad and hope I can help Louisa through this.

I am now quite large indeed. I get out of breath so easily. My chores have been limited to the house, knitting, and some cooking. Ah, that the time would go quickly.

* * *

June 14, 1863
Brandy Station

My Dear Emma,

I received your letter and can tell you did not want me to know the news of town. But you forget there are many fellows here that also hear news from home. Whenever one of us gets a letter, if there is news to be shared, word travels through the company and we are all alerted. I am fearful for myself in this war, but even more fearful for your safety. Please do take extra care - the time for the birth is coming near and I worry for you and for the baby. Have you chosen a name yet? Remember I am amenable to any name you choose, save my Father's.

The days here have been dry as we have not had rain for almost a month. You can imagine the dust in the air with all the horses moving about. I feel dirty all the time. Bugs are everywhere. Not only are they flying around, but populations of them seem intent on crawling all over me. I spend time each night trying to rid myself of them, but they keep returning.

Remember, when last I wrote, I told you we were preparing for a large battle? Up until that time, our cavalry had not fought as a whole. At Brandy Station we were given the chance to show our worth. It was really good that we practiced so long and hard with our sabers because we used them during that battle.

On the ninth, we began the day with much enthusiasm after hearing the bugle sound the order to mount. At Kelly's Ford, about five hundred of us crossed the river, unnoticed by the Rebs, and advanced on Brandy Station where we knew they were camped. A second group, under direction of General Buford, crossed at Beverly's Ford. Leaving the woods, we reached the field and made ready our carbines and charged the enemy. I was filled with the thrill of the battle and, at the same time, anxious for my safety and of those around me. We heard the order to draw our sabers, and we charged again. I rushed up the hill with the others and met the enemy sword to sword. I saw boys fall left and right, and continued on.

We were in such a tangle with the enemy. Fortunately I was able to stay in my saddle and avoided the danger of the enemy sword until the battle was over. After two long hours it was over.

Oh, Emma! You should have heard it. The field was filled with all sorts of sounds, boys yelling, swords clashing combined with the sounds of the horses' hooves pounding the dry ground, generals barking orders, bugles sounding, cannon fire echoing in the trees, and then the disquieting sound of men groaning in pain. Dust and smoke was everywhere making it hard to see where the enemy was on the field.

After so many disheartening engagements, in this battle our 10th did quite well - we did not flee, we did not lose our colors. I do feel sorry for our standard bearers. We lost several good men today

trying to protect our unit banner. The flag is so
important; it is always an easy target. We can't
leave it lay on the ground, so someone is always
ready to pick it up and carry on.

We lost almost a hundred men today, either
killed, wounded or taken prisoner. Our Colonel
Irvine was taken prisoner during the battle.
General Avery was assigned Irvine's place. We lost
four other officers too. From our company Charles
Holdrege was killed. He was from McDonough and
I heard he had five children.

I am so very tired, Emma. Although it was an
exciting day I am greatly relieved it is done and
saddened to know that so many are lost.

Your loving husband,
James

* * *

June 19, 1863
My Dear Emma

Since my last post, we have been on the move
and engaged in battle in several places. After the
Battle at Brandy Station we were again re-
organized into two cavalry units - under General
Buford and under General David McMurtrie
Gregg. Now we are of the 3rd Battalion under
Colonel John Gregg.

On the tenth, we were camped near Warrenton
Junction, but moved again on the fifteenth - this
time going north. The next day, in the afternoon,

we ended up at Aldie. There we were met with the sound of gun fire and quickly moved to the right side of the roadway as another brigade advanced to do battle. During the following two days, we continued marching northward along the road, engaging the enemy each day, ending at Middleburg where the Rebs stopped. There was a stone wall on the sides of the road making it so narrow that we had to squeeze together to get our usual four across. The enemy was in the woods and behind the stone wall. We were ordered to chase them out.

After the battle was done I found out we lost thirty more men, killed, missing or wounded, including three more officers. When we got back to camp I was told the most awful news. Uncle Brunson was one of the officers injured today in battle. They told me a ball struck him in the left side of his chest, near his shoulder, and passed right through his lung. Thankfully I was permitted to see him because he was kin. He could not talk much, so I sat and held his hand. The doctor does not give him good chances, but they are sending him to Emory Hospital in Washington. I wanted to be able to go with him, but was told I could not. I pray that he recovers quickly.

Good night, dear wife. I miss you terribly.

Your loving husband,
James

* * *

June 23, 1863
My Dear Emma,

Poor Uncle Brunson. He passed quietly of his wounds four days ago. I was told he was buried in the Military Asylum Cemetery in Washington. I am terribly heartsick. At times, he was more a father to me than my own. As an officer, he was always so kind and sympathetic to the boys, always giving them encouragement. You will probably be hearing of his death in the town's paper. I wish I could be home with my family at this time. My cousins, Linn, Zerah and Lucy Ann will be grieving terribly. I shall write to them later today. I know you have not yet met them and for that I am sorry. Emma, if something should happen to me, I would ask that you tell our child all about me. Let him know that I am here fighting for our country that he may live in a land united.

I have been receiving letters from my father in recent days, but I am still so angry with him that I leave them untouched. I would welcome news from my little sisters, but from him - no. I cannot think what will mend this rift between us. Right now I fear nothing will. Have you heard from him? Does he even know where you are living now? Perhaps it is well if he doesn't. He might make some trouble for you and I would not want that. If I were there, I could protect you from his rage, but being so far away - it is well to leave things as they are.

We have had more skirmishes in the days since my last post. Today is the first in five days we were able to stop long enough to groom our horses. Poor

Buckley was a dirty mess, but I brushed him carefully and he is much neater and cleaner now.

The countryside hereabouts, near Ashby's Gap, is beautiful, green and hilly reminding me so of Oxford. I tell you, Emma, I am quite ready for this war to be done so that I may go home to you.

In sadness,
Your loving husband,
James

* * *

June 28, 1863
My Dear Emma,

In the time that has passed since my last post, we are back home with our own Cavalry Corps again and much relieved to be so. We had been ordered to report to General Slocum of the 12th Corps and so started out for Leesburg on the 24th. Many of us are not too comfortable with the infantry, having had spent so much time with our own cavalry. After crossing the Potomac at Edward's Ferry we went to camp at Point of Rocks. We continued north and ended up today here, at Frederick in Maryland, camped outside the city. We found some good dry railroad ties and used them to make our cook fires. The land here is beautiful with healthy crops unlike the ones we left behind in Virginia.

Oh, and we have another new leader. No telling why, but General Hooker resigned and has been replaced by General Meade. That makes five different Generals leading our Army since I joined. I pray this one will lead us on to victory.

Your loving husband,
James

* * *

July 1, 1863

When I left Oxford I broke off all ties to James' family. I would have liked to continue to communicate with his sisters, to share with them the news from James, to learn of their growing. I pray the maid who took my place watches over them. They are coming of an age – if Mister B is so inclined they might be in danger of his advances as his was to me. I have Louisa now and have put thoughts of Mister B and the girls aside.

But now I hear of the death of James' Uncle Brunson and am so saddened. If we were living closer, and if I were not so near to birthing, I would take the stage and visit with his wife and family. I know James' cousins are not much younger than he and they were close. I did not have an opportunity to meet this family before James left for the war. Our time together had been so short after our marriage and all we had to do kept us very busy indeed and we had no time.

We do not get the paper here at the farm and my trips to town are not often. When I finally read it, the *article in the newspaper said it right. "Another brave man fallen a martyr in a just and holy cause, doing his duty trying to put down a cursed rebellion against the best government the world ever saw. He was a patriot who gave up his life for his beloved country." Rest in peace, Uncle Brunson.*

They are all such brave men, who fight so far from home. I pray for my James, that he will return safely to me.

* * *

Rachel heard the mantle clock chime the hour again. Eleven o'clock. She had no idea it was so late. *It's so hard to stop reading.* The words had leapt across one hundred fifty years of time with as much impact as if the battles were just occurring. She set the books and letters aside, checked the doors and turned off the lights. Heading upstairs, Rachel discovered how tired she was. After changing into a flannel nightgown, throwing some water on her face, and giving her teeth a cursory brushing, she slipped under the covers. Rachel turned out the light and went to sleep.

She stood at the edge of the road, the hoop skirt of her brown homespun dress billowing in the wind. Grasping the ends of the white shawl, she held them tightly in one hand, the top of her poke bonnet with the other. She felt someone standing beside her, felt a hand on her arm. Glancing to her right, she saw a young girl, belly swollen with child, light brown curls threatening to fall free from hair pins.

Fallen leaves whipped around them as they watched the battle in the distance. She heard the sounds of the carbines and the cannon – saw the horses racing by, sabers flashing in the sun.

One after another they fell. She heard the one standing next to her scream, "James!"

Turning to look, Rachel watched as the scene changed quickly. The girl disappeared. Her hoop skirts were replaced by jeans. Windblown sand replaced leaves. She heard the roar of planes and watched the missiles. She stood there and screamed, "Jon!"

Rachel woke, drenched in sweat, sheets and blankets twisted around her legs, her heart racing, and her breath coming in quick gulps. She opened her eyes, the nightmare quickly fading. Moaning softly, she got up and went to the bathroom to splash cool water on her face. She looked in the mirror and saw in her eyes the remnants of the dream's terror. Rachel went back to bed, straightened her tangled sheets and settled back on her pillows and stared at the ceiling, thinking of Emma, James and Jon. *I'm so sorry, Jon. I let you down.* It was a long while before she fell asleep again.

Chapter 14
The next day

"Julia, time to go. The bus will be here any minute." Rachel stood at the bottom of the stairs, waiting for her daughter to appear dressed for school. "Now, Julia!"

"Okay." Julia's footsteps were heard on the bare wood floor of the upper hallway. She appeared fully dressed. Pink tutu, white tights, pink leotard. Rachel groaned and stomped up the stairs. She was in no mood for such nonsense this morning. The effects of the nightmares of the night before were making her irritable, her head throbbing with a headache.

"Oh, no Missy. Those are not school clothes." She turned her daughter around, and marched her into her room. Opening the dresser drawer she tossed a pair of jeans and pink knit top onto the bed. "Change."

Julia's mouth turned into a pout. She stomped her foot. "I wanna wear my tutu!"

"It's not for school. Now change."

"But I don't want to wear the jeans. I wanna wear my tutu." Julia stomped her foot again.

"They're not for school. Change." She really wasn't in the mood to deal with another tantrum this morning.

Rachel remembered the words from a parenting class she'd taken a couple of years earlier. *When confronted with an obstinate child, be the broken record. Say the same thing over and over and don't get drawn into an argument.* It's times like these, as she watched her daughter, tears beginning to spill down her soft cheeks, that made parenting so hard, Rachel thought.

Julia slowly sat on the floor, removed her ballet clothes, and tugged on the jeans and top. The sound of the bus's horn echoed and Rachel realized they wouldn't make it. She held Julia's shoes in one hand and backpack in the other.

Rachel took a deep breath. "Now I'll have to drive you to school." *This is not a good start to the day.*

Julia finished dressing, followed her mother down the stairs, shrugged into her jacket and followed Rachel out the door to the car, tears still flowing.

Rachel inserted the key and crossed her fingers again praying it would start this morning. Another worry on top of everything else, she thought. The car was the one thing she hadn't taken care of yet. The car started with a screech, and then settled into a dull roar. The noise of the muffler was growing day by day and there still was no money to make repairs. She dreaded driving to town fearing the ticket she might get for the sound violation. *I only need to make it a few more days, please Lord.*

Thankfully, the drive to the school was a quick one, and Rachel only stayed long enough to quickly drop the little girl off at the sidewalk.

"Toodles, Sweetie." She tried for a smile. It didn't quite work. She tried again. "I'll pick you up from school and we'll go to the library again, okay?"

"Okay," she sniffed and said quietly. "Bye, Mama." And off she went, into the school, backpack slapping against her.

* * *

A half hour later, Rachel sat at the kitchen table, completely free of those piles of old newspapers that had covered it for so long. She was just finishing with breakfast, sipping a hot cup of tea, when the phone rang. She didn't recognize the number indicated on the phone.

"Hello?"

"Mrs. Benton?"

"Yes, speaking."

"Hi, this is Roger Colby, Principal of the Forest Elementary School, how are you this morning?"

"Fine, thanks."*What could this be about?*

"I'm calling to ask if you would be interested in a long term substitute position beginning in September. I know you applied for a full time position here, and we regretfully didn't have an opening for you. I'm hoping you are still available and might consider this position."

Rachel's heart raced with excitement. A job! She didn't want to sound too eager and said, "Sounds like a possibility. Can you give me some details?"

"One of my third grade teachers had an accident and it looks like she'll be out for quite a while. I've got it covered for now, but I'd need you to start the school year and keep going, depending on how she recovers. Right now I can't tell how long that would be."

"That sounds like something I'd be able to do." Rachel smiled as thoughts raced through her mind. She could see herself standing before a class of third graders.

"That's great. Can you come in later today or tomorrow to sign the paperwork and I can show you around the classroom. Unfortunately, the teacher, Mrs. Collins, is not available to consult with, but one of the other third grade teachers would be more than willing to lend support to get you oriented to the school and the kids."

"Let's see, I can't today. How about tomorrow? I can be there in the morning."

"That's great. Let's say ten – in my office."

"Ok, I'll see you then." Rachel hung up the phone and whooped with joy and did a little dance. Wanting to share the news, she considered calling MariBeth, but changed her mind. MariBeth would be busy at work. She'd call her later. Energized, headache vanishing, her mind began to consider plans for the school year. She hurried to her room, sat at the desk there and jotted notes down as her mind flew with ideas. It was such a treat to start a school year as a substitute, rather than midyear. The students would treat her as the regular teacher, not a stand-in. She couldn't wait to see her classroom and meet the other teachers.

Yes, things were certainly looking up – a clear and clean house to live in, a job, finally. If she could just get through the next three months financially, she'd be in much better shape than she had been for months, years even. She knew that the money left in her wallet would only last a little while longer. She needed to have something to tide them over until September, but didn't know what.

After a quick lunch, she moved into the living room and spotted the diaries and letters again. She was drawn to the story of Emma and James, even though reading them was giving her nightmares and reminded her of Jon. The events that had taken place so long ago were impacting her today. She certainly empathized with Emma and all that she was going through, married, with no one to help, needing to take care of herself and her child, her husband off to war. She hoped James survived.

Rachel stopped to consider. Did her grandmother keep a diary? So far she hadn't found one. What about her mother? *I never thought about starting one myself.* But with the reading of the words from over one hundred and fifty years ago, she wished she'd taken the time to keep a journal. Not many people kept handwritten journals nowadays. In the era of *Facebook, Twitter, YouTube*, and other social media, many people interacted with others, but not using a medium that would last through the years as a diary would. *What will happen a hundred years from now? No one keeps their Facebook notes – they are here today, gone tomorrow. Will folks from the future who are looking back to today wonder about our society? There won't be anything written to help them.*

She looked at the diary and letters again and realized she was nearing the end of both. Putting aside all else, she fixed herself another cup of tea and made herself cozy. Nonna's chair was something she would keep, she decided. Rachel took the last stack of letters in her hand and began to read.

\

Chapter 15
July - December 1963

July 4, 1863
Gettysburg
My Dear Emma,

   I pray you will bear with me as I tell the tale of the last few days. Since my last post, we continued to travel north. The road was dry and dusty. As I rode behind the long line of horses, there was so much dust filling the air, it made breathing difficult and stung my eyes. That and the heat made riding extremely uncomfortable.
   When we got to New Windsor we stopped for a rest. I spied the Rebs all around the small town, but before we could engage them, they scurried away. The townspeople gave us a rousing welcome

and we were able to get some fresh corn and flour along with good oats for the horses.

We only stopped for a couple of hours and then were on the move again. Three days ago, we paused about noon near Hanover Junction in Maryland. We resumed traveling and arrived at Hanover village at about midnight where we saw the dead horses and torn fences left behind by the Rebs. There was no rest for us though. At three in the morning, the bugle sounded and we continued to ride again toward Gettysburg. We reached a location on the east side of the town, at about noon, after nine hours in the saddle.

Some of our regiment wanted to go into the town. The men that joined in the companies the year before me had spent some time training in this town, and they were looking to seek friends they had left behind. Robbie, from B Company, wanted to go to see Jenny Wade. He remembered the young girl from that time and wondered if she was still there. But, as sounds of battle in the near distance were heard, Robbie and the others determined that going nearer would have to wait.

We traveled onward and by mid-afternoon we reached the intersection of Hanover Road and Low Dutch Road about three miles east of Gettysburg. We sat in the heat of the day, resting along the south side of the road, and waited for orders, our horses nibbling on the sweet grasses.

It didn't take much time. After only an hour, Captain Lownsberry gave the order to dismount. One out of every four of us was left behind to hold the horses. I was one of these and watched as twenty seven men went into the field to clear the sharpshooters that were hiding in the hills and woods. When they got to the top of the ridge they came to a rail fence and were met by the Rebs and chased back. More of the enemy appeared on the ridge, but our guns soon had them falling back again. Rebel infantry came out of the woods and more of our company went forward. It was a terrible clash. Bullets were flying everywhere. The sound of the cannon echoed across the ridge and through the woods. Heavy smoke filled the air. As the day grew short, the Rebs tried again to gain ground, but we were able to repel them. Darkness came over the field. About nine o'clock the firing stopped and quiet settled all around. The only sounds were the moans and cries of the wounded in the field. I finally got the opportunity to rest and find something to eat and learned our Captain Lownsberry and Corporal Dow were both taken prisoner during the fight.

Yesterday morning we were told to stay ready, near the Hanover and Low Dutch Roads. Fighting was fierce and we were ready to do our part again, but did not engage. All afternoon I heard the incredible sound of the cannons in the distance - lasting for hours - and wondered at the battle taking place there. For our part, we did not permit the Rebs to gain ground and even pushed them back into the woods. The bugle just sounded and we are to mount and move out. I must put aside this writing and shall continue when we next stop....

Right after the fighting ended last night, our regiment was put on picket. A thunderstorm came up making our time miserable. It was so hard to stay awake after our hard march, and the two days of fighting. This morning, our Regiment remained on picket until noon, when we all started out traveling through the field of battle of the last three days. Everywhere I could see broken wagons, abandoned muskets, clothing and other supplies. In the fields I could still see the dead and dying. I could hardly look, it was so terrible. Along the road we saw some of the townspeople who had left before the battle making their way back to their homes. Some of them asked if we were the Porter Guard. Someone yelled out, "Yes!" And we were cheered. Seems these people remember our regiment from our time here two years ago.

The Reb prisoners, looking dejected, were moving along, under the guard of our regiment. At one time we had almost three thousand of them. All this time we were very hungry. The Rebs had swept through the area getting all the grain available and there was not much more to be found. We sent out foraging groups but not much was brought back. Today all I ate was an uncooked ear of corn and some birch bark. At one farm the foragers stopped and found a farmer who had hidden some oats under straw in the loft of his barn. He laughed to know that he had outsmarted the Rebs who didn't search behind the straw. So some horses were able to eat better than we did. Late in the day, some of us came upon a cherry tree, filled with red, ripe cherries. We ran and grabbed handfuls and ate them right on the spot.

When we rested for the night, I heard the tale of Jenny Wade, the young girl well known to some of our regiment. Seems she was in her kitchen yesterday, making bread for our soldiers when a bullet crashed through a window, hitting her and killing her instantly. How brave she was! During the battle, she would go to her well and fill canteens for our soldiers even though the battle raged around her. Some of our unit took care to give her a decent burial.

I really have come to hate this killing of men, Emma, even if they are Rebels.

I write these lines now, but do not know when it can be posted. What will tomorrow bring?

Your loving husband,
James

* * *

July 4 1863

Louisa and I went to town today even though my time is near. We did not want to miss the festivities to celebrate the day. Our Society has been preparing for this day for weeks. We hope to raise funds again to send to the front. The US Sanitation Commission is always looking for donations of knitted things. When we got to town, people were all talking of the wonderful news. Vicksburg has fallen to our side.

What a victory that General Grant has had. And where James is fighting near Gettysburg was a victory as well. News today was that Lee's army was again heading back to Virginia with over thirty-thousand dead, wounded or missing. It was said that his hospital train was over twenty-seven miles long.

Flags flew everywhere today, and many homes were decorated in red, white and blue. The band played enthusiastically with everyone fairly dancing in the streets.

The only sadness came when someone missing an arm or a leg passed by, and we realized the terrible consequences of this battle on the lives of our fighting men. I would welcome James home in any condition and pray that it is soon. Louisa has not heard from Charles in weeks now, and worries so about him. We have each other to lean on, but having this war done and our men folk home would be the best for us all.

* * *

July 5, 1863
My Dear Emma,

This morning I was told I will be a scout beginning tomorrow. I have been partnered with Amos. He is the one who shared my hut back in Camp Bayard, remember? We will be moving ahead of our regiment to see where the Rebs are going. Amos and I will be on our own, and we will have to forage for ourselves, until we return to the regiment to report our findings. We will put aside our sabers. They make too much noise. Instead we have been given two pistols each. We will prepare our horses too, removing anything that might jingle. It is good that we are going together. Some scouts travel alone but working together, if something should happen to one of us, the other will be able to report to the General what we discovered.

Wish me well, Emma. This may be my last post for a while since I do not know how much time I will have to put pen to paper. I should still be able to get mail when we meet up with our regiment, so please continue to write. I promise to write as often as I am able. How I long to be with you, especially now that you are nearing the time of the birth of our child. I had hoped that this war would be over by now and that I would be with you at the birthing, but this war is not yet done so here I must remain. It gives me comfort to know that you have Louisa to care for you. Be safe, dear Emma.

Your loving husband,
James

* * *

July 7, 1863

When I went into town, for the last time before the baby is born, I found in the newspaper a speech by our President. I copied his words that I might remember them and share them with James when he returns. I pray that it will be soon, that he might be here for the birth of his child.

"I see in the succession of battles in Pennsylvania, which continued three days, so rapidly following each other as to be justly called one great battle, fought on the first, second and third of July; on the fourth the enemies of the declaration, that all men are created equal had to turn tail and run." Abraham Lincoln

I also read news of the 10th and saw the praise given to James' regiment. They did very well in the battle and I am so proud of him and of his friends.

July 15, 1863

I feel my confinement is very near. I can hardly move with the weight of the babe in me. I waddle so and have long ago lost the sight of my toes. The days are hot and with the weight of the babe inside me, I am so very uncomfortable.

Today, Louisa helped me move some things from my room to the first floor birthing room. It will be much more convenient for me there when my time comes. She is so good to me and I wonder how I might repay her for her kindness.

I fear for James, out alone with just one person with him. It is dangerous enough with a whole regiment around, but traveling through woods where the Rebs might be? Oh, I shudder to think it. Please, dear Lord, keep James well and bring him back *to me safely.*

* * *

Mid July 1863
My Dear Emma,

I have lost track of the days since we've been out on our own. We have managed to stay ahead of the regiment. While they go along roads, we can travel through wooded areas to find those Rebs who have crept away after Gettysburg. Some of them we have taken as prisoner, tying them together to march with us and return to wherever our unit happens to be at the time.

Since the great battle at Gettysburg, our Regiment has been on the move almost every day, searching for Lee's Army. We almost had him at the Potomac, but he was able to escape across the river. We were the first unit to cross, following right behind him.

Emma, I find it hard to believe that we've been all over four states in the past weeks. After the Gettysburg battle we went west to Cashtown, then Chambersburg. We turned south in the pouring rain to Quincy, Waynesboro and Middletown. Then we went back north again to Boonsboro; south to Harper's Ferry; north to Shepherdstown. All this time in the saddle is sure tiring for us, but it is even worse on the poor horses because there is so little food to give them. I've heard many of the regiment's horses have perished during this time. I care for Buckley as I can, giving him as much rest as I dare before moving on. So far he is doing fine.

In the middle of the month, after we got back to our unit to report, we heard about a battle they were involved with. Seems they had been picketed nearby Shepherdstown and had come under attack. All companies had joined together, found cover behind a stone wall and kept up good firing. The skirmish lasted well into the night and before daylight, both sides had crept quietly away from the area, our group going back again to Harper's Ferry. I was pleased to know that I missed that battle.

Our scouting is not without danger though. One night as we were sitting at our campfire heating a pot of coffee artillery fire landed very near, knocking the coffeepot into the fire. Thankfully the shell did not explode and we and our horses were not injured. We didn't have coffee that night, or the next morning, but we did have our lives.

Amos and I continue scouting. Miles and miles we have traveled up and down hills, so much time spent in the saddle, through so many towns either following behind or up ahead of the regiment. We've gone by Lovettsville, Leesburg, Goose Creek, Manassas, Broad Run, Catlett's Station, Warrenton Junction, and Bealton, finally resting for a bit near Warrenton. Much of the time I spend worrying about what might be around the next bend in the road, or what might lie beyond the next set of trees. I am always vigilant, keeping my eyes and ears open to anything that might alert me the enemy is near. Several times, as I keep a keen eye on Buckley, I know the enemy is hidden nearby because of his twitching ears. He can pick up their sounds before I do, which is good for me. When Amos or I spot the Rebs, we record their location and make a report upon our arrival back at our regiment's camp wherever they may happen to be.

I write to you as often as I am able, dear Emma, sometimes I cannot know what more to say. I will post this when next I am near the regiment.

Your loving husband,
James

* * *

July 25, 1863

I am a mother. What an amazing feeling! I lie here abed looking at the babies asleep in the cradle beside my bed. Yes, there are two of them – two dear little girls - just as Louisa thought all along.

The pains began in the early hours of the night and by morning were fierce. Louisa sent for the midwife who arrived mid-afternoon. Or so I have been told. I was in such pain, I could hardly think. It is so good that both Louisa and the midwife, Carley, were here to help me. After the birth of the first, I thought I was done, but the pains, which had subsided for a bit, started again and shortly thereafter another was born.

Now, as I lay here resting, I find myself so indebted to Louisa for all she has done for me - for taking me in, for helping me with the birth, for helping me with taking care of them. I do not know what I would have done birthing and taking care of two babes all alone. I smile when I think it was a good thing Louisa suggested we make some extra clothing. I wish I could think of a way to repay her kindness.

So there they lay, not seeming to mind sharing one cradle until we can get another built. I am feeling pretty well considering, and the babes have taken well to feeding. I hope I continue to have enough milk for the two of them.

James will be so thrilled to hear this news. Oh, how I wish he were here to see them. They both have his hazel eyes and I can see a bit of him in their noses too. Since we left it to me to give them names, one I have named Adelia Jean and the other Cornelia Jane, though who knows, I may just call them Jean and Jane. They look so alike; it would be hard for me to tell them apart except that Adelia, the first, is a bigger baby than her sister.

Oh, please, let this war be over so he can come home to me and meet his daughters.

* * *

July 30, 1863
Madam,

In past weeks, your husband and I have been together scouting the countryside for signs of the Rebel army. Periodically we would return to our regiment to report our findings. It is my sad duty to report that during our last time together, near Unionville in Virginia; James was captured by the Rebels. I managed to escape, but it was close. I nearly lost my own life. James was brave as always. He is, and has always been, an excellent soldier. He did not complain at all whenever asked to do a difficult task, such as this scouting business.

I know you would want to know the details. We was along the Plank Road near Orange traveling eastward back to our regiment to report. Coming upon a crossroads at Unionville, we commenced to take the left fork and went on a short distance when we heard a kindly-looking woman standing in her doorway calling to us. She asked if she could get us some refreshments. Knowing we were in enemy territory James was uncertain as to her truthfulness. I thought she might be one of the Union sympathizers that we had heard about and I encouraged our stop. We had not eaten much in two days, and looked forward to having some warm food. We dismounted, hobbled our horses and entered the house. She had food set upon the table as if she knew we was coming. Our mouths was fairly watering at this point, and we sat to eat. No sooner than we started to enjoy the food then comes down the stairs a Reb in full uniform. James did not see him as his back was to the stair. The fellow grabs James and begins to tie him up.

In seeing this, and knowing my turn would be next, I hustled out of there. One of us had to make our way back to the unit with the important information we had in my knapsack. It was up to me. I untied my horse, mounted and galloped away hearing a shot and feeling the ball pass real close.

That was the last I saw of James - and I gather he is now a prisoner and has been taken to Richmond to one of the prisons there. I will try to find out where he is, though you may hear from him. Sometimes the prisoners are permitted letters, I hear.

When I got back to our regiment, I told the tale and they immediately sent out a dozen men to round up that woman and arrest her. Later I found out that they caught her and burned down her house. They did not find that Rebel who had been with her, though. I imagine he is the one who took James as prisoner to his camp.

I am sorry to be telling you all of this. As we was traveling, James told me that you are with child and I pray that this news does not cause anything to happen. If I can I will make sure that James' belongings are packed and shipped back to you.

Yours in friendship,
Amos B. Martin

* * *

August 10, 1863

Oh my poor James. He is captured and now I do not know where he is or how he is doing. How shall I know? What shall I do? Perhaps one of the other wives will have an answer – I must go to the Society tomorrow and find out if anyone knows more. Louisa says her husband has not written either and cannot add anything to the news. I am beside myself with worry.

It is good that the girls are so easy to care for right now. They eat well, and sleep most of the time. I fear the worry about James will affect my ability to feed, but so far that has not happened. Oh, James, where are you?

September 10, 1863

I have had several letters now from friends of James who were serving with him. William and Harris sent letters and some others whose name I do not recognize. Their words warm my heart in this time of despair.

But there is no word from James.

I find myself crying over the simplest of things – especially watching the girls on the blanket sleeping near each other, knowing what James will miss seeing. Oh, aching heart. If I could turn back the hands of time, I would stay his hand and force him to remain here instead of signing those enlistment papers.

Louisa learned about her husband today - he is returning home. She hadn't heard from him for so long because he was in the field hospital. He suffered a bullet wound that has left him disabled. While I am happy for her, I am also jealous and try my best to hold back the tears of frustration while she rejoices.

I am not sure she will want me to remain here with her when he arrives. Is there a place that will take wives of soldiers – a place that will be safe? How can I ask someone else to take me in? So far Louisa has not said anything and I will not bring it up.

* * *

October 10, 1863

Dear Madam Beardsley,

After reaching the safety of the Union army, I was told I would be able to send a letter in the next post, so I am putting pencil to paper and writing you these few lines. I was recently paroled from Belle Isle, one of the more fortunate souls. I knew your James, as we were both prisoners there.

It is with painful regret that I must inform you of his death on the third of October. Until his demise he spoke often of you. He told me if anything should happen to him I was to send along news to you. I also include his ID tag, for this is something I know you would want. He was sickly for a long while, and slipped away during the night two days before I left.

If you forgive my ramblings, I would share with you some of what it was like at Belle Isle, a name that means Beautiful Island. Not a proper name for it, I must say. It is a small island in the middle of the James River, right across from Richmond. Perhaps it was once a beautiful place, but it is no longer.

After I was captured, I was led there after having had to march for days without much rest or food. As with all prisoners I was marched across a long, low bridge, over the James River, from Richmond to the island. As soon as we all arrived on the island, they took all our things, our knapsacks, our money, our writing implements, letting us keep only our hats and blankets.

I looked around in dismay at what I saw. The only buildings were a bake house made of wood for the rebels, and tents for the guards and a hospital, of sorts. There is a graveyard nearby the hospital, a constant reminder of those who did not survive the place. There are no buildings on the island to protect the prisoners from the weather - just a large penned area surrounded by a ditch about three feet wide and eight feet deep. When the Rebs dug the ditch they tossed aside the dirt thereby creating a mound five foot high, almost like a breastwork. When my fellow prisoners and I got there, we were told never, never to go near that ditch. They called it the dead line. Anyone who crosses is shot without warning.

We did not get much to eat, just a block of hard corn bread and maybe some spoiled meat.

Fights often erupted over even the bugs in the food. An occasional rodent or other animal became part of our meal for the day. The surrounding river was divided into parts; some we used for drinking, some for bathing, and some for a latrine.

All around there were thousands of prisoners, sleeping, resting, and waiting - all living outside. At one time, I was told there were tents for the prisoners, but that was before I arrived, before there were so many of us. I saw men that looked very much like walking skeletons. They were all skinny and I saw their bones quite clearly. Their eyes were bleak and they didn't talk. At night, though, I heard those poor souls cry out in their suffering. Some died of disease before they starved to death. I suppose it was fortunate such was the case with your James. I cannot imagine dying of such extreme hunger.

The weather was nice at the beginning, the days and nights still warm. Again, I cannot imagine what the conditions would be like there in the winter. I could not see much in the way of warm clothing, or many blankets, and the frozen ground will take any warmth from a body. I am so thankful that I was released before that time.

I know that James was in despair when, after he took ill, he knew he should not see you again. He often told me about you and wondered about the baby. He was such a kindly chap, and until he came down with the illness that took him, we would spend hours together talking. How unfair that some were released, as I was, and some had to remain. I assure you, if it were humanly possible, I would have begged for James to be one of the fortunate ones. Perhaps if he had been, he would have gotten the medical treatment he needed to be well. It is sad that such a kind and affectionate person ended his days in that rebel prison. I am so sorry.

Yours,
Duncan Talbot

* * *

October 15, 1863

Oh, wretched day. I received a letter in the post today that fairly tore my heart in two. My James is no more. He died a horrible death – so far from home – apart of all that he held dear. He will never hold his daughters and they will never know the loving arms of their father. I am so terribly miserable and depressed. If it were not for those precious babies, I do not know what I would do. They are my only connection with their father now. I have to be strong for them. But oh, it is so difficult.

* * *

My Dear Emma,

I can only write a few lines, my time is short. I have been ill for much of the time since I was brought here after I was captured. I know I will die in this place, that I will no longer see you or

hold you in my arms. I weep to know that I did not
get to see the birth of our child, to hold him in my
arms, to watch him grow. Was it a boy - I pray so.

I know that I served my country well, Emma. I
fear that I served you less so and regret our time
together was so short. I send these lines to you
filled with my love for you, forever. Remember me,
my love.

I am forever yours,
James

* * *

October 30, 1863

*Another letter today – this one penned by James,
just before he died, I believe. I shall cherish these
words forever and keep this letter and all the others
for my daughters to read when they are older, that
they might know of their father. I must be careful
reading this, should my tears mar the precious
writing.*

November 5, 1863

*Cornelia Jane has taken ill with the influenza
and I worry so. The doctor has come and applied
poultices and leeches trying to save her young life. I
stay with her, tending her as much as I am able, and
yet little Jean seeks my attention too.*

November 10, 1863

How much sadness can one person take? Cornelia Jane died in my arms today. She looked so small, so frail at the end. I held her for a long time, smoothing her hair, kissing her, before allowing Louisa to take her from my arms. We buried her under the tree in the yard by the back garden. When I get some extra money together I will have a proper headstone made for her, but for now we put a simple cross there. Little Jean does not know what to make of it all. She keeps crying for her sister and is too young to understand that she will never be with her again.

There is so much tragedy, so many families affected by this war that there is hardly a one that has been saved from it all.

November 11, 1863

I cannot do it - I cannot continue with this diary. There is too much sadness on these pages and I shall not want to be reminded of them in days ahead. So I shall pack these away, along with all of James' letters and the ones that came to me from his friends in the regiment. I received the bundle of letters that he had saved from his father – still untouched. I shall not open them either – but store them with the rest.

* * *

Rachel sighed, silent tears streaming down her cheeks as she read the last entry in the diary. Closing the small book she set it carefully down on the end table beside her, alongside the letters from James. She felt an even closer connection with Emma. *We are sisters in sorrow – spanning years. Both husbands died as a result of their service to our country – poor James in a prison camp, and my poor Jon by his own hand.*

She felt as if she had just finished a well-written novel. Today's reality had disappeared because she had been so engrossed in the lives of James and Emma. She really didn't want the story to end, but knew that there was no author there to write another chapter.

She glanced at the mantle clock and was amazed. She had been so engrossed in reading, the hours had flown. It was time to pick up Julia from school. Brushing the tears from her eyes, she grabbed her jacket, dashed out the door, and into the old Chevy. She grimaced again at the engine's sound. As she drove down the road, her mind was back in the Civil War with Emma and James.

Chapter 16
The next day

The next morning the sun shone into the bedroom windows and into Rachel's eyes, waking her before the alarm went off. She heard the sound of the birds chirping in the branches outside her bedroom window and smiled. Waking to the harmony of spring sounds was much better than hearing the blare of the alarm. She heard Julia down the hall already getting ready for school. The day was starting on a much better note than yesterday.

The morning routine went off without a hitch, Julia hopping on the school bus and waving through the window. Rachel waved back, and blew her young daughter a kiss with a smile.

She felt full of energy as she anticipated her meeting this morning. Dressing quickly in a black skirt and powder blue blouse, she paused as she saw herself in the free-standing mirror in the corner of the room. Certainly not glamorous, she thought. But then, she never wanted to be. Take it or leave it, was her motto. She'd always sped past the beauty counters at the department store on the way to the casual clothes. That is, when she went to one, which was rare. More often than not, with her very limited income, she shopped at discount stores and thrift shops. The *Goodwill Store* was her friend.

As she passed the desk in the corner, she gathered the notebook in which she'd prepared a list of questions to have answered at her meeting. She was anxious and at the same time enthusiastic about her upcoming position.

Rachel drove to the school to meet with the principal at ten. The bustle of the building was evident with children walking the halls in line led by a teacher. The library, just inside the main door, was busy with boys and girls cheerfully choosing books to take home. Three boys were already in line at the checkout station, scanning their cards and books.

Rachel smiled and walked into the school's main office and was greeted by the secretary.

"Good morning. May I help you?"

"Yes, I'm Rachel Benton. I have an appointment with Mr. Colby.

"Welcome to Forest Elementary, Mrs. Benton. Please take a seat and I'll let him know you're here." The secretary walked down the hallway and returned almost immediately followed by an older man. His hair and neatly trimmed beard were both sprinkled with grey. He wore navy pants and a light blue shirt, but what caught Rachel's eyes were the yellow smiley faces adorning his tie. Perfect for an elementary school, she thought.

"Mrs. Benton, glad you could come in today."

She reached for his extended hand and shook it noting his firm grasp. "I'm glad to be here."

He turned to his secretary and asked, "Could you call Mrs. Riley to the office, please." Turning back to Rachel he explained, "She has a free period right now and can meet with us. Then you can go back with her to her class, so you can get a feel for what goes on here."

Moments later they were met by a young teacher, Frances Riley, casually dressed in slacks and a knit top,

"Frances, this is Rachel," he said. Then turning to Rachel he said, "I'll meet with you later, Mrs. Benton, if you have any more questions after you talk with Frances."

Rachel nodded, and then followed Frances who walked down the hall quickly, eager to get back to her classroom. She pointed out the different classrooms along the way, chatting the whole time.

Rachel stayed two hours with Frances. She learned where her classroom would be, the layout of the school, and the procedures involved in getting students through the school day. *So much to remember.* Rachel was excited to have this opportunity and yet the butterflies in anticipation of a classroom filled with eight year olds were beginning to churn in her stomach. She still had three months to prepare – to plan for each school day. Hopefully once the school year started those same butterflies would have found their way someplace else.

* * *

Leaving the school, Rachel turned her face up to the sun and felt its warmth for the first time since arriving in Oxford. She noticed the tulips were emerging and the air smelled of early spring blooming trees. California seemed so far away and a lifetime ago. Never would she have imagined six months ago that today she would be walking the streets of this small town. The air seemed cleaner somehow, the streets friendlier. Taking care of her grandmother for those first few weeks took all her time and she hadn't had the opportunity to explore the town or meet anyone else but MariBeth and her daughter's teacher, until now.

Walking down the bluestone sidewalk, she was reminded she wanted to research more of the town's history. As she drove to the library she thought again of Emma and James. She never had a strong interest in history, but after reading the diaries and letters, she was drawn to learn more of their time, their experiences. More research was needed, she thought. She parked and made her way up the sidewalk to the library. She noticed new baskets of flowers hanging from hooks along the library's balconies.

Jen Frasier was in her usual position behind the circulation desk. Rachel went up to her. "Hi, Jen."

"Hi, Rachel. Good to see you again. May I help you with something?"

"I hope so. I want to do some research on someone who was in the Civil War. How do I get started?"

Jen smiled, "That's a hot topic since it's around the one hundred fiftieth anniversary of the Civil War. There are several free government web sites that have information. If I were you, I'd start with the National Park Service website. They have something called the *Civil War Soldiers and Sailors System*. At that site you'll be able to do a search on a particular soldier or sailor, regimental histories and their battles, and cemeteries."

"Thanks so much." Rachel moved across the room to the computer work stations. The area was not as busy as her previous visits. There were only two people, connected to the computers with earphones, who looked like they were playing video games. She logged onto a computer and went to the website, *www.nps.gov/cwss*, and typed in James Beardsley. Up came his information. He was indeed in the 10th NY Cavalry, Co K. Another link in the website brought her to the regimental history and she saw all the battles the 10th NY was involved with during the four years of the war. She noted the names of the places that were mentioned in James' letters. His descriptions made the story come to life – rather than this list of dates and places.

On a whim, Rachel typed James Beardsley into the Google search engine and found more. It said he had enlisted in August and mustered in on October 29, 1862. Captured in Unionville in Virginia in July 1863, he died a prisoner of war at Belle Isle on the 3rd of October, 1863. He is buried in the Richmond National Cemetery, Section 3A, #981. *Oh my, he was only nineteen years old! So young!* She printed the information to take home. *I still want to know why*

Nonna had the letters and diaries. What's the connection?

Rachel realized she wanted even more information. She went back to the librarian and asked, "How can I learn about genealogy and doing research on an individual?"

Jen reached under the counter and handed Rachel a flyer and said, "There's a class starting soon on the basics of genealogy research. It's right here at the library. You can sign up by calling the name on the flyer. But hurry, it's pretty popular and usually fills up quickly."

Rachel took the flyer, thanked her and left the library. Once outside she reached for her phone and made the call to Maggie Birch, the genealogist listed on the sheet.

"Hello, Maggie speaking." The voice sounded familiar.

"Hi, Maggie. This is Rachel Benton."

"Hi Rachel," she paused. "...wait didn't I meet you at the grief group meeting last week? How are you?"

Rachel hadn't made the connection, and smiled when she thought of the woman she'd met.

"Oh, I'm doing fairly well, I suppose. I have good days and not-so-good ones."

"That's the way it goes. It's the same for me. And how's that sweet little girl of yours? Julia, right?"

Rachel smiled. Maggie was so easy to talk with. "That's right. She's doing as well as can be expected. She still has tantrums off and on, and yet there are days when she's all smiles and acts like nothing happened."

"I can imagine how difficult it can be to deal with a little one grieving as well as dealing with your own. I give you a lot of credit for moving to a new town and all."

"Thanks, but it was unavoidable. We had nowhere else to go." Rachel continued. "I'm just glad we ended up here. I really love this little town and I'm getting to know people since Nonna died and I can get out some more."

"Well, give me a call whenever you want to chat."

"I'll do that. But, I really called to ask you something else. I didn't even know it was you I was calling at first," she chuckled, then continued. "I got this flyer about a genealogy class from Jen Frasier at the library. I'm interested and would like to sign up. Is there still room?"

"You're in luck, Rachel. There was a cancellation earlier today, so there's one slot open. I'll put your name on the list."

"Thanks. Is there anything I need for the class?" Rachel wondered if she was getting in over her head.

"No. I'll be bringing all the materials to the first session. We'll be using the library's computers, unless you want to bring your own laptop."

"Okay." Rachel realized she didn't know if there was a fee involved. "Umm. Maggie? Is there a charge?

"No. It's a free class through the library service."

"Fantastic. I'll see you then." Rachel snapped her phone shut and, with a spring to her step, made her way to her car and drove back to Nonna's house.

Pulling into the drive she looked at the house and realized she still didn't feel like it was her home. *At least not until the estate is finalized. And I still haven't heard from Neil Walker.* If she didn't hear by tomorrow, she was going to have to give him another call and nudge him along. She smiled as she thought of him and what he was wearing the last time they met in his office. Perhaps she would take Julia to the Renn Fair, if only to see him in action in his SCA gear. Just the thought of him sent a tingle through her. In her heart and mind, she knew she wasn't ready for any kind of new relationship, but her body was certainly responding to him.

She turned the key in the lock and entered the back door into the kitchen. Taking a deep breath, she realized that the smells had finally disappeared, replaced by the clean smell of lemon polish and floor cleaner. Noticing the light blinking on Nonna's old answering machine, she tapped the key to listen.

Neil Walker's voice said, "Mrs. Benton... Rachel... this is Neil Walker. I've got good news. The court has appointed you administrator and issued the necessary letters testamentary. That means that you now have the right to manage, spend and distribute the assets of the estate. In short, you now have the authority to do what you need in order to pay bills and take care of yourself. Don't forget to do the inventory. If you have any questions, please don't hesitate to give me a call. You still have my cell, right? I look forward to hearing from you."

She listened to the message again, just to be sure she'd heard correctly. Rachel felt relief wash over her. Then she smiled, remembering Neil, and the outfit he was wearing the last time she saw him. A warmth spread through her.

Today was certainly a good day. Feeling full of new energy and inspired by Neil's news, Rachel went from room to room with an eye on the contents. There was one more place in the house she hadn't yet explored. A place that might prove to be a treasure trove of items worth selling, as well as storage spaces where other important documents might be found. She climbed the stairs, past the second floor bedrooms, to the doorway that led to the attic. Unlike most modern attics that could only be reached by crawling through a small space in the ceiling of a closet, this old house had a set of stairs leading to the top floor from a door down the hall from her bedroom.

Once there, Rachel found a large, dry, bright space. Full length windows were on all four walls, the roof rafters were tall enough that she could stand easily and the floor was solid wood. Just as Rachel thought, the space was filled with old furniture, chairs, and trunks stacked everywhere. Boxes of books and magazines were interspersed throughout the attic space. *Okay, more trash to haul. At least this is the last of it.*

In the corner sat a spinning wheel and a yarn winder, discolored yarn still attached. Nearby was a Singer treadle sewing machine. Rachel could imagine Nonna or her mother using the machine. *I wonder if it still works.*

On a small table sat what looked like a jewelry box. She went to it and opened the lid. She was wrong. It was a music box. She carefully pulled the lever to wind it and listened. The round cylinder had raised bumps. As it spun, the bumps plucked the comb with metal teeth making the soft music play. What a lovely sound. *Nonna, you have such treasures. Now why would you hide this in the attic?*

The music continued to play as she crossed to a beautiful roll-top desk. This looks valuable, she thought. Looking around she realized again that she didn't have the skill needed to make a decision on the value of the things in this house. She began to feel overwhelmed again. The house contained so much that could bring her the money she so desperately needed, but she didn't want to make mistakes in valuing the items. *I'm going to have to bring in an expert.* Again, she thought of MariBeth. Rachel flipped open her phone, took a picture of the desk, and emailed it to her friend with a message to call as soon as she got it.

Ten minutes later her phone buzzed.

"Ah, hello, MariBeth. That was quick."

"I was just having lunch and saw your message. What is that picture you sent me?"

"I'm in the attic at Nonna's house. You won't believe all that is up here. There's furniture everywhere and old trunks, a music box. Help!"

MariBeth laughed. "I'm not busy right now – I can come over after I finish lunch and see what you have there. Have you been making a list?"

"No, not yet. I've been much too busy working on just getting the place cleaned of the junk. And I've been doing some research at the library. I'm curious about the history of the house."

"Well, I'll be there as soon as I can. Don't touch a thing."

"See you in a bit." Rachel snapped the phone closed, and felt her stomach grumble. It had been a long time since she had a small breakfast.

Rachel went down to the kitchen for a quick lunch, and looked around for something to write on to start the inventory.

A short time later, she heard a knock at the door. Rachel opened the door to let her friend enter. "Come on in. I'm so glad you could come today."

The day was a warm one. Rachel saw MariBeth was wearing a pale blue short sleeved lacy blouse with a linen skirt. She glanced down at her own second-hand clothes and felt second best once again. *Can she tell where I get my clothes?*

MariBeth seemed oblivious to Rachel's discomfort. "I'm so excited to see what you've found up in the attic. The picture you sent has me intrigued. I've only seen some of the other rooms of the house."

"Yes and those rooms were filled with junk so you could hardly see what was there. I've made huge progress, but decided today was the day for the attic."

They made their way to the top floor and when MariBeth saw the contents, her eyes widened. "Oh, Rachel, this is fantastic!"

Rachel watched as MariBeth walked around the room, stopping at different pieces, hand caressing the antique wood chairs. "I think the desk is the best piece up here, what do you say?"

MariBeth crossed to the large desk that Rachel had noticed earlier. "Rachel, do you know what this is?"

"All I know is that it's a desk and it's old. That's why I asked you to come. You're certainly more of an expert than I am."

"This oak roll top desk looks to have been made around the 1870s, I think. Look at all the details." She caressed the smooth surface, and then gently rolled open the lid. "See – there are two trays that pull out on each side of the center drawer. And the cubby drawers are fantastic. Look how many there are! This piece is in great shape, too. All the original hardware is in place." She pulled open one of the side drawers.

"Two little keys. Did you see these?" She picked them out of the drawer.

"Yes, I found them earlier." Rachel was beginning to feel as excited as her friend.

"Have you tried to open it yet?"

"No. I called you right away. Here, let me." Rachel took them from MariBeth's outstretched hand, inserted one key into the lock, and opened the center drawer. Inside was a collection of old pencils, pens, useless rubber bands and rusty paper clips. In the back of the drawer she found an envelope. A quick glance inside showed her grandmother's birth and marriage certificates. *I'll need these for the estate.* She set it aside without looking at the details. In another drawer, stuck way in the back was another packet of papers tied together with twine. She drew them out and noticed the date stamped on the top envelope.

Rachel exclaimed with joy, "Oh, this is fantastic. More letters from the 1860s!" She whirled and showed the packet to MariBeth then realized she hadn't yet shared the other letters she'd found and read. "I haven't told you about what I found. Remember those boxes in Nonna's closet?" MariBeth nodded and she continued, "In one of the boxes I found letters tied with a ribbon, and two little diaries. I've read all I've found so far. It's such a sad tale of a soldier named James and his wife, Emma, during the Civil War." She paused and glanced at the new bundle of letters in her hand. "Maybe these will add to the story."

"Rachel, do you know how valuable anything from the Civil War is? I hope you're being careful with them."

"Of course I am." The hurt in her voice was unmistakable. "I may not know much about history or antiques, but I know that these are old and should be treated carefully." She looked at the letters and other documents in her hand and put them aside to bring downstairs and read later.

"I'm sorry, Rachel." MariBeth put her hand on Rachel's arm.

Rachel nodded without speaking. Then, pointing to the desk, she asked, "So, what do you think this piece is worth?"

MariBeth frowned in thought. "Well, I'm not sure." She paused. "Without doing any research on it, I'd give it a ballpark figure – five to six thousand."

Rachel voice squeaked in disbelief. "Wow, that's amazing."

"I told you there were valuable things in this house." MariBeth's eyes swept around the room again, and then she looked down at her watch. "Sorry, I have to get going pretty soon."

Rachel was confused. She thought MariBeth had said she was free the rest of the afternoon.

"Oh, okay. Thanks for your help." She looked around the attic space. "I just have to decide whether this is something I want to sell. Then, I still have to go through the rest of the attic and rooms below. That inventory is much more important now."

MariBeth gave Rachel a quick look, and then her eyes scanned the room. "When do you think you'll get started?"

Thinking of all she had to do in the next day or so, Rachel responded, "I'll need to clear this space of the junk first, and then I can start with what's on this floor, but the rest of the house? Oh, probably not for a couple of days."

"I'm not going to be able to help. I have a lot of work at the museum to get ready for the new toy exhibit."

"MariBeth, that's all right. You've done enough for me already. And I should ask my lawyer what to do. If you're not sure of the value of things, it sounds like I may need a professional."

"If that's what you decide, there's a list of appraisers at the museum. We use them all the time and they have good reputations. Let me check and I'll get back to you. Just remember, even though I say this piece might be worth six thousand, you still have to find a buyer for it. Someone who wants to pay that much. Ultimately a piece is only as valuable as the market demands. There may not be a local market for this desk." She glanced at her watch again. "I have a couple minutes yet, let's check out the rest of the furniture on this floor."

MariBeth pointed to the nearby tables and chairs. "Those mismatched chairs are in fairly good shape, except for the caning in the seats. That will need to be replaced. I'd guess about a hundred-fifty for the four of them. The tables? Hmmm, I'd say between three hundred and five hundred each. The steamer trunks vary quite a bit in value and they may have something in them."

Rachel lifted the lid of one domed-shape trunks. A musty smell hit her nose. The trunk was filled with old clothing. Trunk after trunk yielded the same result. "Oh, my. I guess I'll have to get some air freshener up here before I take those things out of their trunks."

MariBeth wiped her hands on her skirt. "Vintage clothing has value, depending on age and condition. Have you ever been to an antique show?"

Rachel shook her head. "I've never had an interest in old stuff before."

"There's one tomorrow at the Community Center. You should go. It'll help you as you look around the house at the things that are here. Dealers come from all around the region and most of them buy as well as sell, so you might find a buyer for something you want to sell. Oh, and you should come to the museum too. You might be interested in seeing the kinds of things that are on display there."

Rachel nodded. *More things to think about.* She had never been interested in history. She'd hated the way it was taught when she was in school. Memorizing lists of names and dates had no meaning for her. Daylight was beginning to dim, and Rachel realized that they'd been at it for an hour. Julia would be home soon from her play date with a school friend. She looked around the room one more time. *Too much to do and not enough time.* "Let's stop here – this will keep for another day."

They walked downstairs and MariBeth left saying, "Give me a call next week."

"Okay." Rachel wondered about her friend. She was acting odd today. *What changed her mind – why did she have to rush off so quickly?*

Chapter 17
Later that evening

Later that evening, after dinner and putting Julia to bed, Rachel settled in her own bed, and reached for the bundle of letters she had discovered earlier in the attic desk. She thought she had read all the letters from the 1860s. These were dirty and torn in places, held together with twine. Untying the dirty twine, she discovered five letters. Rachel saw that four of them were addressed to James Beardsley in various places in Virginia. The return address had no name. It just said Oxford, NY. Rachel noticed that not one of them had been opened. *Why would James keep the letters in his knapsack all that time, unopened?* Only the top letter, addressed to Emma, was opened. Rachel carefully took this out and read.

Dear Madam Beardsley,

I am writing these few lines and send my deepest regrets for your loss. I realize you must have heard from many others in our company by now. Before James left on his last scouting mission, he handed me this packet of letters, and asked that I send them to you, if anything should happen to him. I know he kept your letters with him, as he read them over and over. They brought him so much comfort. James was a good soldier - a good friend, and I, for one, shall miss him terribly.

Yours,
Harris

* * *

Rachel returned the letter to the envelope. She seemed to recall the name Harris from one of James' letters to Emma. Wasn't he the one whose girlfriend died in the fire? Curious, she took her letter opener and carefully slit the first of the unopened letters. Again Rachel was swept back to 1863 as she read the letters to James.

* * *

Dear James,

Sometimes a father's words are harsh. Sometimes a son responds with harsher words. At the time, I thought we might have more time to put aside those words and come to some understanding. You have always been headstrong, knowing what you want, and going out to get it. I remember a time when you were just a lad. You had it in your mind that you would go fishing. Without a word to me, you set off with your small pole and a few worms. Hours later, after your Ma and I searched for you everywhere, a neighbor returned you to us soaking wet.

Seems you had reached too far and fell in the river. The current swept you downstream. Lucky for you that farmer was there at the time, spotted you and pulled you to shore. I almost lost you that day. Do you remember that?

When you said you wanted to join the cavalry and fight in this dagburned war, I fought like heck to keep you with me and safe. But no, off you went. And without us saying goodbye, as you did when you were that lad going off fishing.

Months have gone and now I find that I need to try to put aside the hard feelings between us. Can you find it in your heart to do that? I certainly forgive you and hope you can do the same.

Please let me hear from you. Your sisters would like to know that you are well.

Your Father,
Asa

* * *

Oh, no, Rachel thought. Asa was James' father. Remembering the diaries and earlier letters, Rachel recalled that James and Asa had a severe falling out before James left for the war. Here, it looked like Asa was trying to make amends. She slipped the letter back into its envelope and opened the rest, one at a time and read each one.

* * *

Dear James,

I have not yet received a reply from my last letter. I hope that you are still doing well. Here we read the news of the army, and sometimes one of the other fathers will tell the news of their son in the same regiment as you, so I know a little of what you are doing. But I would like to hear your words. Have you not forgiven me?

Your Father,
Asa

* * *

Dear James,

I have tried to find your wife, Emma. Yes, I finally admit that you and she are husband and wife. She left so suddenly, without telling where she was going. I am still hoping I might find her and ask her forgiveness as well, but have not been successful yet. Just as you and I parted angry, I must admit I was much more so with Emma. She really did no wrong, though, at the time, I felt she had overstepped her bounds as a servant in my employ. Knowing how gallant you are, son, I find it hard to imagine how she could not have fallen for you. But still, at the time I couldn't see that, just as I couldn't understand you wanting to leave me, and her.

Your sisters are doing well, growing tall. They miss you and Emma. I would bring the dear girl back if I could only find her.

Your Father,
Asa

* * *

Dear James,

Weeks and months have gone by without a word from you, no response to any of my letters. I fear my letters are not reaching you. I fear too, that you are dismissing them and that you don't know what has been happening. I hope that is not true so I will take a few lines to tell what has been going on.

Quarry work has been good to me lately. I have become a partner to Sirus Johnson. I do not think you know of him. Together we have created a new Quarry Company. We have orders for our bluestone from many places - even as far away as New York City. Some of the stone is being used for sidewalks, and some for buildings. We have done so well financially that I have decided to set aside some money and put it in a fund for you and for your children, should there be any. I have placed it in the bank in town and will leave it there for when you return. If something should happen to me, the bank knows what to do.

Ah, James. It would do my heart good to have a letter from you. I hear word of the great battles you have been in and I live in fear you will be *injured or killed. Can we not set aside our differences? Please do write.*

Your Father,
Asa

* * *

Rachel, feeling the tightness in her head and chest, was close to tears again, reading about James and Emma and now Asa. Such as tragic story. Father and son. Husband and wife. Rachel reached for Emma's box and put Asa's letters with the others from James. She was curious about the mention of a fund that was established. *I wonder what became of it. That's another question that will probably remain unanswered. Oh, this is so frustrating.*

She set Emma's box back on the nightstand next to another one she'd not felt like opening until now. It contained mementoes from her marriage to Jon that she'd brought from California. She'd had to let so much go, but had kept this.

Opening the box she rifled through the contents, remembering the good times, the wonderful times, she'd had with Jon. A small ribbon and pressed flower from her wedding bouquet, a post card from their honeymoon, a picture of Jon in his uniform holding a newborn Julia, and a tiny pink baby bootie were all carefully kept with the letters Rachel got from Jon when he was first overseas. Rachel smiled as her mind was flooded with memories.

She'd be sure to keep these, and share them with Julia to help her remember her Daddy. Rachel replaced the memento box next to Emma's.

Chapter 18
The next day

It was a warm Saturday and the parking lot was filled when Rachel pulled in to the Village Antique Show. Walking toward the building, Rachel realized she was finally able to be outside without a jacket. Up until now she'd thought she would never be warm again, but spring finally arrived, spreading warmth and beauty across the town. There were so many more trees here on the East Coast, it seemed. And now many of them were blooming, pink and white and purple flowers gracing their branches.

Rachel had never been to a show like this and had no idea what to expect. She spotted several people returning to their cars with a variety of odd objects in their arms. With Julia in tow, she entered the large warehouse building and paid the small admission fee. When they rounded the corner, Julia's eyes widened, "Wow!"

Rachel agreed and paused to take it all in. The huge room was filled with row upon row of dealers. Each had a space artfully decorated with their wares. People were wandering up and down the aisles, stopping at the various booths, haggling with the dealers for the best price on an item they found interesting. Hand in hand, Rachel and Julia slowly went from booth to booth, admiring the items that were displayed. Pausing at one, Rachel spotted some crocks and old bottles.

Julia pointed, "Look Mama, I saw those kinds of bottles in the basement, remember?"

"Yes, I remember." Rachel turned over the price tag on one small brown bottle, and gasped. She was amazed at the price. Seventy-five dollars for one old bottle! She remembered seeing at least a dozen in the basement.

When Julia started to reach for another Rachel scolded, "Don't touch. If you break something, I would have to pay for it, and we don't have the money." Julia frowned but kept her hand down. They moved along down the row.

At another booth, Rachel spotted some neatly folded linen and again was astonished to see the price tag on the one she picked up. They looked similar to some that she'd found in Nonna's house. During the next couple of hours, as they wandered the booths, Rachel jotted prices in a small notebook she always carried in her purse. *This will sure help with making decisions. But, MariBeth was right. I need an appraiser. I don't know enough about this and, before*

I throw something away that might be valuable, I need an expert's help.

At the end of a row, near the exit, she spotted a sign at the booth. *Sam's Appraisals*. A woman sat in a chair behind a table with an assortment of items displayed. Rachel saw her name tag said Samantha Matthews. She was neatly dressed in a retro forty's style dress with a shawl covering her wide shoulders. Long braided hair hung down her back and her half glasses hung from a chain like a necklace. She was working on a counted cross stitch sampler. A teen boy sat nearby, earphones inserted, fingers rapidly moving as he played a hand-held video game. He ignored her when Rachel stopped.

"Can I help you," Samantha asked setting aside her hooped sampler.

"Yes, perhaps you can," Rachel replied, reaching across the table to shake hands. "I need an appraiser and saw your sign. Are you available?"

"I am. Do you have the item here?"

"Um, no. I need more than one item appraised." Rachel explained about the death of her grandmother and the need to make an inventory for the estate."

Sam took a card from a small stack on the table and handed it to Rachel. "Here's my phone number." Her dark eyes narrowed, "I'm very familiar with what's needed for an estate appraisal."

"How long have you been doing appraisals?" Rachel asked.

"I have ten years experience." She glanced at Rachel, and then looked at the boy. He glanced up at Sam, but continued to ignore Rachel. "I've done appraisals for estates in the area." Rachel remembered

MariBeth had a list of good appraisers, but here was one handy. *Should I hire Sam? I can't wait for Maribeth.*

"Um...how much do you charge?" Rachel asked.

Sam paused, thinking. "The initial consultation will be free. After that, the cost will be determined once I assess the contents of the house, to get an idea of how much work I'll need to do."

"Okay, but I don't have money up front for your fee. You'll have to bill Nonna's estate. Will that be a problem?"

"No, that's fine. Most estates work that way."

"So, what will you need to do?" Rachel had no idea what would be involved in the process.

"First, I'll need to meet with you at the house to get an idea of the contents. Then we can go from there. Most of the time, the work I do is after I take photos and make a list. It takes a while for me to find the value of each of the items." Sam smiled, as her eyes again shifted to the boy.

Rachel was curious about the unspoken exchange she observed, but ignored the uneasiness she felt. "That's sounds good. The sooner I get this done, the happier I'll be." She paused, looked at Sam's card in her hand, and made a hasty decision. "I'd like you to do the appraisal."

Sam nodded. "That's great." She took out a date book from beneath a pile of papers, glanced at it and said, "How does a week from Friday sound? That's the earliest I can do it."

"That'll have to do then." Rachel gave Samantha her address and directions to Nonna's house and they shook hands again.

Taking Julia's hand, the two wandered away, looking at other booths. Rachel continued to make notes. *I'll use the notes to see what the appraiser tells me when she looks at Nonna's things, to compare prices.*

When Rachel left the show two hours later, she felt like she'd learned a great deal, and she had an expert to help with what she didn't know.

Unfortunately, she didn't overhear the muted conversation between the woman and the boy after she walked away from their booth. "I think we got a good one," the boy said. Sam nodded in agreement.

Chapter 19

A week later

Rachel drove to town dreading the upcoming meeting. Patsy Lee, from her lawyer's office, called and said he needed to meet with her as soon as possible. This was the earliest appointment she could get. The day was a warm one with clear blue sky and puffy white clouds. The spring flowers were in full bloom. The Square was now a riot of color. Earlier blooming tulips and daffodils were now joined with .forsythia and lilac. A crab apple tree boasted dainty white flowers. Such a beautiful day should not bring bad news.

She parked her obnoxiously loud car, walked into the bank and up the stairs to the lawyer's office, fearing what she may hear. Reaching for the door handle, she paused to take a deep breath, trying to release some of the nervous tension.

Again she was greeted by Patsy Lee, who today wore all black. Her nails, her lips, and even the large bow in her hair were black. Rachel wondered how Neil Walker could have such a person working as his secretary. Maybe appearance doesn't make a difference in client relationships. Glancing at Patsy again, she shook her head.

"Hello, Mrs. Benton. Mr. Walker will be with you in a minute." Rachel nodded, her eyes falling to a framed photo on Patsy's desk she didn't remember noticing before. Three people were pictured. Two older, a man and a woman, and a younger girl, about six years old, dressed in a beautiful white dress. Rachel guessed it was Patsy and perhaps the other two were her parents. Now what could make a beautiful girl decide to change her appearance so? Rebellion? Patsy saw Rachel's focused eyes, pointed to the photo and said, "It was taken five years ago."

Rachel was confused. "Sorry, I didn't mean to intrude."

"No, it's okay," said Patsy with a touch of sadness in her voice. "That's my daughter with my ex-husband's parents.

"She's adorable."

"Yes, she was." The pain was now evident in her eyes. "Caren died shortly after that photo was taken."

"Oh, I'm so sorry." Rachel couldn't imagine the pain of losing a child. The deaths of Jon and Nonna were painful enough... but Julia. She felt her stomach clench with the thought.

Patsy gave a weak smile, "It's all right. You couldn't know."

"What happened? If you don't mind my asking,"

Rachel's voice was quiet.

"She was visiting with my ex. He was on the way to bring her home to me, driving on the highway, when a tractor trailer blew a tire right in front of them. The resulting crash killed them both." She paused, and then continued, "I pretty much lost it – for a long time." She paused. "And then I met Neil Walker and he gave me a chance. I've been working here ever since – still trying to gain some stability in my life. I must admit, it's sure been hard." She looked up and gave Rachel a wan smile.

"I'm so sorry, Patsy," Rachel repeated, not knowing what else to say to the woman. She felt embarrassed as she realized how much she had misinterpreted Patsy. She wasn't as young as she looked; not nearly as frivolous. *How could I have made such a terrible mistake?*

"I've had this photo put away until just last week. This office has been a place to put aside the past, but now I'm strong enough again to face Caren here as well as at home. At least that's what my therapist told me." The sorrow was clearly evident in her voice as she turned back to her computer keyboard and began typing, topic dismissed. "You can sit while you're waiting."

Rachel sat, again taking a magazine. Rifling through its pages, her mind wandered. She thought about Patsy and then wondered again why Neil had called for her. She didn't have long to wait. The door opened and Walker poked his head out and motioned her to come into his office. Her heart skipped a beat when she saw him.

Today he was impeccably dressed in a grey linen

suit. His cream shirt was set off neatly by a striped tie. Inside his office, Rachel noticed the ever-present sword was in its usual place guarding the end of the lawyer's desk. She smiled at the memory of him standing there, sword in hand, the last time she was here in his office.

He seemed to notice her glance and returned the smile.

"Nice to see you again, Rachel. Have a seat." He sat in the chair behind the desk and shifted the stack of papers in front of him.

"Good to see you too." She realized she meant it. This man surprised her each time she saw him and today was no different. She hesitated, started to say something, and coughed slightly, choking on unspoken words.

"How are you doing?" His forehead furrowed with concern.

"Oh, as good as I can be, I suppose," she replied.

"Well, I'm glad you were able to find time to meet with me so quickly."

Rachel squirmed in her seat, smoothed her nervous hands down the front of her black slacks, and then began to twiddle her ring. "It sounded like an emergency so I made the time. What is it?"

"Um, I don't think this is going to come to anything at all." He looked at the file in front of him.

She frowned, not liking the tone in his voice, sounding like impending disaster.

He saw her face and tried to calm her, "I don't think you'll need to worry."

His words generated a new flock of butterflies that fluttered in her stomach, "What is it?"

"Okay." He took a piece of paper from the file on his desk. "I received this letter in the mail yesterday from a lawyer in another town." He glanced at the letter. "This states that he's representing someone who is claiming to be a closer relative of your grandmother."

Rachel was shocked. "But that's ridiculous! There is no one else, just me," Rachel paused, uncertain if what she said was true. "At least that's what I was always told." She frowned, thinking, trying to come up with anything she might have heard differently.

Walker interrupted her thoughts, "Because you are now the administrator of the estate, appointed by the court, we'll need to address this right away. That's why I called you in. I'm sorry this is happening. I know you are anxious to have the estate finalized. This will only extend the process."

"Who's making this claim?"

He glanced down at the letter again. "Sorry. The letter doesn't say. It just mentions a client."

"So what do we do now?" Rachel's stomach was churning with this new development.

"We have to reply to this letter with one of our own. Preferably with something that will prove in some way that you are your Grandmother's only descendant. Can you do that?"

"I think so. I've found Nonna's birth and marriage certificates in the attic. There may be something else at the house in all the paperwork I've yet to get to." She paused, "Oh, and I've been thinking of doing some genealogy research, would that help?"

"Anything you have that can prove your case will be very helpful."

"How much time do we have?"

"I can respond to this query from the lawyer with one of my own. That will give us some time. Once I hear we'll need to work more quickly. So, I would say probably two or three weeks."

"Okay. I'll get started working on this today." She stood and extended her hand to shake his.

He walked around the desk, put a hand in hers and said, "Don't worry too much about this. I don't think they have much of a case."

Rachel felt his other hand covering hers, its warmth flowing through her, "Thanks for the encouragement. I don't know if I can stop worrying. It seems that's all I have been doing for a long time."

Slipping his hand along her back, he escorted her to the door. "This will be done soon and you can get on with your life."

The nervous butterflies were joined by a fluttering of something growing between them. His hand on her back sent comfort and something else. She didn't want to think about what it all might mean.

"I appreciate your help with all this. I certainly will be happy when the estate business is all done and Julie and I can move forward and leave all this uncertainty behind us."

Rachel left the office and, walking to her car, noticed the skies had turned grey during her meeting. A storm threatened. What happened to the beautiful spring day?

She ran the list of things she had to do in her head. *I need to finish searching the house to find a definitive connection to Nonna. I have the birth certificate but will that be enough? Now I need to do some genealogy researching as well. Oh, and the appraisal needs to be done right away so I can sell some things quickly.* The money in her wallet was dwindling rapidly. The car needed fixing, the refrigerator and food cupboards were quickly emptying, and all Nonna's bills still needed to be paid.

She drove home feeling like that cartoon character who always had a gloomy cloud hovering over his head.

* * *

For the next two days, Rachel searched all the nooks and crannies of Nonna's house looking for anything that might assist in making her case for the lawyer's report. She found copies of her mother's birth certificate but nothing else. Gathering all the important papers in one spot, she would take them with her to the genealogy class on Monday. *Maybe I'll learn enough there to be able to get enough information for Neil Walker. Maybe the instructor will be able to help.*

Chapter 20
The next day

It was a damp, chilly Monday morning when Rachel walked up the steps to the library. *Where did spring go? I'm so tired of being damp and cold. Days like this make me want to pack up and go back to California!* She pulled open the door and was grateful for the blast of warm air. *At least they still have heat on.*

She eased into a chair at one of the library's computer stations, set her notebook down, and glanced around. Ten people sat at nearby computers. Some were already busy exploring a variety of websites. Others sat patiently with notebooks by their side ready to take notes. She recognized some of the younger ones. They were often here. She wondered at their interest in genealogy.

Rachel watched as the instructor stood, back to the group, and fiddled with the connections to hook up the laptop to the projector. When she finished, the screen behind her lit up with the first image of her PowerPoint presentation.

Taking her notes in hand, she faced the group of students and smiled when she spotted Rachel.

"Hi, Rachel, I'm so glad to see you again. You're looking good."

"Thanks, Maggie." Rachel felt embarrassed to be singled out, even though she'd known that Maggie was the instructor of the group, tonight she was just a student like the others. "I'll talk to you after the group, okay."

Maggie nodded, and taking a deep breath, started the class. "Welcome, everyone. My name is Maggie Birch. I started working on my own family tree fifteen years ago and got hooked and now I'm a professional genealogist. I also volunteer to teach this basics class in genealogy. You're all here because you have an interest in finding more about some of your relatives and don't know how to get started. I'm here to help with that." She looked at the group and saw she had everyone's attention.

She passed out a packet of information. "If you look on the first page, you'll see a list of some of the most useful websites."

Rachel listened intently, taking notes on the packet as Maggie proceeded with her presentation. It was all fascinating and a bit overwhelming at the same time. *I'm going to have a hard time getting up to speed fast enough to gather the information I need for the court in the time-frame required.*

Maggie finished her talk two hours later, "Feel free to stay and try out some of the websites. If you need some more help, or want someone to do the searching for you, please give me a call." She handed everyone her business card.

After taking care of the computer and projector and gathering her things, she stopped by Rachel's station.

"I'm sorry, Rachel. I can't stay to talk right now. Give me a call, okay?"

Rachel nodded and watched Maggie leave the library.

Well, how hard can this be? Rachel opened the internet connection and typed in the first site on the list. When the LDS site opened, she typed her grandmother's name in the appropriate slots. Up popped a census report. *Okay, now what?* She traveled the link and tried to see the actual census document but found she would need to pay for access to the site. She couldn't go that route, she had no credit card. *This is not good.* She decided to try another website from the instructor's list.

Her fingers tapped the keyboard as she typed in *Cyndislist*. As the name indicated, it turned out to be a website that provided a list of links to other sites that had genealogical information. After clicking on some of them, she noticed that some were free, but most others requested she sign up and pay for the information. *I'm not getting anywhere fast.*

Next she tried a site called *RootsWeb*. She wandered that website and again input her grandmother's name in the spaces provided. And she was promptly asked to start a free trial, for membership, for a credit card. *Oh, this is so frustrating!* She remembered what her lawyer had said when she asked if she should hire a genealogist. "I think that's a great idea," he had said. "That would provide a professional's opinion of the legitimacy of your claim as well as negate the other person's claim."

She logged off the computer, gathered her notes, and left the library. Once outside, she took out her phone and dialed the number on Maggie Birch's business card.

"Hello?"

"Hi, Maggie? It's Rachel."

"Rachel, I'm glad you called. I'm sorry I had to leave in such a hurry."

Oh, no problem," Rachel paused, and then continued. "Listen after the class I stayed a bit and tried some of the sites you talked about in the class."

"Did it work?"

"Well, yes and no. I was able to get to the sites, but then when I wanted more information, I was asked to sign up for a service with a credit card. I don't have a card so I'm pretty stuck."

Maggie laughed. "Yeah, that can be frustrating. So, how can I help you?"

Rachel took a deep breath, "Here's my situation. You know about my grandmother and that I'm the administrator of the estate. Well, I found out that there's someone out there making a claim to be one of Nonna's relatives. I don't know who it is, but my attorney has said that if I can prove that I am the sole heir, then this person wouldn't have a case. I'm really under a time crunch. I thought I'd be able to do it on my own, after taking your class this morning. But then when I tried to get anywhere, well…I need your expertise.

"I can certainly help," said Maggie. "Listen, my office is in my home and I'm not busy at the moment. Can you come by now?"

Rachel checked her watch. Julia wouldn't be home for another two hours. "Sure, I just have to grab a quick lunch. I'll be there as soon as I can."

"No, no. Come on over and I'll fix us something. We can talk as we eat."

"Okay, that sounds great. Where are you?"

Rachel listened as Maggie gave directions to her house, snapped her phone shut, and hurried to her car. The drive took just twenty minutes, taking Rachel into a part of town she hadn't been to before. The houses she was passing were set far apart and farther back from the road. Large lawns and landscaped gardens seemed to be the rule here. It all spoke of money.

Rachel pulled into the long driveway that curved to the front of a three story home perched on a hill. Built in the same era as Nonna's house, this one was in much better shape. Baskets of flowers hanging from hooks on the front porch made for an inviting feel. She made her way along the red brick sidewalk to the front door. Before she could knock, Maggie opened the door with a warm smile and a quick hug.

"Hi, come on in."

"Thanks for seeing me so quickly." Rachel followed Maggie down the hall to the kitchen, where she saw Maggie had laid out luncheon at the table. "Mmmmm. Smells good."

The two ate lunch as they chatted about a variety of topics. Neither one seemed to want to talk about recent deaths, so they talked about Julia. Rachel told Maggie about exploring the basement and finding the gravestone.

"I still don't know how it came to be there. Another of the many mysteries I've discovered in the house so far. And it doesn't look like I'll find out – that's not something that can be looked up in a book at the library."

Maggie laughed. "Oh, you are so right. I always find it amazing how families don't talk about things until it is too late and those with the information in their heads are long gone. I've always encouraged my clients to sit down with their older relatives and record the conversation. Ask them about their youth, ask them about some of the things in the house, pull out the old family photos and ask who is in them, and what their story is. That's what makes a family history so rich. I have the ability to get the names and dates and in rare occasions, there's a letter or other information about the people, but for the most part it's just the bare bones."

"I've come to realize I should have spent the last month while I was caring for my grandmother talking to her, instead of just taking care of her health needs. I was so young when my mother and father died, and had little interest in family history – I lost out there, too." Rachel felt the missed opportunity settle on her like a heavy blanket.

After lunch, Rachel followed Maggie into her office. It was a large brightly lit room to the right of the entryway. Yellow wallpaper and crisp white curtains added to the cheerful look. A large, oak desk was centered along one wall. Matching bookshelves, neatly filled with binders labeled with family names, lined two more walls.

Seeing Rachel's glance, Maggie explained, "Those binders are the result of the fifteen years of work on my family's history I mentioned in class today."

"Fifteen years? Wow, I had no idea researching a family history would take that long." She frowned. "I don't have that much time to find the information I need!"

Maggie chuckled. "No problem. It sounds like you are looking for specific information for a limited time frame. It shouldn't take as long to research."

"I just spent several hours at the library getting nowhere. I found many of those sites required a credit card. Like I said, I don't have one, so I got stumped pretty quickly. It was very frustrating."

"Well, I have access to all of those sites. They are well worth their cost, if you are interested in searching for your family history. It should only take a week or two to find what you need for the lawyer."

"That's fantastic." Rachel paused, wondering if she should tell about those Civil War diaries and letters. She was so curious about the people in them. Was she connected to them in some way? She decided it couldn't hurt to ask Maggie to explore beyond her grandmother.

"Maggie, there's one more thing. I found some diaries and letters dated 1862 and 1863.

"Wow, Rachel, that's great. Primary source material is always so valuable for gathering information. And Civil War era letters are even more precious."

"I have no idea why they are in my grandmother's house or why she would have them. I've never heard my mother mention them and certainly my grandmother didn't before she died. I can't help but think that perhaps I might be related to the people in some way too. Is that something you can find out for me?"

"I certainly can. I'll just go further back – as much as I can. I might take be a bit longer to gather that information, but I can do it."

"Awesome! She paused, "But, I can't pay you right away. Not until the estate is settled. Is that okay?"

"Sure thing." She reached for a new file folder and a pad of paper and gestured to a nearby chair. "Okay, have a seat. I just need as much information as you can give me right now, so I can get started."

Over the next hour Rachel shared what she knew, showing the information in the files she'd brought to the library, then stood. "Thank you so much!"

"No problem. I'll give you a call when I have the report done."

"Thanks again…for lunch, for your help, for your friendship." She paused. "I'm so glad I met you, Maggie." Rachel gave her new friend a hug and left the house. Relief spread through her and she took a deep breath of the chilly air. *Perhaps things will all work out.*

* * *

She started the car, heard the loud roar and moaned. *Please, car, last a little bit longer.* She drove slowly home, listening to the loud, growling engine when she spotted a sign. *Will buy junk cars.* Now there's an idea, she thought. She remembered Nonna's Pinto still sitting in the garage. She'd driven it a few times. It was a newer car and it ran better than her own. For now, anyway. *Now why didn't I think of this before?*

She pulled to the side of the road, took out her cell and dialed the number on the sign. Half hour later she pulled into Nonna's driveway followed by a tow truck.

The driver stepped out of his truck and followed Rachel into the house. After signing some papers, he handed Rachel an envelope with four hundred dollars. He hooked up her old rusty, noisy car and drove it away. She felt relieved to have money in her pocket again. *Now, I won't have to worry about a noisy car falling apart and I can get some groceries.* Her food cupboards had gotten very bare in the last three days.

Chapter 21
That same night

"Daddy? Mama? Mama!" Julia screamed from her room. Rachel woke with a start and glanced at the clock. It was just three o'clock, the middle of the night. Grabbing her robe, she raced down the hall to find Julia, sitting in her bed, sniffling, clutching Bear close.

"What's the matter, sweetie. Did you have another bad dream?" Rachel put an arm around her daughter and found her nightgown clinging to her shaking body.

Julia nodded, still sobbing. Rachel put a hand to Julia's head. *No fever.*

Rachel drew her daughter onto her lap, caressed her long hair and murmured, "Shhh. It's okay. I'm right here." These nightmares, that had once been more frequent, still came unexpectedly, and Julia often had trouble remembering what it was that caused her to cry out in the night. With all that has happened to her, to them both, in the past several months, Rachel was amazed she didn't have more issues. For the most part, she seemed to be handling things well, with only the nightmares and the occasional tantrums to mar the serene daughter Rachel knew. Only time will heal, although she knew the scars would be there forever. She still mourned her own parents and she'd lost them as an adult.

When Julia's sobbing quieted, Rachel went into the bathroom and dampened a washcloth with cool water. She returned to Julia and pulled off the wet nightgown. She wiped Julia down with the cool cloth and helped her into a clean, dry pair of pajamas. Julia looked up at Rachel with sad eyes. "Read me a story, Mama," she begged.

"Okay, one book and then you need to try to go back to sleep." Rachel read one of Julia's favorite books as Julia snuggled next to her. By the time she'd finished reading, Julia's eyes were closing. Rachel rescued Bear from the floor and tucked it under the blanket with her daughter. After gently rubbing Julia's back, Julia saw that the little girl had finally fallen asleep.

On the way back to her own bed, Rachel envied her daughter's ability to fall asleep so easily. *I wish I could go back to sleep as quickly,* she thought. Once awakened, she often tossed and turned for an hour or more before sleep claimed her again. Rachel had begun to fall into a light doze when she came awake with a start. *What was that?* Clutching her blankets, she held her breath hoping it would help her hear better. *Was it an animal?* What she heard didn't sound like the typical creaking of the house settling in the night. She listened intently, frozen in her bed. There was one place in the floor in the hallway from the kitchen to the living room that creaked when it was stepped on. She heard that sound now. Then she heard a crash, something fall to the floor with a bang, and a mumbled curse.

Someone was in the house. Her stomach tensed. Nervous sweat sprouted on her forehead. *Where'd I put my phone?* Fumbling in the dark, Rachel's hands found the cell phone on her nightstand. She speed dialed and waited for the response, listening carefully for the footsteps that might be climbing the stairs.

"911, what's your emergency?"

"I need the police," Rachel whispered. "Someone's broken into my house."

"What's your name and address, Ma'am?"

Rachel responded, her voice shaking with fear, "2101 Meadow Lane. The house is set back from the road. But the mailbox has a flag on it."

"Okay, I've sent a call to the police. I'll hold on the line until they come. Where is the intruder?"

"On the ground floor, in the living room, I think. I heard footsteps and something fall."

"And where are you?"

"I'm in my bedroom on the second floor. My daughter is down the hall in her bed. Hurry please!"

Rachel heard the sirens getting louder and sighed in relief. At the same time, she heard her back door slam open. She got out of bed, grabbed her robe again and ran to Julia's room. Her daughter was sound asleep, thank goodness. With the phone in her hand, she said quietly, "I think he left. I heard him at the back door."

"Stay put until the police arrive, Ma'am."

"Okay."

The doorbell rang and Rachel flew downstairs, robe flying. She peered through the peephole and saw the two officers standing there. One had his back to the door, watching the yard around the house. The other stood facing the door, eyes scanning the area.

She opened the door. "Thank you so much for getting here so quickly. I think he ran out the back door! Hurry, you might find him," she said in a rush.

The taller one said, "Bruce, run around back that way. I'll go this way."

The night was dark, and the single bulb at the back door would do nothing to light the expanse of the yard. Rachel watched as the two officers took out flashlights, split and ran around to the back of the house. She waited in the doorway, anxiously twiddling her ring and then jumped as she felt someone touch her arm.

"Oh, goodness, Julia! I didn't hear you come down the stairs." Julia leaned against her, holding Bear and the lovey blanket she hadn't used in a long time.

"Mama? I'm scared."

"It's okay, I'm here." Rachel snuggled the girl close until she saw the two men returning.

"We didn't see anyone, Ma'am. Can you tell us what happened?"

Rachel read the names on the tags pinned to their lapels. Harry Schmidt was the tall one with dark brown hair, balding on the top. His uniform fit snugly, with a too-many-donuts belly folding over his belt. His partner, Bruce Roberts, was shorter, younger, slim and fit. He had sandy hair and a boyish face. Two opposites – in appearance anyway. She explained what she had heard.

Roberts asked, "Can we come in to look around?"

Stepping aside, she waved them in and turned on some lights. The two men quickly went from room to room, upstairs and downstairs, checking in closets and behind doors for any intruder that might still be there.

Walking back into the living room, Rachel noticed a book on the floor. Pointing she said, "That must be what I heard fall."

"Do you see anything missing?" Schmidt walked to the bookshelf where an empty space was found.

"No, I don't." She explained to them her circumstances. "This house belongs to my grandmother. We were staying here when she died. I've worked on cleaning up the house, and met with the lawyer. I've just become the estate's administrator, and I'm in the process of creating an inventory for the estate – but I've not started yet.

"Has anyone been in the house recently?"

"Um." She tried to remember. "My friend, MariBeth Logan. Do you know her? She works at the museum and has been invaluable to me so far. She helped me clean up and came over a couple of days ago to look at some things in the attic." Rachel stopped as she heard herself babbling. She took a deep breath and continued, "Oh, and earlier today a car dealer came in to give me money – I sold my car to him."

Schmidt paused, jotting notes in his little book, looked up and glanced at his partner, who nodded. "Hmmm. Well, we'll have another look around outside again."

"Help yourself," Rachel said. At her side, Julia sneezed and leaned on her. "Come on sweetie. You need to get back to bed." Hand in hand they started up the stairs. Over her shoulder she called, "I'll be down again in a minute."

Schmidt said, "Take your time. We'll be outside. We'll check in again with you before we leave."

Rachel took Julia to her room and, while waiting for her to settle and go back to sleep, she stood by the window watching the two policemen in the back yard.

The yard was large, the lawn ending at the back in a wooded area, and beyond that a small alley to the canal. Fences extended on both sides, but not in the back of the yard along the tree line. With flashlights in hand, Rachel saw Schmidt scouring the yard. Looking for signs of recent footprints, she thought. She watched him reach the tree line, bend over near a pile of leaves and scratch away debris. *Now what could he be finding way back there?* Rachel glanced at her daughter and realized she'd fallen asleep. Tiptoeing out of her room she went down the stairs to the back door where she found Roberts checking the doorframe and locks. He looked up as she approached. "I found marks on the lock. Looks like it was jimmied," he said to her. Then he turned and called out to his partner, "Harry, I found something."

Schmidt turned quickly and hurried to have a look. As he neared the back door, his flashlight caught something else, "There are smudges of a footprint, too. Call the lab and get a forensics team here. Maybe we'll get lucky and find a print. This sure doesn't look like a very professional a job."

"Agreed. We've had some unusual break-ins lately. This seems like one of the same."

Ten minutes later, another car pulled up to the curb and a forensics team walked around the house to the backyard. Schmidt showed the two, Logan and Carter, what he had found and let them get to work. Within an hour they were packing up their equipment.

"Carter, what'd you find?" Schmidt asked.

"We took a cast of the partial foot print and we found a smudged fingerprint on the window next to the door. Sloppy work, on the part of the thief, in my opinion. Looks amateurish."

"Yeah, that's what we thought – in keeping with the others happening in the area lately."

"We'll take it back to the lab and let you know if we get a hit."

Rachel joined the group at the back door. "Ma'am, we're just about done here." Schmidt pointed to his team. "They'll process their findings and once I find out anything, I'll give you a call."

Arms wrapped tightly around her, Rachel said, "Thanks again."

"Ma'am, I suggest you get some sort of alarm system. We've had several thefts and attempted thefts in the area lately – you're kind of out of the way here and it would be best if you had security."

"I'll check into it in the morning. Thanks again."

Schmidt turned to leave, walked two steps down the sidewalk, and paused. He turned and said to her,

"Oh, by the way. When I was in the back yard, I noticed an area where leaves had been pushed to the side. Beneath the leaves was a small marble stone. It was broken and the rest looked to be missing. Maybe it's a small cemetery. Did you know about that?"

She frowned, "No, I hadn't gotten that far in the yard."

"You might want to check it out. Don't know if it means anything to you."

"Thanks." He turned again and left.

* * *

She shut the door and leaned against it, thinking. *This is such a small town. How can this be happening?*
Now five in the morning, she gave up trying to sleep any more that night. Rachel went into the kitchen for a cup of tea.

She took her tea and walked over to the living room bookshelf to look at the book that had fallen and those around it. The book that dropped was a Dickens. It didn't look much different than any other old book on the shelf. What could be so important about this one? There were about a hundred books on the shelves which, by the look of the bindings, varied in age. Some were recently written with authors like Patterson and Coulter. But, Rachel knew, some of the others were very old. *I wish I had more knowledge of antiques. I am way over my head here!*

She shook her head, and then remembered what the policeman had said. *A graveyard in the backyard? How can that be?* Rachel found a flashlight in a kitchen drawer, and went out to look. The sky was beginning to brighten with the early dawn. The air was chilly and she pulled a jacket on over her robe.

She found her way to the very back of the yard and saw the small area the police had mentioned and the white stone. It was lying on its side, as if thrown there. She searched the area and didn't find any sign of other markers. *Hmmm. I don't think it's a cemetery. Looks more like a trash pile. But why would this be here?* She bent to look closer and rubbed at the stone. Hidden under the dirt and rotted leaves she read the words, "*daughter of Emma and James 4 mos*"

She remembered the other stone Julia found in the basement. This one looked like the other half. Connecting the two stones, the engraved message would read, "Cornelia Jane, daughter of Emma and James, 4 mos."

Rachel recalled reading in the letters about the twin daughters of Emma and that one of them had died. *But why would this stone be here, broken in half? Another mystery. It's so frustrating not to have answers to these questions. Oh, Nonna. I wish you were still here.*

Rachel shivered in the early morning dampness. Not finding anything more, she returned to the house.

Chapter 22
Later that morning

An hour and a half later, Rachel managed to get Julia off to school without squabbling. Thank goodness. She was really tired. Julia didn't say anything about the events of the night before. *She's a pretty resilient child. That's for sure.* But there were days when the turmoil in her young life was evident. The tantrums and the nightmares were interspersed with days of a bright and cheerful child. Rachel never knew what she would discover when she greeted her daughter each day. With her own emotions a wreck, Rachel wondered how they were surviving.

Armed with her second cup of coffee, Rachel took the phone book and paged through it looking for a good security company. She found a likely one and gave them a call.

"Apex Security."

"Hi, yes, my name is Rachel Benton and I need a security system put in a house as soon as possible. Can you do that?

"Yes, Ma'am. Let me check..." She waited for him to continue. "Okay, I can have a technician out this morning to see what is needed. Will that work?

"Sounds good, I'll be here." Rachel gave her address and hung up, relieved that the work could be done so soon.

Rachel grabbed a quick shower and changed into her work jeans and a comfortable sweatshirt. She pulled her bedding in order, did the same to Julia's room and did a quick tour of the house making sure nothing else was touched by the intruder of the night before. Nothing seemed out of order, except for that book that was knocked off the shelf. She wondered if perhaps that had scared the thief before he got what he came for. Interesting though, Rachel's purse was nearby and wasn't touched. *What could he have been after?*

The doorbell rang, and Rachel hurried to answer. Pausing to look through the peephole, she saw a tall, thin man in a white uniform shirt and navy slacks carrying a brief case. The sign on the side of the white van parked in the driveway said Apex Security. Rachel opened the door.

"I'm Joe from Apex Security, Ma'am. Here to see what can be done for you."

"Thank you. Come right in."

Standing in the foyer, Joe said, "So, what are you looking to get."

"I want the doors and windows secure. Someone broke in last night and tried to make off with something. Seems I might have some very valuable things here. I don't feel safe anymore."

"We can certainly take care of that. I need to look around and see what needs to be done and let you know what the cost will be. He reached into his briefcase, took out a brochure and handed it to her. "While I'm at it, you can look at this. It gives an idea of what the system will do for you."

Rachel took the brochure and glanced at it while following him around the house. They went in the basement first, and then the first floor. When he was done they returned to the kitchen and sat at the table.

Joe removed other papers from his briefcase and said, "Okay. Here's what I think you need. You should have the basement and the first floor wired for security. That means a central unit will be installed with sensors on each door and window. The unit will be activated using a touchpad we'll put near the door you use the most, but you'll also get a key fob to use for either door. That way you can activate and deactivate the unit when you're outside. In the basement I also recommend you get a sensor that would detect water and gas in case the furnace is working improperly or your water heater springs a leak."

"All that sounds good, but what does it cost?"

"There's an installation fee, and then the monthly fee would be forty-three dollars."

Another expense – but it was desperately needed. I need to think about Julia. Her safety is my primary concern. And I can't have things stolen from Nonna's house. I'm responsible.

Rachel hesitated. "I sure need the system. But I

can't afford to pay you outright. Can you bill the estate? I'm the estate's administrator, and the estate is being probated right now."

"I'll have to ask my supervisor, but I think it'll be okay. Just a minute and I'll give him a call." He took out his cell and punched in the numbers. His supervisor answered his questions quickly and he snapped his phone shut.

"Just as I suspected. Billing the estate is not a problem."

"Great. When can you install it?"

"The earliest appointment would be this Friday."

"Nothing sooner?" Rachel felt uneasy. The break-in had unnerved her, and she didn't feel secure any more in the house. She wanted the system installed now.

"If someone were to cancel, then I could squeeze you in sooner, but no, that's the earliest I have."

"Well, that will have to do then."

He pushed a triplicate form across the table and handed her a pen. "Just fill out the top for me and sign the bottom."

Rachel walked him to the door and saw him out. Closing the door behind her she leaned against it and sighed. One more task done. This one made her feel much better. After last night, she wanted to make sure that she and Julia were safe. She didn't think such a small rural town would have this kind of crime. She remembered Nonna's friends at the diner, talking the other day about some thefts that were taking place in town. Now it had come here. *I should have listened more carefully to them.*

* * *

After a quick lunch, Rachel decided another trip to the basement was in order. She wanted to check the other part of the stone that Julia found. She returned to the basement, armed with a flashlight and a rag – to take care of those ever present cobwebs. *I hate cobwebs. Why are basements always so full of them?*

She went immediately to the little room in the back, lifted the broken stone and carried it to the stairs, where she set it down. Her eye caught sight of the ladder she'd noticed before. This time, she was determined to explore. She reached the ladder and started up the rungs, making sure to carefully test each before putting her full weight on them. No telling how old the ladder was. *It wouldn't be good to fall with no one home.* The ladder reached through the ceiling and ended at a trap door. It seemed like she was now on the main floor of the house. The small trapdoor opened on rusty hinges. She climbed out and found herself in a small dark space, like a closet. The flashlight showed there was no door exiting into a room. Just another ladder. *Where in the house is this?*

She climbed the second ladder and found herself on the second floor, again in a small closet without a door. The next ladder took her to the third floor and emptied into a room. The room was tiny with just enough room to stand upright. One small window let in meager light. She walked to the window and saw she was indeed on the attic floor – toward the back of the house.

On the floor was a moldy mattress with a torn quilt on it. Nearby the makeshift bed was a wooden crate, and on it a candleholder with the remnants of a candle. A chamber pot sat nearby. On a small table in the corner there were chipped dishes and a fork and spoon, along with a tin cup. Several three-legged stools were scattered around and another small hand-hewn tabletop was engraved with a checkerboard pattern. Rachel saw several small circles in wood that must have been used as the checkers.

Looking around there seemed to be no other exit other than the ladder down to the basement. *That can't be very safe. What would happen if that candle caught the mattress on fire – there would be no way out. It would be a death trap.*

She remembered the information she'd gotten from the book at the library. *Oh my goodness. This must be the place where the escaping slaves stayed. A station on the Underground Railroad. This house is amazing. I wonder if Nonna knew about this.* She imagined an escaping slave family running from house to house and stopping here as they made their way north to Canada. They might spend the night or several days, waiting until it was safe to begin the next leg of their journey.

Her curiosity grew as she looked around the small room. She noticed an object on the floor next to the mattress. Bending down, she discovered it was a corn husk doll. She imagined a little slave girl leaving this behind. Or perhaps some other young girl used this room as a playroom. *I need to do more research! I'm finding all of these mysteries quite fascinating. I wonder why I never liked history before. Once all this estate business is taken care of, I'm going to have to research and try to find the answers to these questions.*

She yawned. The events of the night before were

catching up with her. Leaving the small room to ponder later, she descended the ladder and ended up back in the basement where she picked up the headstone, bringing it up to the kitchen table. She ended up snuggling into Nonna's chair in the living room for a quick nap.

Chapter 23

The next day

The town's police station was located in a converted 1890s three-story house. The front entry had a make-shift handicapped ramp winding its way up to the front door ten steps above street level. Inside the foyer, one set of stairs led to the courtroom on the second floor and another went down to the police offices at the basement level. A wheelchair lift, between the two sets of stairs, made the building ADA compliant and accessible.

Downstairs, the room was cramped with desks strewn around haphazardly, and work spaces piled high with paperwork. Phone lines and computer wires crisscrossed the space, making it dangerous to walk without paying close attention. At one end of the room, an office was delineated from the rest of the space with a chest-high room divider. From there emerged Sergeant Miller.

Miller was a tall, large man. Like Schmidt, his uniform should be one size larger to fit properly. He denied that fact, however, saying that the dryer had shrunk his pants. His grey hair was thinning on top, and he wore a comb-over that fooled no one.

Schmidt and Roberts were huddled over several pages of notes. Behind them a white board listed dates and locations of the recent robberies. Miller slowly approached the two and asked, "Fill me in. What do we know?"

Schmidt pointed to the notes on the robbery at Rachel Benton's house. "We thought right; the robbery was very similar in nature to the four others in the area. All the robberies were in older homes with no security systems in place. In each, the more obvious things to steal were left behind. TV's stereos, purses were all left untouched."

Roberts indicated the information on the white board. "At the first robbery, Mrs. Marshall said the only thing taken was a cut-glass vase and bowl. Miss Herbert's house was next. She said the thief took a cameo and other antique jewelry she had on display on a table in her living room. At Mr. Johnson's house, some old photographs done on glass were taken. Apparently they were really valuable because they used an old process called ambrotype – like was used during the years of the Civil War. The rest were daguerreotypes. At the last one, the thief made off with several paperweights. This latest, the Benton house, is where the thief left before grabbing anything."

Miller looked at the list and frowned. "Looks like all the robberies took place at houses located in isolated locations. Houses set away from the road, with yards that back up to wooded areas or, like the Benton place, to the canal."

"Yep," Robert nodded. "And in all of them, small, easily removed antiques were missing."

"Wasn't something taken at the museum, too?" Miller asked.

"Right again." Schmidt walked over to his desk and rummaged through the pages, found the one he wanted. "Says here that several small items were missing from a display case one day last month. The display had been rearranged to disguise the missing items, but an employee noticed it and reported to us. They think it might be an inside job, but with the rest of these thefts, we can't be sure. You took the report, right Roberts?"

Roberts nodded again, "It's all there in the report." He leaned on his desk, obviously disgruntled at having to recap it all for Miller. Why couldn't Miller read the reports for himself, he thought.

Miller turned to Schmidt. "What about forensics?" Miller was one who wanted to have everything wrapped up in a neat and tidy package as soon as possible. He was in line for a promotion and having this case closed would help tremendously when he went in front of the review board.

Schmidt responded, "At the Johnson house, a hair was found. The DNA report says that there's no hit in the system. The partial footprint left at the Benton house was on the small size. It could be male or female. Fingerprints were too smudged. Basically, there's nothing conclusive."

Miller crossed his arms and frowned. "So where do we go from here?"

"I've been watching those houses, patrolling them every night. Especially the Benton place. Maybe the perp will return there considering he or she didn't get anything last time."

"Good idea. Let's hope we get lucky." Miller walked to the door, then stopped and turned his head. "Keep up the good work and let me know what you find."

"Sure thing," Roberts mumbled. He sat back down at his desk, turned to his computer, and began typing.

Chapter 24
Two days later

Friday morning, after Rachel finished a quick breakfast, she straightened the bedrooms and cleared the areas near all the windows on the first floor. Just in time. The doorbell rang. Peering out, she saw the Apex van and opened the door. A different technician stood at the doorway with a tool kit and satchel filled with equipment. He was fairly young, early twenties, tall, thin. His curly hair was secured under a ball cap with the company logo on it.

"Good morning, Ma'am. I'm here to install your security system."

"Yes, come on in. I've tried to get things ready for you."

"No problem. It'll probably take all morning to do this, but I'll be as quick as I can. I heard you want to have this unit set up and ready to go."

"I do. I'll be working in the kitchen, if you need me."

"Sounds good." He set his satchel down, rummaged through, and, taking out his tools, got to work.

* * *

Earlier Rachel had decided to take advantage of the time. Needing to decide what had to be paid immediately and what could wait, she gathered all the bills and assorted paperwork from her grandmother's desk, and brought them down to the kitchen table. Her meeting with the appraiser was that afternoon and she wanted an idea of how much money was needed to get by until September when her job would begin. How much was she going to have to sell?

She remembered her daily trips to the mailbox at the end of the long driveway while her grandmother was still alive. She'd dutifully brought the mail to Nonna, only for it to be set aside unopened. She'd found other mail in various places in the house and wondered how long it had been since Nonna had been aware enough to take care of her bills. It had taken days for Rachel to find it all and gather it in one place.

Walking to the table, she sat and started through. At the bottom of the pile was a series of unopened envelopes from a local bank. Rachel shook her head in dismay. How did I overlook these? And, more to the point, what was her grandmother thinking? Didn't she want to know how much was in her accounts? How could she live like that? Rachel always took the time each month to balance her checking account, verifying her book with the monthly statement. She knew that in this day and age, many people had long ago discarded the paper path and went to online banking but Rachel was still old school. She didn't feel comfortable relying on electronics to take care of her business. Apparently Nonna either didn't care, or was not able to keep up with her mail.

* * *

"Ma'am?" Rachel jumped. She almost forgot there was a technician in the house working on the alarm system. "Sorry, I didn't mean to startle you. The system is installed and ready to go. Let me show you what I've done."

He walked her around the basement and first floor, pointing out all the sensors on the windows and in the corners of the doors. They stopped at the keypad and he showed her how it and the key fob worked. She tried it herself a couple of times to make sure she understood and then nodded.

"That's pretty easy. Thanks."

He left the customer programming guide and said, "Remember you also have a panic mode here. If you find someone in your house, say someone comes in when you are here and the alarm is off, then you can just punch the button and an alert will be sent to the police. They should respond within ten minutes."

"Fantastic. Thanks again." She watched him leave and felt a huge sense of relief. No more middle of the night entries from would-be thieves.

* * *

The day was flying by. Rachel grabbed a quick sandwich and an iced tea. She had just finished cleaning up when the doorbell rang again. This time she knew it was Samantha Matthews, the appraiser, who had arrived promptly at the appointed time. *Things are coming together quickly today.* Rachel opened the door and Samantha smiled, extending her hand to shake. She wore a blue peasant top, a long flowing floral skirt and had a large tote bag hanging from her shoulder.

Rachel reached out and took her hand, inviting her inside. "Thanks for coming today. I am so overwhelmed by all that's here in the house. As I told you, I need to have an inventory done for the estate. I've started making a list, but I realize I don't know how to properly describe some of the older things and how to value them. And I need to know what some of the things in the house are worth because I need quick money to pay some bills."

"Sure thing. Let's have a look around." Rachel watched her eyes taking in all that was in the living room, the bookshelves, the tables, the small figurines on the mantle. "Where do you want to start?" Sam asked.

"Why don't we start in the attic? There are some things there I can sell quickly, I think. My friend, MariBeth, has already given me an idea what she thought they were worth. I want to see if you have the same idea. Is that all right with you?"

"It's as good a place to start as any."

"This way."

Rachel led Sam up the stairs to the attic doorway. As they passed each of the second floor bedroom doorways, they paused and glanced in each room. Rachel saw Sam's eyes widen as she saw what was there and wondered what the woman was thinking. Reaching the attic door, Rachel opened it and they climbed the last set of stairs. She paused at the top and waved her arm toward the clutter, indicating all the furniture stored there. "This is it. What do you think?"

Samantha stood at the top of the stairs, taking in all that was before her. Her eyes spotted the desk across the room. "Oh that's a beautiful piece!" She walked quickly to it and stroked the polished surface.

"It looks to be in excellent condition. Are you sure you want to sell it?"

Good question, Rachel thought. What do I want to sell? She responded, "I'm not sure right now. That's one of the reasons I have you here. Just tell me what you think it's worth and I'll make a decision later."

"Right." Sam walked slowly around the piece, opening drawers, and noticing the hardware and the dovetailed corners. She looked behind and underneath where she found the furniture maker's stamp. "I would have to take some time to do some research, but I believe this piece could sell for at least six thousand, maybe as much as ten. Of course, that assumes there's a buyer in the area."

Just what MariBeth thought. Rachel said, "Okay. Let's assume I want to sell everything that's here in the attic – the desk, tables, chairs, the trunks, and the spinning wheel. What could I get for all of it?"

"Let me take some pictures, make some notes, and I'll get back to you. I'll also start making a list of what you want to sell." She took a notebook out of her large canvas tote bag, jotting down the items she saw. She snapped a few photos of each piece of furniture.

Half an hour later, she turned to Rachel. "Have you checked inside the trunks?" There were ten of them scattered throughout the attic space, a variety of shapes and sizes.

Rachel shook her head. Sam opened the first dome-lidded trunk and began removing the clothing she found. The musty smell and dustiness soon had them both sneezing. Rachel had forgotten the air cleaner. She covered her nose as her eyes started to water.

"Ah, these are marvelous." Sam said, lifting a gown from the trunk. The clothing seemed to be in fairly good condition. "What handiwork. Look, this is all hand stitched. See the boning in the bodice? It's designed to augment the corset the woman would be wearing. See the drop shoulder, full sleeves and the full, gathered skirt. It looks to be silk and there's not much damage. It's typical of a Civil War era gown. This is wonderful."

Rachel looked at the beautiful green, silk gown in wonder. *Could this be the kind of dress worn by Emma? Look at the tiny waist.*

Sam and Rachel opened the rest of the trunks. Clothing from all eras seemed to be represented. Turn of the century blouses with leg-o-mutton sleeves, flapper dresses from the 1920s, and even a World War II uniform were soon spread around the room.

Rachel reached the last trunk in the corner of the room and discovered a hand stitched quilt. As she carefully lifted the quilt from the trunk, a draw-string bag fell to the floor. It jingled as it landed. Rachel picked it up and untied the strings. Inside were coins. She retied the bag, and slipped it into her pocket.

With clothing and quilts carefully displayed on the floor, Rachel turned to Sam and asked, "So what do you think about the value of everything up here?"

"Well, again, I'll have to go back and do some research, but my first impression? Hmmm. Perhaps about ten to fifteen thousand. But remember, that's only if you can find a buyer."

"That's fantastic." Rachel was relieved. Except for that gown that Emma might have worn which she'd keep for sentimental reasons, she had no need for any of the clothes or other furniture. If she could sell them quickly, she would be able to pay most of the bills.

Rachel waited and watched as Samantha took photos of the clothing and recorded each item in her notebook. When she finished with each piece, Rachel refolded and carefully placed them back into the trunks. Her eyes were itchy and nose was running; the musty smells attacking her allergies. *I'll be glad when these are taken care of.*

Sam gathered her tote bag and paused to look around the room one more time. She nodded to Rachel and said, "I have enough information here."

"Okay, let's go down to the bedrooms," Rachel said. They crossed to the attic stairs and descended to the second floor. "My lawyer said, for the inventory, I need to make a list of the valuable items in each room."

"That's fine. Shall I point out the more valuable items to you as we go along?

"That's great." They entered Nonna's room. It

was now perfectly cleaned and orderly; smelling of the rose sachet Rachel had lain out in bowls on the dresser. Rachel had rearranged the furniture and remade the bed with freshly laundered linens so that when she entered she would no longer see her grandmother lying there dying. Room after room, Rachel was beginning to make the house her home.

Sam pointed out Nonna's antique four poster bed, handmade quilt, drop-front desk, and the three antique paperweights on it. They moved to the other four rooms. There was nothing outstanding in Rachel's room. Julia's room contained a child's roll top desk and small rocking chair. In the spare room Sam noticed a stack of linens in the closet and a box that, when opened, revealed another twelve-tune cylinder music box like the one Rachel had found in the attic. Sam indicated it might be very valuable and continued to make notes and take photos in each room.

They went downstairs and into the kitchen. Here Sam pointed out some Depression glass, and cut glass vases and bowls stored in the cupboards. In the dining room, behind the doors of the china closet, she noted a silver tea set and other silver pieces. They ended in the living room.

Samantha walked to the fireplace mantel. She pointed to the photographs. "Is this your family?"

Rachel crossed the room and stood beside her. "That's my Grandmother and Grandfather. The little girl standing with them is my Mom. I think she's about five years old there, the same age as my daughter. Julia looks a lot like her grandmother."

Rachel reached for one of the figurines next to

the framed photo. "What about these?" She handed the small figurine of a little boy holding a paint brush and palette, and watched as the appraiser turned it over.

Not looking up, Samantha hesitated, "Uh, not sure." She took a picture of the dozen that were on the mantel and then moved to the other side of the room, stopping at the two recessed, white bookshelves.

Sam reached out and took a book from the top shelf. She riffled through the pages, stopping to look at the title page in some of them. She replaced each book back on the shelf. Rachel caught Sam's brows furrow as she glanced through the book. *First Maribeth is curious, now Sam. What's with those books?*

Sam continued, "There's not much of antique value here." She turned and looked around the room again, eyes taking in all the contents. "But there's a lot in the house that is. I'll get back to you when I finish my research.

Rachel sat in the nearest chair. She was overwhelmed with all that was in the house, "I can't believe it. I had no idea."

"My dear, it was good that you asked me to help you, especially if you intend to sell any of these things." Samantha had gathered her notebook and camera equipment into her tote bag and moved toward the front door. "It'll take me a couple of weeks to do the research so I can place a value on the things on the list."

Rachel suddenly jumped up, "Wait, I almost forgot. I didn't get to show you the diaries and boxes of letters. MariBeth thinks they are valuable too. Just a minute, wait here, I'll be right back."

Looking around the room again, Samantha nodded, "I'll wait." She stood by the shelves in the living room.

Rachel dashed up the stairs, and quickly retrieved a few of the letters from Emma's box on the nightstand in her room. With her eyes on the letters she was shuffling through, she carefully made her way down the stair. "I've got them," she said. She looked up and found Sam missing. "Sam? Sam, where did you go?"

Hearing no response, Rachel moved toward the front door. She didn't hear the footsteps approaching from behind her, but felt the sharp pain as something heavy connected with the back of her head. She collapsed to the floor, darkness overtaking her.

Chapter 25
A few minutes later

Moaning, Rachel woke, and felt the back of her head. *Pain.* Her hand felt damp and she found blood smeared across her fingertips. Dizzy from the knock to her head, she carefully stood up and hit the panic button on the newly installed security system, then sank back down to wait.

It only took ten minutes for the police car to come screeching to a halt in front of Rachel's house. She was sitting in the open doorway, holding her head, and waved to them. They were the same two from the previous visit.

Schmidt hurried up the sidewalk to her, "Ma'am? What happened?"

"I'm not sure. I think someone hit me in the head," Rachel stammered. Roberts took a step down the brick sidewalk and looked up and down the street. Not a single person was in sight.

Rachel slowly stood and leaned against the doorframe with a moan. Schmidt reached for her arm. "Whoa. Are you all right?"

"Yeah, I think."

"Ma'am? Can we go inside?"

"Yeah. Sure." Rachel groaned and Schmidt kept his hand under Rachel's arm as they slowly made their way to the living room. She sank into a chair and put her hand to her head.

"Can I fetch some ice for you?" Schmidt still hovered over her, expecting her to collapse at any moment. "Maybe we should call the paramedics."

"No ambulance. I'll be okay. But I will take the ice. Thanks." He moved to the kitchen, rummaged around for ice and a cloth, and returned to her. He handed her the ice and she applied it to the back of her head.

Roberts took out his notebook and asked. "What happened, Ma'am?"

"I think she's the thief. I went up the stairs to get something. I wasn't gone that long. When I came down she was gone. Then I got hit in the head. I must have passed out." Rachel was babbling. She felt confused and angry.

"Wait, slow down," Schmidt said. "Who is she?"

"Samantha Matthews. I asked her to do an appraisal of the things in Nonna's house. She acted like she knew what she was doing. I thought she was legitimate. I did notice her looking at everything but I thought that was part of her job. Little did I know."

The words came tumbling out as she sat looking

around the room.

"Are you sure she was the one who hit you?"

Rachel thought for a minute, "Well, no. When I got downstairs she wasn't in sight so I called out to her. She didn't answer though and no one else was here. At least I don't think anyone else was here."

"Did you happen to notice the kind of car she was driving?"

"Sorry, no."

"Okay, I'll call it in." He called dispatch and put out a BOLO, a notice to be on the lookout, for Samantha Matthews.

Rachel groaned again. There was just too much going on! First the attempted break in – now this. Just when she thought she was making progress, something came along to set her back.

Roberts walked over and stopped in front of her. "Ma'am, could you tell if there's anything missing this time?" he asked gently.

Rachel looked quickly around the room. She noticed ten figurines missing from the mantel and then noticed that there was a space on the bookshelves. "The Dickens!" she cried.

"Excuse me?" Roberts looked puzzled.

"She stole some books that were on the shelves over there," She waved in the general direction of the shelves. "And there are some figurines missing too. I don't know what else."

Roberts handed her a piece of paper. "Could you make a list, please?"

Rachel took the paper and pen and began to write. Schmidt joined Roberts saying, "I don't think there's anything else for us to do here. We'll send the team to get fingerprints."

Roberts nodded. "If it was this Samantha, we know she was here. It would just be corroboration for the courts and help us with the other thefts in the area. Maybe we'll be lucky and she's the one who did them all."

"Ma'am?" Schmidt turned and placed a hand on Rachel's shoulder. She looked up from her list making and saw his sympathetic look. She wished he hadn't done that, she was trying hard not to break down and cry in front of them. Now tears spilled over and coursed down her cheeks. She bowed her head and covered her face, trying desperately to get under control.

Schmidt knelt in front of her. "Ma'am?" he repeated, "Are you sure you're all right?"

Rachel slowly nodded.

"We're going to leave now. Don't forget to set your alarm after we leave. And if you happen to spot Samantha, give me a call." He handed her a card. "It has my cell phone one it. Call anytime."

"Thanks," she mumbled. The two officers left quietly talking to each other. After a few minutes, Rachel was able to get up and set the alarm.

She felt so tired, and so disgusted. How could she have trusted that person? *What kind of judge of character am I?* First Patsy Lee, now Samantha. She was beginning to doubt her abilities – what about standing in front of a classroom of children. She settled back in the chair and closed her eyes.

* * *

Banging at the kitchen door startled her awake. "Mama? Mama!" Julia screamed.

Rachel glanced at her watch and saw that it was three-thirty in the afternoon. She'd forgotten she had locked the doors and set the alarm. It was something she was going to have to remember – and to tell Julia about. Rachel ran to the door, disarmed the alarm and opened it. Julia flew into her arms, terror in her eyes.

"It's okay Julia, I'm here." Rachel knelt and soothed her daughter.

Julia cried, "I knocked and knocked and you didn't come. Why did you lock the door? I couldn't open it." Tears were streaming down her little face. Oh, what a pair we are, thought Rachel, wrapping her arms around her daughter until she quieted.

"Here, let me show you something, Julia." She stood, walked her daughter to the nearby alarm panel and explained how it worked to the child. Julia tried it, successfully turning the system on and off. Rachel showed her the panic alarm too.

"You press this button and the police will come," She explained.

Julia's eyes widened, tears forgotten. "Really? Can I try it?" She reached for the button.

Just in time, Rachel stopped her hand. "No, Julia. That's just for a real emergency. Not for fun." She turned her daughter away from the panel and to the kitchen table. "Sit here and I'll get your snack."

They sat chatting while making ants on a log. Rachel spread the peanut butter on the celery and Julia giggled as she carefully placed the raisins on top. Again, Rachel noticed how easily her daughter was able to pass from tears to smiles.

Julia sneezed and Rachel reached into her pocket for the packet of tissues she usually kept there. She felt something else and drew it out. The bag of coins from the attic.

"What is it, Mama?" the ever-inquisitive girl asked.

"I don't know, let's see." She dumped out the coins on the kitchen table and spread them out. "Look! Here are some silver dollars. They are very old, from the middle of the 1800s. Here are some quarters, and dimes. And look here, the nickels have buffalos on them. All these are very old and probably very valuable."

As she pushed the coins around, and Julia picked up one of them.

"This one is different than the others, Mama."

"Let me see."

Julia handed the coin to Rachel. It was the size of the silver dollar but bronze in color and engraved on both sides. Rachel's finger traced the writing. *J. Beardsley* curved on the top and underneath *Co K 10th Reg N.Y.S.V.CAV.* Flipping the coin over, she saw, in the center the Union shield with stars in the upper field and vertical bars below. Surrounding the shield were the words *Against Rebellion 1861.*

Chills raced up her arms. *Can it be? Is it possible?* "I'll be right back, Julia." The pain in her head forgotten, she dashed down the hall and up the stairs to her room. Not wanting to take the time to find the right one, she grabbed the diaries and letters and, stopping at the table in the living room to get the ones she had intended to show Sam, took them all to the kitchen.

She looked at her daughter. Julia had been busy sorting the coins into neat and tidy piles.

"Scoot over, Sweetie. I need some space." Julia grabbed coins in two hands and sat on the floor with them. They would keep her occupied for a while. Rachel spread the letters on the table.

Let's see, where was that entry? I think it was somewhere at the beginning. Rachel was so excited. She impatiently opened the diary and glanced through the earliest pages of the 1862 book. Not finding what she was looking for, she began looking through the letters, starting with the first ones in the packet.

She finally found the correct passage. It was in the February tenth letter from James. She read the words he'd written, "This morning we were given our pay – going back to the end of October. Three months pay, about forty dollars. I am keeping some to pay the sutler for some sundries and an ID tag. The small bronze disk has my name and regiment on it. Many of the boys are getting them to wear under their shirts – just in case."

She was right. The disk was the same ID tag that James mentioned in his letter. This was his ID Tag. *How did it come to be in the little bag of coins?* She shook her head in disbelief. It was if the past were reaching out to her. Again she felt sadness at missed opportunities. If she had only known all of this – the letters, the diary, the headstone and now the ID tag, she would have sat with her grandmother and asked her about them. Now she would never know for sure. She had no one in her family left to ask. *Oh, unless this other person is really related.* She had almost forgotten the court hearing that was coming up.

Chapter 26
A week later

Rachel was anxious to have this whole court thing done. During the past week, she was so often on edge; it was beginning to wear on her nerves. It was also beginning to show in her behavior toward her daughter. She lost patience quickly and found herself snapping at the little girl. Julia would run from the room in tears. Rachel really hated to feel this way, hated the endless tension, endless worry. How easy it would be to follow in Jon's footsteps. But that wasn't an option for her. *I have to be strong for Julia.*

The following Monday, Rachel entered the library with Julia in hand. "Go to the children's room, Sweetie, and I'll join you there in a bit." Mindful of her mother's mood, Julia quickly made her way across the floor.

Rachel spotted Maggie sitting at one of the tables along the side wall of the library, away from the noise of the children's room. She noted the comfortable jeans and knit top Maggie was wearing. *I love the way she dresses, just like me. Not like the pretentious clothes that MariBeth seems to wear. I always feel second hand around her. But not Maggie.*

Maggie waved in greeting, smiled, and stood as Rachel approached. "Hi, how are you doing today?"

Rachel gave her a quick hug, and then sat. "As good as I can be, I guess." She really was not in the mood for small talk at the moment. "Did you find anything for me?"

Maggie seemed to understand and quickly removed a stapled report from her briefcase. "Okay, you've told me what you know about your mother's history and a bit about your grandmother's, but it wasn't much. That's what you told me when we met in my office. Are you ready to hear more?"

Nodding, Rachel listened intently as Maggie told her what she had discovered.

"Working our way backward, here's what I found. Bear with me while I go through this. Some of it you already know. But I want to put things in context." She shuffled the papers in front of her.

"You were born in 1976 in Oakland. Your mother was born Lynn Thornby in 1952 in Oxford, NY. She married your father, Bruce Morton, when she was nineteen years old, in 1971, five years before you were born. They moved to Oakland, California after their marriage. You have no other brothers or sisters. Your father died in Vietnam when you were three. Your mother died ten years ago. With me so far?" Rachel nodded again. This information was not new to her. She shifted restlessly, waiting to hear the answers to her questions.

"Okay, let's go back another generation on your mother's side to your grandmother. You called her Nonna, but her real name was Eleanor Rachel Palmer. She was born in 1923. I found her listed in a 1930 census report." Maggie passed Rachel a document and pointed. "She's listed there with her family on line twenty-nine."

"I didn't know I was named after her." Rachel reached for the document, and looked at the highlighted line, amazed at what Maggie had been able to discover. She nodded and handed the document back to Maggie.

Maggie continued, "In 1949, when Eleanor was twenty-four years old, she married Roger Thornby. She had your mother three years later, in 1952. Again there were no other children. Your grandfather died in 1960, when your mother was eight years old.

"This report contains documentation of sources for all the information I just presented to you. It should prove to the court that you are the sole beneficiary of your grandmother's estate."

Rachel was overwhelmed with relief. She felt the tension of the past two weeks begin to drain. She sat back in her seat and smiled. "Maggie, I can't thank you enough for this."

Maggie chuckled. "Oh, you'll get my bill. Research like this doesn't come cheap, but in your case it is well worth the money spent." She stood and gathered her papers. Here's your copy of my research."

Rachel took the report, "I'll make an appointment to see my lawyer tomorrow." She stood and gave Maggie a quick hug. "Can I treat you to lunch? I'd love to hear more about your research."

Maggie glanced at her watch, "I'd love to. I have time before my next appointment, as long as we make it a quick one."

"I just have to go get Julia. She's in the children's section. Lunch with her is always quick." As they walked to the children's room, Rachel had a wide smile on her face.

* * *

The three sat in a booth by the window at Margo's Diner, Julia nibbling on her hot dog and French fries.

Rachel set her coffee mug down and asked, "How did you get started with genealogy?"

Maggie sipped her iced tea and sat back. "Well, that's a long story. But, in a nutshell, it started with someone in my family giving me a document at a family reunion. It was the bare beginnings of a family tree. I was intrigued and started to look further and, after months, was able to take that branch of my family tree back to the 1600s. It was so much fun. I loved the research, the detective work involved. As I said, with so much now on the Internet, searching has become easier. Then, I began talking to others, at the library and elsewhere, and found people, just like you, who wanted to find out about their families but didn't have the time or the inclination to do the searching themselves. So, I began doing genealogies for them. As I went along, I took some classes and became certified and here we are!"

"That's fantastic. You're doing something you love, and are getting paid for it too."

"Yes, I'm very lucky."

"Once the estate is finalized, we're going to have to get together again, so I can learn more. I'd love to do more research on my own, not just for the court, but for myself. I think the older I get, the more I find knowing about my family and its past is important to me. I've focused on my mother's side of the family for this court case, but there's my father's side too.

"Let me know when you're ready and I'll help as much as I can. I love to teach people who are enthusiastic about their past!" Maggie leaned forward, "I'm curious, Rachel, how did you end up here, in Oxford?"

Rachel smiled and told her story to Maggie, though she carefully edited portions, mindful of her daughter sitting beside her. She skipped much of the details of Jon's suicide and the turmoil of losing her home. "…so once the bank decided to foreclose, I contacted Nonna and she welcomed us. And here I am." She looked down at her daughter. "It's been so hard these past months. For both of us."

Maggie reached across the table and placed her hands on Rachel's. "I'm so sorry. But remember I know something about what you're going through. My cousin was in the National Guard and took his life after he returned from Iraq. At the time there was very little in the way of a support system for military wives and families. We just seemed to have to wing it, find our own way. It was so frustrating, at times."

"I know what you mean." Rachel agreed. "I wish I could have talked with someone, found a group or something to help us get through it. Jon didn't want help, refused it, but I could have used the help, if I had known how to find it."

"Certain places have chapters of *Operation Homefront*. Have you heard of that group?"

"No. What's that?"

"It's a fairly new non-profit organization that started in Texas and has spread to other states. But not every state has a chapter, unfortunately. I often wish there was one in this area – we could certainly use it with so many families locally affected by the wars in Iraq and Afghanistan – and other places too." She paused, looked off, thinking.

Rachel waited, and then asked, "So what did you do? After…"

"Well, my cousin and his wife didn't have any children so she went back to live with her mother. It was good for her to have someone close by.

As for me, I've kept in touch with her periodically, but have been on my own. After my brief marriage ended, I came back here where my parents lived at the time. I've lived in this town for the past ten years. My parents gave me their house and moved south two years ago. Now they're living in a gated retirement community in Naples, Florida. They love it there, and I love going down to visit with them as much as I can, especially during the cold winters here. Being self-employed and with the kind of job I have, I can take off whenever I like, and take my work with me. As long as I don't need to be at a local resource, like a church or court records, I can do much of the research I need using the Internet. It's amazing what's available online."

"I saw that. After the class, I spent some time on the websites you had listed and did some searching. Unfortunately I needed to use a credit card – most of them seemed to require membership of some sort, so I didn't get very far. That's why I got in touch with you."

"Yes, that can be frustrating. There are a lot of libraries that have sites such as *ancestry.com* as part of their services, but our town doesn't."

Rachel smiled, finding it so easy to talk with Maggie. She felt a growing friendship with her and looked forward to learning more. *If my history teachers could only see me now.*

Maggie said, "I should have the rest of your mother's tree done in a couple weeks. I'll give you a call when it's done."

"I look forward to it."

Chapter 27
The next day

The phone rang in the police station. Answering the phone, Schmidt listened to the caller, and then slammed the phone down.

"Roberts, grab your things, we've got a house alarm – just went off." They hustled out to the squad car and took off down the road, lights flashing, sirens blaring. It only took fifteen minutes and they pulled into the long driveway to a house set back from the road, front yard covered with trees. Roberts exited the car first, his slim agility giving him an advantage over his partner. Schmidt was not far behind, yanking up his pants.

They approached the front of the house, and Schmidt indicated with a wiggled finger for Roberts to go around back. Waiting for thirty seconds,

Schmidt knocked on the front door. It moved open. "Police! Anybody there?"

He heard a shout from the back of the house, turned and ran. The half acre yard in back of the house was neatly mowed, gardens in bloom. A white stone walkway stretched from the brick patio to the gazebo centered in the yard. Schmidt spotted his partner racing past the gazebo and saw a figure in a dark sweat pants and hoodie running ahead of him, a tote bag slung over the shoulders.

"Stop, police," he shouted.

The race continued, but as Schmidt puffed behind, he watched Roberts run through the yard after the fleeing person. One after the other they jumped the wooden fence and ran toward a parked car. Drawing closer and then with a final lunge, his partner tackled the runner. Schmidt lumbered over the fence and, racing to the pair, stood there gun drawn, breathing deeply. Roberts reached behind for his handcuffs and snapped them on the thief's wrists.

Schmidt removed the tote bag, turned the intruder to face them, and removed the hood that disguised his face. It was a teen male, looked about five foot six, trim and athletic. His long brown hair was braided, her brown eyes shifted from one officer to another. He panted, working to catch his breath.

"What's your name?" Schmidt asked. The boy didn't respond.

"No comment, huh. Okay, we'll take it to the station." The two officers took his arms, marched him to their car and locked him in the back.

"Was anyone home?" Roberts asked Schmidt.

"No one answered when I called."

"I'll wait here while you check."

"Better call for back up. Just in case he had an accomplice."

Roberts walked across the lawn to the front door which had remained ajar. He called in, "Anybody home?"

Without backup, he was reluctant to go inside. He pushed the door completely open and took note of the living room. It seemed untouched, and there was no one in the room.

Another squad car pulled up in front. Two men got out. One went over to Schmidt. "You okay here?"

"Yeah, just go help Roberts clear the house. We don't know if anyone else is inside." He leaned against the car, keeping an eye on the teen in the back seat.

The two joined Roberts at the front door and they quickly went through the rest of the house, finding it clear. The owners were not home and there was no other person in the house. They couldn't tell if anything had been taken and wondered what the thief had wanted in the house.

Roberts said to the two. "Thanks for the back-up. We can take it from here." He turned and shut the door, walking down to Schmidt.

"Okay, let's get this one to the station." They drove off in silence, the rider in the back seat slumped against the door."

* * *

"Is he talking," asked Roberts?

They had returned to the station and Schmidt had been interrogating the boy for the past hour. "He's not saying a word," he said. "There's no ID on him either."

"He hasn't asked for a lawyer?" Roberts asked in disbelief.

"Nope. I read him the Miranda rights, but he just nodded that he understood."

"Well, I checked the contents of the tote bag he was carrying and another one we found in the car. In the car's tote bag I found some books, ten small figurines and a couple of paperweights. Oh, and there were some old photos in metal frames."

"Sounds like some of the things from the Benton house. Maybe we can get her down here to make an ID and see if the things are hers."

"I'll give her a call." Roberts moved to his desk across the room and, after a brief conversation with Rachel, turned and said, "She's on her way."

Rachel hung up the phone. With nervous butterflies dancing in her stomach, she drove quickly and parked near the station. She hurried along the sidewalk, feeling anxious as she walked into the police station. She didn't quite know what to expect. Roberts had just said they had someone in custody. She really didn't want to see Samantha again, but she was willing to help the police catch the thief. Not only for herself, but for the others the thief had stolen from in recent weeks.

When she got to the basement offices, she was met by Schmidt who reached out to shake her hand. "You're looking better than the last time we met."

Rachel shook his hand, and then felt the back of her head. There was a small lump still there, but it didn't hurt as much as it did. "I feel much better.

Thanks. Why am I here? Have you caught the thief?"

"Yes, but I want you to look at something first. Come with me." They walked down to a small office. Scattered on the table were a variety of items.

Rachel immediately recognized the books. "Those are mine! And look, there are the figurines from the mantle. You caught her!" She felt so relieved.

"Not so fast. We caught a young teen with these, not Samantha."

Rachel frowned. "But I thought..."

Schmidt asked, "What is so special about these books? Do you know?"

"I'm no expert. Let me see." Rachel took one of the books from the table. She recognized the book from the shelf in her living room, but hadn't picked it up until now. It was *The Pickwick Papers* by Charles Dickens. She felt the cover. Burgundy in color, it felt like leather, but she could be wrong, she thought. The book was in excellent condition, didn't even look like someone had read it. She gently opened the cover to the title page and glanced at the bottom of the page. London: Robson & Kerslaker. 1882. First edition. "Wow!" she exclaimed.

"What?" Roberts entered the room joining Schmidt and Rachel.

"It's a first edition Dickens!" Energized now, Rachel began examining the other books.

The second book she picked up was really beautiful. *Edwin Drood,* another one by Dickens. This one was royal navy blue with silk pages and gilt accents. On the bottom of the spine, the publication date was stamped in gold, 1870. Her fingers trembled as she turned the page to find the words she was seeking. She found them, First Edition. She remembered reading somewhere that this work was actually done in monthly parts. This book looked like it had the original works in their wrappers bound together. "This is amazing!"

She reached for the third one, also by Charles Dickens. Again it was bound in antique leather, the spine having embossed decorative ribbons. She very carefully turned the pages of the book and again saw the words – First Edition. She found illustrations in this one. There was an engraved title page and she counted over thirty other illustrations.

Three more of the Dickens books looked to be a set. The title was *Master Humphrey's Clock, With Illustrations by George Cattermole and Hablot Browne* – yet another first edition. Bound in leather, it had gold bands on the spine. Again, Rachel recalled what she knew about the book. Master Humphrey's Clock was a book that originally contained both short stories and two novels, *The Old Curiosity Shop* and *Barnaby Rudge*. In later publications, the short stories and the novels were separated.

Rachel gestured to the Dickens books, "These are all first editions. They're probably worth quite a bit of money. I don't know how much for sure." Picking up the last book on the table, she said, "I don't recognize this as one of mine."

She took *The Godfather,* by Mario Puzo, in her hands and again looked at the copyright date. "Yep, I'm right; this one is a First Edition too. Seems like that's what the thief was after. I wonder if my house has any more of these. I haven't checked all of Nonna's bookshelves too closely. For the most part, I just dusted the tops of the books!" She grimaced, thinking of what she had overlooked.

Roberts asked, "So what do you think these are worth? Ball park figure."

"Do you have a computer I could use for a minute?"

Schmidt pointed to the one on his desk in the other room. "In there. But what are you going to do?"

"I'll do a quick check on Ebay and see if any of these are listed for sale. I've come to realize that it makes a good source for estimating values of things. Problem is it's hard to find items sometimes."

Schmidt, tugging at his sagging pants, walked with her to his station. She sat, fingers flying on the keys. Minutes later she sat back. "Well," she said, "I was right. They are worth money. Lots of it!"

"How much?" Roberts asked, joining them at his partner's desk.

"Well, I just checked with one website and I know the values can vary. Just that one book, *The Pickwick Papers*, is worth about fifteen thousand dollars. It said that other one, *Master Humphrey's Clock*, published in 1840 is a rare book, even for a first edition. So, rough guess, I'd say between twenty and thirty thousand for the lot of them."

Roberts whistled and glanced at the books in the other room. "Well, now we know..."

Rachel interrupted. "The figurines are going to be harder to find. The paperweights too."

"That's okay." Schmidt said. "We need you to look and see if you recognize the person we have in custody. Can you do that?"

Rachel hesitated and frowned, "Will he see me?"

"Nope, he's behind one-way glass in the interrogation room."

Relieved, Rachel agreed. He led her down the hallway and they stopped at a window. Rachel looked and saw the boy sitting there slumped in the chair. Her eyes widened. "Oh, yes! I know him – except I don't know his name."

"What?" Schmidt was confused.

"He was at the antique show, at the booth with Samantha. I don't know his name, or his relationship to Sam, but I do recognize him and Samantha should know who he is."

Schmidt smiled, and gently squeezed her arm. "Thanks, Ma'am."

"Please, call me Rachel."

"Rachel, I'm going to have to keep the books and other things for evidence. You'll get them back once we're done with them. Thank you so much. You've been a great help today."

She shook his hand and he walked her to the door. She drove home, stunned with what she had learned. She was also anxious to get back to look more carefully at the rest of the books at the house.

* * *

Rachel sat on the floor of the living room, amazed, astonished, and in awe of the collection strewn on the floor around her. In the time since arriving home from the police station, she had begun taking the books down from the shelves one by one and now had them organized into several piles. She had found several more first editions and many, many books with publication dates in the late 1800s and early 1900s.

After carefully checking each book, she entered the details into a database she'd started on her laptop so she could take it to the library and check the values. She remembered what MariBeth had told her. A collector would pay a premium for similar books or ones that make a series. The value of the books will increase with their condition. Most of the books around her looked untouched.

Did her grandmother collect them? Did she read them? When did she do this? Why? What kind of woman was she? *I really missed getting to know her as I grew up – and now it's too late. All these questions will probably remain unanswered.* Rachel felt a certain sense of disappointment.

Reluctant now to hire anyone else to help, having been burned by Samantha Matthews, she was determined to do as much as she could on her own. She'd have to remember to ask Neil Walker if she needed to have a professional. Maybe MariBeth would help her, or perhaps Maggie. The two friends were so different, but each had helped her so much in recent weeks.

"Mama?" The back door banged announcing the arrival of Julia.

"In here, Julia,"

Julia ran into the room and stopped short. "Whoa. What are you doing?" She continued into the room, stepped around the piles of books and sat in her mother's lap. "Look at all the books."

Rachel gave her daughter a squeeze, laughed and said, "Yep, lots of books, lots of important books. Not for you to touch, okay?"

Julia looked disappointed. Her love of books gleamed in her eyes, and Rachel could tell she was yearning to look at them, but she knew the little girl would be disappointed in most of them. No pictures of princesses.

Chapter 28
The next week

The day was a beautiful one, with bright clear blue skies and birds chirping as they sought food for their newly hatched babies. Rachel and Julia walked into the library armed with books and videos to return. Julia placed them in the return slot one by one.

"Julia, you know the routine – go get some books and a video and come back to me. I'll be over there by the window."

"Okay, Mama." Off she went, her hair escaping from her pink hair band.

Rachel sat and connected her laptop to the library's internet service and began to search for the values of the books she'd listed in the database. After an hour, she sat back in her chair, amazed at the prices she'd discovered. Just as she thought, the books would bring a tidy sum, if she needed to sell them. She remembered seeing several book dealers at the antique show and figured she'd be able to work with them when the time came.

Sensing someone approaching, Rachel looked up and saw Maggie walking toward her. The genealogist had another stapled report in front of her. Rachel stood and gave her a warm hug. "Good to see you, Maggie."

"Hi, Rachel. How are you?"

"I'm doing much better than the last time we met. Things have been progressing quite nicely, I must say." She told Maggie about the theft of the books and the capture of the teen. "I think the boy is Sam's son, but when I was at the police station, he hadn't talked yet. I haven't heard from the police since, so I don't know for sure. Oh, and I gave your last report to my attorney but he's not gotten back to me yet either."

"Well, you sure have been busy!" She sat down at the table. "Are you ready to hear the rest of the report?"

Rachel smiled and leaned forward. Will the report answer any of the questions that have been swirling in her mind, she wondered. "Oh, I sure am. I've been waiting to see what you've discovered."

Maggie chuckled and pointed to the report. "It's all here. I was able to take it back to the people you are interested in finding more about." She opened the report and began.

"The last report ended with your grandmother. We're still following your maternal line, so this next set refers to your grandmother's mother – your great-grandmother. Her name was Irena Ashford, born in 1893. She married Benjamin Palmer in 1918 at the end of World War I. I found out he fought in World War I and I'm guessing they married when he returned. I couldn't find any source material on their marriage. After they married they must have moved into the house you're in now, according to the census report. It's where your grandmother was born in 1923. Again, your grandmother was the only child. Irena died in 1964 when she was seventy-one." She paused. "Are you following so far?"

Rachel nodded and Maggie continued, "Now back another generation, again focusing on your great-grandmother's mother. Her name was Adelia Jean Beardsley..."

"Wait," Rachel interrupted. "I recognize that name. It's one of the babies from the diary."

"That's right," Maggie continued. "Adelia Jean and Cornelia Jane were born in July, 1863. Little Cornelia Jane died when she was four months old."

Rachel said, "The headstone I found in the basement."

Maggie nodded, "Right again. Adelia Jean lived though, and married Thomas Ashford in 1887 when she was twenty-four years old. After they got married they moved to Chenango Forks. I found them in the 1890 census report. They had three children, but unfortunately all of them died in childhood. The fourth child was Irena, your great grandmother. Adelia was thirty years old at the time.

Now back again to the final generation in your letters and diaries you've been reading.

Your two-times great-grandmother was Emma Wells. She was born in 1845 in a town not too far from here called Smithville. When she was fourteen, she was hired as a domestic in the household of Asa Beardsley. In the 1860 census, she is listed in that household along with James, who was just a year older than she, and the two younger girls, Ida and Ella and, of course, the father. According to what you read in the diary, Emma fell in love with and married James in 1862. I was able to find a website documentation of their wedding. James enlisted and went off to war, and she was left behind, moved to Union Center to live with her cousin Louisa, and had twin girls she named Cornelia Jane and Adelia Jean.

"Wow!" Rachel sat back stunned at all the information she had learned. "This is more than just names and dates on a piece of paper. This is my family. I'm shocked that there were so few children that survived. I feel so lucky to even be here."

"Yes, you are. It wasn't unusual in the 1800s for families to have a lot of children, because not all of them survived. Did you know that in some families, if a child died, the next child born of the same gender got the same name as the dead child? Seems an odd fact, but true."

"Genealogy is amazing."

Maggie smiled at her. "It's like a treasure hunt. A mystery to solve. And you are the detective. Yes, it can take hours, months, and even years, to find all that you are looking for, but at the end of the day, it's your story."

"Well, I really appreciate your doing the rest for me. It makes all the things I've read in the diaries and letters even more personal. I knew I felt a connection to Emma and now I know why. I can't wait to find out more about my family tree. There are boxes and boxes of letters at the house, and perhaps I'll be able to read through those now and discover the stories behind all those names and dates you just gave me."

"Give me a call if you get stuck and want some help."

"I sure will. Thanks so much, Maggie. I'm sure glad I met you at that counseling group. When this court business is done, let's get together for dinner to celebrate." The two stood and after a quick hug, Rachel left Maggie, and went to collect Julia from the children's room, genealogy report in hand. Rachel drove back to her grandmother's house in silence, pondering all that she had learned from Maggie.

* * *

Rachel pulled into the driveway and stopped at the mailbox. Reaching in, she pulled out several envelopes. Riffling through them, and looking at the return address, she noticed several more bills, and another from the bank. She remembered the others from the same bank and realized she hadn't done anything with them. Too much had taken place and they were forgotten.

Back in the kitchen, with Julia safely occupied at the laptop, Rachel sat, opened each bank statement and put them in chronological order. She saw that her grandmother had been receiving her social security money directly deposited. She also noted something odd. One month, in addition to the checking account interest, there was a notification labeled, Trust. Each month after, the statement mentioned the same thing.

The trust was ready to be enabled. In the accompanying letter, Nonna was alerted that she needed to stop in at the bank and complete some paperwork in order for the trust to begin its distribution to the beneficiaries. Apparently she never did. There was no indication of additional deposits being made in the subsequent months.

If she were in such need of money to pay bills why would she ignore this? Rachel leaned back in the chair and shook her head thinking of all that Nonna had left untended in the last weeks of her life. Perhaps if I had lived closer I could have helped her. She stared at the pile of bank statements, when she suddenly sat up straight. Something clicked in Rachel's mind. The letters! The ones written by Asa to his son. Her mind raced. She thought of the bank statements and the term trust, and of Maggie's genealogy report, still fresh in her mind.

Rachel dashed upstairs to her bedroom, gathered Asa's letters and flew back down the stairs. She put the letters together with the bank statements. She remembered that Asa had been trying to tell James about a trust he had established for James and for James' children. James never opened those letters and when Emma got them, she just put them aside unopened too. Rachel realized no one knew of the trust because no one had opened the letters. *Could it be? Could the bank statements be referring to the same trust? If it is, the money must have been sitting in the bank gathering interest all this time - since 1863. What could it be worth today?*

Unable to sit still, she grabbed her phone, called the bank listed on the statement and made an early appointment for the next day.

Chapter 29
The next day

The next morning, Rachel showered and dressed in her navy slacks and white cotton blouse. Tossing a white sweater over her shoulders and slipping on her comfy navy shoes completed the outfit. She tied her hair back with a gold barrette, applied a touch of lip gloss and she was ready to go. Julia was getting dressed for school in her room and the two met in the kitchen where they had a quick breakfast. Julia nibbled her breakfast cookie and banana.

As Rachel sipped a quick cup of coffee, she wondered when she'd hear from Neil Walker, her attorney, about the report she'd sent. *It's been a few days.* She figured she'd give him another day or two then call him.

Her cell buzzed in her pocket. She removed it,

looked at the screen. *Well, speak of the devil.* It was Neil Walker. She snapped it open, "Yes?"

"Hi Rachel, how are you doing?"

"Oh, pretty well. I was just thinking about you. I can't stop thinking about the unfinished business with that other claimant to Nonna's estate. Did you get the genealogist's report I sent you?"

"Well, that's what I called you about. I received the report and it looks really good. I presented the information to the other lawyer, but he hasn't gotten back to me yet. This may not need to go to court. If his client doesn't have clear proof, well, it would be in his or her best interest to drop the claim."

"How much more time do you think it will take?" Rachel wondered.

"Don't know. Could be a couple of days, could be a week. I'll certainly let you know the minute I hear anything."

"I can't wait to have this finished. It's really wearing on me."

She heard him moving papers and then clear his throat, "Umm, Rachel?"

"Yeah?"

He hesitated, stumbled and said, "Would you... would you have dinner with me when this is all done?"

She was speechless. She couldn't deny she felt a certain attraction to him, but it was much too soon. The hurt from Jon's death was still too raw for her to get involved with another man. "Oh Neil," she hesitated, "I don't know what to say."

"Rachel, I'm sorry, it's much too soon. Forget I asked," he said, embarrassment in his voice.

"Don't be sorry, Neil. I must admit I feel attracted to you, but… you're right, I can't even think about it. There's still too much hanging over my head right now."

"I understand. Hopefully this will be done with soon." He paused again. "Well, I'll call you when I hear from the other lawyer."

"Thanks, Neil."

She closed the phone and returned it to her pocket and sighed. *Oh, please let this be done with soon.* She turned to her daughter, "Let's go Julia." When they reached the back door, Rachel paused and reminded Julia about the alarm system.

"Can I do it, Mama?" Julia asked, reaching for the keypad.

"Go ahead." Rachel watched, amazed, as Julia hit the keys in proper order. "Good job, Julia. That's just right."

System armed, they both exited through the door and waited outside in the warmth of the morning sun for the school bus. When it arrived, Rachel blew a kiss to Julia and went to Nonna's car. Rachel drove to the bank in the next town, her mind spinning with thoughts of Neil, Jon, Nonna, the will, the estate, and now this trust business.

Twenty minutes later, Rachel stopped and parked in the first available slot, anxious to get inside and speak with the bank manager. She didn't want to get her hopes up, but felt there was something huge about to happen. Just as she was about to open the car door, her phone jangled. Rachel answered "Yes?"

"Hi Rachel, its MariBeth. I haven't heard from you in so long. What's going on with you?"

Rachel laughed again. "Ah, quite the story! I have so much to tell you, but listen, right now is not a good time for me to talk. Can you come by tomorrow night?"

"Sounds intriguing. I'll be there after dinner."

Rachel slipped the phone into the purse slung over her shoulders. She walked into the bank, tote bag slapping against her thighs. In the tote bag, she had the bank statements and the collection of letters from Asa to his son, James. *My great, great grandfather.*

Her eyes searched the interior for the office of Philip Marino, the trust officer of the bank. Finding it, she crossed the lobby, her shoes snapping on the marble floor. Marino's office had a glass wall looking out into the lobby. He noticed her arrival and motioned her in. She opened the door and entered the small, efficient office space. The set of furniture all matched – oak desk, chair, file cabinet and shelving unit. Marino sat behind the desk in the grey swivel office chair.

Marino was dressed in a steel grey pinstriped three piece suit, with a pale green shirt and matching tie. His eyes were brown, hair graying at the temples. There was certainly nothing about him that would make him stand out at a bankers' convention.

As she entered, he rose and extended his hand. She reached across the desk and shook it. "Welcome to First City Bank, Mrs. Benton. Please, have a seat."

Rachel sat in the small wooden visitor's chair, the only kind that would fit in the small office. "I'm glad you were able to see me so quickly, Mr. Marino."

"That's what we're here for." He leaned forward

in his chair and leaned his arms on his desk. "I understand you are confused with some bank statements."

She reached into her tote bag and removed the letters and bank statements. "Yes. As I told you, I'm the administrator of my grandmother's estate. Since being appointed, it's taken me several weeks to go through all the mess that was in her house. I finally gathered all the bills and bank statements and other important documents and began to sort through them. Most of them were pretty straight forward. Bills for utilities and medical and such I set aside."

"So what brings you here?" He fiddled with a paperclip and shuffled the papers on his desk, impatiently waiting to hear the rest.

"Look here." She shoved the bank statements across the desk to him. He read the first one and saw the lines that she had highlighted. Sorting through the stack, each statement had lines highlighted.

"All those lines in yellow say much the same thing. It's a reminder to my grandmother about resolving a trust fund. What does that mean?" She leaned forward to point to additional letters. "Those were included in each bank statement."

"Hmmm, let me read this a minute." He took the page and sat back in his comfy chair. After a few minutes of silent reading, he looked up at her. "This is pretty straight forward as well. It refers to a trust fund your grandmother has been ignoring all this time. The letters were written to get her to come in to the bank and sign the paperwork required to begin getting the funds into her account."

Rachel shifted in the hard wooden chair. She

thought it was purposefully uncomfortable in order to get visitors out the door quickly.

"I brought along something else that also refers to a trust fund. I recently found out that I am related to this person."

Again, Rachel slid the letters across. This time, she didn't have anything highlighted. Mindful of the historic and monetary value of the Civil War era letters, she had inserted in the envelopes the notes she had taken referring to the contents of the letter. In that way, she would only need to remove the letters he needed to read.

"Which one refers to the trust fund?" He fidgeted in his chair and looked at his watch.

She was beginning to get upset with his impatience. *Isn't he in the customer service business?* "Here's the one that refers to the trust." She took the rest back.

He slipped the note out of the envelope and quickly read. *"We have done so well, that I have set aside some money to put in a fund for you and for your children, should there be any. I have put it in the bank in town and will leave it there for when you return. If something should happen to me, then the bank knows what to do."*

Marino didn't say a word, but turned to his computer and proceeded to type, waited for it to respond and typed again. He frowned at the screen, moved to get a closer look, then his eyes widened. He sat back from the screen and looked at her. "This is unbelievable."

"What is it?" Rachel couldn't stand the suspense. "What did you find?"

"Well, I read the bank statements and the notes and then checked with our accounts department. It was just confirmed. You are a very lucky lady."

"Yeah, how?" Rachel was becoming as impatient as he had shown to be.

"Mrs. Benton." He looked at his computer screen again. "The trust fund is now worth one million, five hundred six thousand, nine hundred seventy-seven dollars and fifty cents."

"Oh my God! How is that possible?" Rachel's heart was pounding, her stomach clenching in excitement.

"Well, there wasn't much when the trust was established about one hundred fifty years ago, but over the years it's been building interest, compounding annually. And it adds up. Especially if the principal isn't touched at all, and this seems to be the case here."

Rachel was speechless. She leaned forward, clasped her hands together and, grinning widely, finally said, "What do I need to do?"

"We'll get the necessary paperwork together. It'll take a day or so, then you'll sign them and the money is yours or, to be more precise, the money goes into your grandmother's estate. The beneficiaries will share the money according to her will."

He stood and moved from behind his desk. "Mrs. Benton, should you need, I'd be pleased to help you invest the money here in our bank."

Rachel stood, gathered her papers and put them in her tote bag. "I will certainly consider that, thank you."

"I'll give you a call when all the paperwork is

ready."

"Thanks again. Oh, really thank you!" Rachel couldn't stop grinning. She felt like shouting to the world, like dancing in the streets!

She left the bank, got into her car. *What a day.* The money was an amazing discovery. And so was finding out that Neil might have feelings for her, just as she was beginning to have for him.

Rachel was extra careful driving slowly down the road, knowing excitement was hampering her reactions. Reaching the gates, she turned in and parked. Walking down the gravel path, she found the spot and knelt. The headstone read, "Eleanor Palmer, loving mother, loving grandmother." Rachel put her hand on her grandmother's grave.

She whispered as if her grandmother could hear, "I wish I had known you better, Nonna. I missed so much, living so far away. There are many things I would have asked you. But most of all I would have said, I love you. And thank you, from the bottom of my heart."

She sat for a while, recalling the words of the bank manager. Her heart settled in its regular rhythm again and her mind wandered. *Oh, my God.* Her stomach did another flip-flop. She remembered. The issue with that other person who had come forward has not yet been resolved. She still had a court date. If he, or she, had a legitimate claim, then Rachel would have to share the house, the contents, and now this money. *There was enough for two, that's for sure.* But she still wanted to get the whole thing settled so she could plan for the future. *For me, and, more importantly, for Julia.*

Chapter 30
The next day

The next night, Julia was seated in front of the TV watching a Disney movie when the doorbell rang. Rachel walked across the room to the front door, saw that it was MariBeth and hit the keypad to disarm the system. She opened the door with a smile and let her friend in.

"Hi, I'm glad you could come over. Want a cup of coffee?" Rachel pointed to Julia and led them into the kitchen.

Understanding, MariBeth said, "Sure." Rachel poured two cups, set them on the table and the two sat.

"I haven't seen you in so long, so much has happened." Her voice quiet, Rachel told MariBeth about the intruder, the theft of her books and figurines, and her visit to the police station to identify the teen. "I got a call from the police yesterday. They caught Sam."

"Who's that?"

"She's the appraiser I hired and the mother of the teen who hit me. I went to that antique show you told me about and she was there. She looked legitimate, so I asked her to do the inventory and appraisal. Little did I know," Rachel shook her head, hand moving to feel the lump.

"Wow, Rach, I had no idea."

"The police seem to think that he was stealing small items, ones that would fit in a tote bag, from isolated homes in the area so that his mother could sell them at the antique shows and to her dealer friends. Apparently her job has been slow with this economy, she needed extra money and they thought it would be an easy way to make some quick."

MariBeth leaned forward, "Do the police think they stole from the History Museum, too?"

Rachel shrugged, "The police are not sure. They're sending a report to the head of the museum. They told me they didn't find the items that were stolen from the museum, so I suppose they're still investigating."

"Sure can't tell about people, can you?" MariBeth looked at Rachel as if to say more. She sat back in the chair, her hand covering her eyes.

Rachel leaned forward and placed a hand on MariBeth's arm. "You okay?"

MariBeth said nothing and Rachel continued, "I also heard from the genealogist I hired."

MariBeth dropped her hand, looked at Rachel

with a surprised expression clearly visible, "You hired a genealogist, why?"

"My lawyer learned that someone was claiming to be another relative of my grandmother and needed me to prove that it was a false claim. He encouraged me to hire a genealogist and so I did. She worked quickly and I met with her a few days ago. She had the report all finished and I sent it to my lawyer. He called yesterday and told me he'd gotten it and would be contacting the other person's attorney." Rachel sighed, "I've been really anxious about the whole thing. I just want to have this business done."

MariBeth looked down at the table, not saying a word. She stood quickly, looked at her watch, and said, "Rachel, I've gotta go."

"But, you just got here!" Again Rachel was baffled by Maribeth's behavior. *What is going on with her?*

Without a word, MariBeth opened the back door, and exited, slamming the door behind her, leaving Rachel standing with her mouth open. *What just happened?*

Rachel realized she didn't even get a chance to tell MariBeth about the trust.

Chapter 31
Three days later

Rachel was seated on the front porch in her comfortable sweats, idly swinging in the wicker glider, sipping a glass of lemonade. The warmth of the June sun shone on her, making her feel quite mellow. Occasionally, through the trees, she could see a car pass by. The cardinals and blue jays were at the feeder, fighting over the sunflowers seeds she'd put there earlier. Her cell phone jingled its song. Rachel leaned forward and snatched it from the small wicker table nearby.

"Hello?"

"Rachel, its Patsy Lee, Neil Walker's secretary. How are you doing today?"

"Hi Patsy, I'm doing pretty well. Is there anything wrong?" She was still waiting for news of the court case, and the call brought to the surface again the anxiety she felt for the ordeal to be over.

Patsy's voice was cheerful, as usual. Rachel could almost see her sitting at her desk in a different odd outfit – perhaps perky pink this time! "No, no," she said. "Mr. Walker wanted to meet with you today, if possible. Perhaps this afternoon?"

"Hmmm," Rachel thought quickly. With the school year ending, today was a half day for Julia. She'd need to wait for her to get home from school, get her some lunch, and then drive to the lawyer's office. Mentally calculating the time it would take, Rachel finally said, "I can't meet before one-thirty. And I'll have to bring Julia along. Will that be okay?"

"That's fine. Julia will be no problem – she's a delight. She can sit with me while you're meeting with Mr. Walker. I'll put you down for 1:30."

"Thanks," Rachel snapped her cell phone shut, wondering if the news will be good or bad. If it was good news, wouldn't he be able to tell her on the phone? The mellow mood gone, she picked up her glass and went inside, the screen door slamming behind her. Looking around the living room of her grandmother's house, she took a deep breath and slowly exhaled.

Gone were the piles of garbage that had littered the room. Now the air smelled fresh and clean, with a hint of the lemon furniture polish she had used. The stacks of books were replaced on the white shelves, neatly organized according to their value – just in case Rachel needed to sell them. She had spent hours on the internet at the library researching the titles. EBay and Amazon had been helpful websites in finding what the books might be worth. Rachel had also found library books on antiques. A couple of them had helped her value the books and some of the other items in the house. She was learning.

On the cleared tables on either end of the floral print sofa, Rachel had placed fresh cut flowers from the gardens in the yard. She'd spent more time there, raking the yard, mowing the lawn, and pruning the flowering bushes. The spring flowering bulbs had come and gone, replaced by the summer daisies. She enjoyed working in the yard. Her old place didn't have a yard – just a small fenced-in patio. Rachel never realized how relaxing working in the dirt could be.

After cleaning the yard, she'd placed the two pieces of Cornelia Jane's headstone together under the willow tree in the far corner of the back yard. Rachel knew the baby wasn't buried there. Unfortunately she probably would never know how or why the headstone made its way from Chenango Forks to this yard, but she would keep the memory of that young child in the small plot she'd created under the tree. The summer bulbs she'd recently planted there were beginning to emerge from the mulch-covered ground.

With Maggie's help, Rachel continued to research her own past. She was enjoying Maggie's company more and more, their having so much in common. Although she was several years younger, Maggie was much more knowledgeable about genealogy and researching the past. History. It was certainly something Rachel hadn't thought she would ever enjoy. But, history seemed to be entwined with everything that had happened in the last three months. Learning about the Civil War through the eyes of James and Emma made that era come alive.

She had learned about antiques as well. After discovering how easy it was to use Craig's List, she'd taken all of the chairs and tables from the attic, the jugs and bottles from the basement, and posted an advertisement on the list. She'd had to wait only a couple of days before the calls came. She continued to be amazed at the people who would want the old furniture. The items had sold and Rachel was able to pay some of the bills that Nonna had long overlooked. She was making progress.

Yes, she felt an attachment to the house now, so close to feeling like it was hers. She had made so many changes in the other rooms as well, thinking that if she was forced to sell the place to share the estate with the other claimant, at least she'd have it ready to put on the market. In the process, though, she'd made it into a comfortable home. Somewhere along the way, she'd realized she really wanted to stay here. The little town didn't seem so odd any more. The world she'd left behind months ago seemed so foreign, like it belonged to someone else. Jon's death was not as raw. She was slowly healing.

Rachel took her half-empty glass of lemonade into the kitchen. It was nearing lunchtime, but her stomach was churning again, and she didn't feel hungry. Glancing at the clock on the wall, she realized that Julia would be home in a half an hour.

She needed to get cleaned up for her afternoon

appointment with Neil Walker.

Ah, Neil. Her mind flew back to the last she'd seen him – the night of Julia's kindergarten program. She had been seated in the auditorium, waiting impatiently for the play to begin. She'd seen Neil enter the room, look around, and finding her, smile. Nervous warmth spread through her body, as she watched him walk toward her. She was surprised to see him there, and so very pleased that he'd shown up for her daughter's program. He'd politely asked if he could sit next to her. She agreed, and they'd chatted quietly until the lights dimmed and the program began. Afterwards, they'd gone to the diner and had treated Julia to a much-deserved ice cream. Neil was playful and quickly had Julia giggling. She felt so torn, knowing the feelings for him were growing, thinking of Jon.

She shook her head at the memories, set her glass on the counter and went upstairs to change.

Pausing at Nonna's room, she glanced around and smiled at the accomplishments she had made. She had stripped the old faded rose print wallpaper from the wall and replaced it with a fresh coat of pale yellow paint. In place of the old, pink, heavy drapes were now hanging white, lacy sheers. She'd discarded the pink chenille bedspread and replaced it with a simple white blanket until she had enough money to shop for a new bedspread.

Moving down the hall to her own room, she changed into a decent pair of navy slacks and slipped her favorite pale blue knit shirt over her head. She felt the need for comfort clothing for this meeting. She ran a comb through her hair and then twisted it into the familiar ponytail. A touch of lip gloss and she was ready. Hearing the bus pull up, and the door slam below, she realized Julia was home.

"Mama? Where are you?" Rachel could hear her running steps – the familiar sound when she came home from school.

She called down, "I'm up here, Julia. Be right down." And she hurried down the stairs where her daughter met her with a big hug.

"School's done, Mama. And guess what? I got a prize!" Julia wriggled out of Rachel's arm, turned and reached into her tote bag which was bulging with all the papers and folders from cleaning out her school desk. She found the page, and shoved it into Rachel's outstretched hand.

"What's this?" The certificate said that Julia was now a first grader. *How cute.* "This is wonderful, Julia. You're not in kindergarten anymore."

"Nope, I'm a big girl." Rachel gave her a squeeze and Julia squealed in delight.

"Yes, you are – you're getting so big. How about we celebrate and go to the diner for lunch."

Julia whooped with joy and twirled around the room. "Yeah! Can I have dessert too?"

"We'll see. Oh, and after lunch, I have another meeting with the lawyer. Remember Mr. Walker? I'll bring your sticker book to keep you busy while I'm in the meeting, just like before." Rachel's smile fell with the reminder of the upcoming meeting.

She told her daughter, "Go wash up and then we'll go."

"Okay, Mama." And off she went.

* * *

The diner was crowded, but not with the usual businessmen. They seemed to know that mothers would be taking their children for the end-of-the-school-year treat. Rachel and Julia slipped into a vacant seat at the table by the window. The town square was a spread of green grass. The manicured gardens around the gazebo and at each end were ablaze with summer color. A father and his two young children were playing an improvised game of keep-away with a soccer ball. Even from behind the window, Rachel could hear their squeals and calls to each other.

A younger, college-age waitress came to take their order. Rachel's stomach only permitted toast, but Julia wanted a hamburger and fries. When the food arrived, Rachel grimaced as the smell reached her nose. *Maybe this wasn't a good idea after all.* She took in shallow breaths, trying to keep her stomach in order. She reached into her purse for the roll of Tums she kept handy. The emotional roller coaster she'd been on for so long was beginning to get to her. She really needed it to end.

Julia finished her burger and asked for dessert. Rachel looked at the time and realized it was getting late.

"Not right now, Sweetie. Maybe after my meeting." *Depending on how it goes.* Rachel paid the bill and they left, hand in hand, and walked across the Square, around the ball game, and to the bank on the other side.

Once inside, Julia tugged out of Rachel's hand and scurried up the stairs. "I know where it is!" she shouted down. Rachel followed, footsteps dragging.

Much as she wanted to know, she was dreading the news and slowed, trying to postpone the meeting.

Rachel found Julia at the door struggling to turn the knob. She slipped her hand around Julia's, opened the door and again, they were greeted by Patsy.

Patsy wasn't wearing perky pink today. No, she was wearing blazing red. From top to toe! The ends of her hair were tipped in red. She had on red lipstick and nail polish. On her feet were red socks and red, striped sneakers. The red jacket she wore had gold buttons, but that was the only other color on her today.

Seeing Julia enter the room with Rachel behind, she welcomed them with her usual warm smile, "Hello Rachel. Good to see you again. And you too, Miss Julia." Reaching into a side drawer of her desk, she pulled out a lollipop and handed it to the young girl.

Julia reached out to take it, and then turned to her mother, "Can I, please?"

Nodding, Rachel said, "Yes, go ahead."

Patsy cheerfully said, "Sorry, but he's a bit late with his last appointment. It should only be a few more minutes. I'll let him know you're here." She buzzed the inner office.

"That's fine." Rachel sat in the chair and took the same magazine she'd tried to read the last time she was here. Julia sat on the floor, pulled out her sticker book, and, with lollipop in her mouth, worked on peeling stickers.

Ten minutes later the inner door opened and a man walked out. He was another non-descript businessman in the ever-present three-piece suit carrying a leather briefcase in his right hand. He nodded to Rachel and left the office.

Neil Walker motioned to her and she stood, "I'll be back in a few minutes, Julia. Be good for Patsy." She entered the Neil's office, her stomach a chorus-line of butterflies. For some reason, she couldn't tell from his expression if the news she was going to hear would be good or bad.

Today he was dressed formally, matching the appearance of the man who had just exited. She took his outstretched hand, shook it, and then took a seat.

"Good to see you again, Rachel," Walker said, giving nothing away in the tone of his voice.

Rachel nodded, not trusting her voice.

"Well, I can see that we're going to be all business again." Neil said sadly. "All right. Do you want the good news or the bad news first?"

Rachel grimaced. She needed some good news before she could deal with any more bad. "Good news," she said.

"The lawyer who just left represented that person who claimed to be a relative of your grandmother. He told me that the claim is being dropped. The other person can't provide the necessary proof." He smiled for the first time. "So that makes you the sole heir. The estate, the house and all the contents are yours."

Rachel felt the butterflies begin to settle. "And the trust fund?"

"What trust fund?" Neil looked puzzled.

Rachel leaned forward, "That's right, you don't know about it yet. Seems my great, great, great grandfather started a trust fund a long time ago. It's been lying dormant all this time in a bank in the next town. I just found out about it the other day." She paused, and then continued, "It's worth a little over a million and a half dollars! Can you believe it?"

He whistled, "Wow, that's great news for you."

"Yeah, it's pretty amazing. I still can't believe it." She paused. "And now you say it's all mine – I don't have to share with anyone?" She was trembling, the butterflies doing a different dance now.

"That's right." His voice hinted at other news to come.

Rachel sat back, and steadied herself, that roller coaster getting ready to take another dive. "So what's the bad news?"

He rose from his chair, came around the desk, and stood in front of her, leaning his back against the desk.

"Rachel, how well do you know MariBeth Allen?" he asked softly.

She frowned. Why was he asking about MariBeth? "She's been a really good friend. She's helped me a great deal with the house and with Julia, with Nonna, why?"

"How did you meet her?" he continued, ignoring her question.

"Let me think." She paused, remembering. "Oh, yeah. It was in the diner. She came to me one day about a week after I got here and introduced herself. She told me she worked at the museum. Neil, why all the questions about MariBeth?"

"Rachel, I hate to tell you this, since you seem to consider her a close friend and all, but she's the one who claimed to be the relative. I just found out from the lawyer who left here a few minutes ago."

"What! No, you've got to have that wrong. It couldn't be her." Rachel's eyes filled with tears and the sense of betrayal settled on her like an oily blanket.

Neil took a handkerchief from his pocket and handed it to her. "I'm sorry, Rachel but it's true."

The tears that had been threatening now spilled down her cheeks and she quietly wept into the handkerchief. She felt Neil place his hand on her shoulder. She wanted him to take her in his arms, but knew the time was not right. She wasn't ready. Rachel looked up at him, eyes red, and gathered some inner strength. With trembling voice, she said, "Thanks for telling me – both the good news and the bad." She drew away from him and walked to the window.

He watched her face and saw the emotions changing her expression, sadness, joy, relief, confusion. He walked around behind the barrier of his desk, sat and waited.

She finally released a sigh, and returned to her seat. "I'm so sorry. I seem to be a basket case each time I'm here. What must you think of me?" Rachel looked across the desk into his warm eyes.

"Rachel, you needn't apologize. None of this is your fault. You've been through a great deal in the last weeks, I know."

"Hmmm." She hung her head, not trusting herself to say something she was not ready for. The distance between them widened again – and not just physically.

Neil sighed and pulling a piece of paper from the

file on his desk, he slid it across to her. "I just need you to sign your name on the bottom and this controversy will be behind you."

She took the pen from his hand and signed her name. "Is there anything else?" He turned to the machine, made a copy of the document she'd signed, and returned it to her.

"No. Enough time has gone by to allow any other person with claims on your grandmother's estate to come forward. You still need to finish paying the estate's bills, and at the end of the year you'll have to file taxes, but that will be it." He stood again, rounded his desk and reached out his hand to her as she rose from the chair.

"Congratulations, Rachel." He seemed to want to say more, but kept the words to himself.

Rachel took his hand, squeezed it gently, and covered it with her other hand. With a warm smile, she said, "Please, be patient with me. There's something happening between us, but I'm not ready."

He squeezed her hand in return, and with a wink, "I'll be here, whenever you want."

She turned and left his office. She gathered Julia from the waiting room, waved to the all-in-red Patsy, and let the office door close behind her.

They paused at the sidewalk. Rachel glanced down at the document in her hand and she smiled. What a war of emotions. But now she'd come to the end of the roller coaster ride she'd been on for so long. She took a deep breath, let it out, and with it all the tension she'd kept inside for so long flowed from her.

Julia tugged at her hand, "Mama?" Rachel realized they'd been standing there for a couple of minutes. The park had emptied of the family playing their ball game and the older couple at the gazebo.

"You ready for that dessert now?"

Julia clapped, "Yippee! Can I have a sundae?"

Rachel took her hand, "Whatever you'd like."

They crossed through the Square once more and went into the diner. Rachel ordered and while waiting for their sundaes to arrive, her mind wandered. Then she heard the name MariBeth and realized the two women in the booth behind her were talking about her friend. Her former friend, that is. She couldn't help but listen in to the conversation.

"I can't believe it either," the first woman said. "How could the museum make such a mistake in hiring that person?"

The second woman responded, "Well, I heard that MariBeth lied about her past experience. She had never even worked in a museum before. She'd arrived in town only a short time before getting hired, having moved here from across the state. The director was concerned that MariBeth didn't seem to know some of the things she should and the truth came out. Thank goodness she's been dismissed. She's left town, too, it seems. No one knows where she went."

So that's that, Rachel thought. I have no way of getting in touch with her. Rachel realized that MariBeth always called her, never the other way around. It was MariBeth who befriended Rachel, MariBeth who asked to help in the house. And now it was MariBeth who claimed to be the other relative and MariBeth who was telling lies. What a friend she turned out to be.

Although Rachel felt betrayed, she knew the museum director and all those who worked there with her did too. MariBeth had been able to convince the people around her that she was someone she wasn't. Rachel felt a bit better knowing that it wasn't just her. But still – what was her motivation, other than money. That is a great motivator, Rachel realized. She thought back to Samantha, who tried to steal from her. As poor as I was, I never tried to steal, manipulate, or lie.

Spotting her grandmother's old Ford parked outside, she realized she wouldn't have to worry about the car falling apart any longer. She could either get it fixed, or maybe even get a brand new car! What a wonderful thought. Rachel smiled again.

Rachel looked across the table at her daughter. *Julia's getting so big, and she's so happy here. The move across the country and all the turmoil that has taken place in the last months has all turned out for the best.* Glancing out the window, she spotted Neil Walker looking down at her from his office window. He gave a wave, and this time she waved back and smiled. Yes, this town is all right.

After the two finished their desserts, Rachel paid the bill. They left the diner, got in the car, and snapped their seatbelts. Rachel turned to her young daughter and said, "Let's go home, Julia."

Epilogue
A year later

Rachel turned onto the gravel driveway under the stone arch. Wrought iron fencing marked the boundary. A small office building was on the right; red roof, green siding, and white trim making it look like something for Christmas. Nearby, along the sidewalk was a sign indicating the hours the office was open and a phone number. A plaque held part of a poem written by Theodore O'Hara.

> The muffled drum's sad roll has beat
> The soldier's last tattoo;
> No more on Life's parade shall meet
> That brave and fallen few.
> On fame's eternal camping ground
> Their silent tents to spread,
> And glory guards, with solemn round
> The bivouac of the dead.

Another plaque indicated the names and locations of all those buried in this National Cemetery. Rachel parked the car and got out, grabbing her umbrella and the floral arrangement she had purchased at a nearby farmer's market. It was chilly in the dampness, the early April drizzle sneaking down the back of her jacket. But she would not let this misty rain deter her from her mission today.

Looking at a small piece of paper in her hand, Rachel looked around her. She realized that the numbered plots were neatly organized and the sections were labeled and in order. All throughout the cemetery, the headstones were alike – simple granite stones about two foot by three foot with rounded tops. Many of them, too many, had the words *two unknown soldiers* or *three unknown soldiers.* Rachel's heart was heavy with the knowledge that so many had died and were buried here and no one knew who they were.

Julia unsnapped her seatbelt buckle and joined her mother. They wandered around searching for section 3A.

"See if you can find it, Julia," Rachel encouraged.

"Here's section one, Mama. Oh, and here's section two. It's gonna be next," Julia hopped, excited to be near their destination.

After months of searching, months of yearning to find the truth behind those diaries and letters she'd found in Nonna's house, Rachel felt drawn to this place. To the one whose life so impacted hers – her three times great-grandfather.

The two walked hand in hand in the morning quiet. Spring birds were calling to each other in the trees. There was no one else in the cemetery. Stones crunching under their feet made the only disturbance to the silence.

"Look, here it is," Julia's voice was hushed, as if she understood the solemness of the occasion.

They stopped and looked at the stone. Under the number 981 was his name, James Beardsley, in raised lettering arching around the state, NY.

The drizzle had stopped and the sun peaked from under the grey clouds. Rachel closed the umbrella and laid it on the ground. She bent and touched the stone, tears again threatening. Carefully placing the flowers in their container to the left of the stone, she made sure she didn't obscure the name engraved on the marble. Earlier she had prepared a small card with James' name and picture on it and secured it in the arrangement. Now, when someone came here, they would not see just another faceless grave. They would know a little about a young man who gave his life, his all, for the welfare of his country, and for them all.

"Oh, Mama, look!" Julia's voice was hushed, but excited. She was pointing to the sky at the far end of the cemetery.

There, arching over the trees was a bright rainbow. Rachel stood with her hand in her daughter's and they watched the rainbow. She felt it all in her heart, sadness and joy, a sense of wonder and awe. She heard the car door shut, and felt him approaching. Neil wrapped his arm around her. She gazed into his eyes, found there the depth of his love for her and smiled.

Notes from the author:

I've been an avid reader since I was a young girl, reading under the blankets with a flashlight after my official bedtime. Over the years I've read many books in different genres. Some of them left me wondering more about the characters, where the author came up with the ideas. What was truth, what was fiction? So I figured I'd share my thoughts about *My Dear Emma*.

I came to write this book because of a small bronze disk that I found in my father-in-law's estate. My husband, the executor, and I were going through the contents of his house of thirty years and came across a small box of coins. Among the coins was the ID Tag that is described in the letter written by James. Initially thinking nothing of it, I put it aside. Months later, I picked it up again and became intrigued. I started researching what was inscribed on the tag. Unfortunately no one in the family had any idea as to the tag's history and how it came to be in my father-in-law's coin box.

Months and years have gone by and I've collected notebook after notebook of research on the person named on the ID tag, Addison Beardsley. I've read regimental histories, visited libraries, museums, and civil war battlefields, watched videos and re-enactments, interviewed historians and Civil War store owners, and endlessly searched the internet. At the *U.S. Army Heritage & Education Center* in Carlisle, Pennsylvania, I found the regimental history book written by Nobel Preston. When I found Addison's photo, chills ran down my arms. He looked so young!

For the past fifteen years I've also been involved with gathering information on our family genealogy, both my side and my husband's. His is much more easily researched and detailed, and therefore, I've been able to trace the four branches of his family back to the 1600s. With the help of my membership in *ancestry.com*, I was finally able make the connection from Addison J. Beardsley to my husband. They are third cousins, four times removed!

Again using *ancestry.com* I found the 1860 census, Oxford, New York, showing the household of Asa Beardsley, Addison's father. Asa was a farmer, and then did work in the bluestone quarry. Asa died December 24, 1894. Addison had two sisters, Ida and Ella and a brother, Arthur, whom I don't mention in the story. Addison was sixteen at the time, and a girl, Frances E. Squire, fifteen, was listed as a domestic living in the household. She was the inspiration for Emma.

Yes, Addison enlisted 31 August 1862 when he was eighteen, in Oxford NY, mustered in on 29

October 1862 at Elmira, New York into the 10th NY Cavalry, Company K. He experienced the major battles of Fredericksburg, Brandy Station and Gettysburg and the minor skirmishes in between. According to the regimental history (pg 517 Preston's regimental history), he was a scout. Yes, he was captured in Unionville in July 1863 (pg 457 Preston's regimental history), although exactly how, I don't know. I also couldn't find out why he was so far removed from the rest of his regiment at the time of his capture.

He was sent to Belle Isle. The descriptions of that place as a prison of war camp are terrible. A recent visit there shows the field that was the encampment surrounded by mounds of dirt. How Addison died, I have not been able to discover but the cemetery, where he was originally buried is still noticeable.

Yes, Addison is now interred in the Richmond National Cemetery in Richmond VA, Section 3A plot 981. If you do a Google search, using *Find a Grave,* you'll see the flowers my husband and I placed there with the card giving his name and details.

Brunson Beardsley was born in Coventry, NY 17 September 1816. He was raised on a farm and was a teacher and married Antoinette M. Thayer. and had three children whose names I used in the story.

He enlisted at the age of 44 in June of 1862. He was a sergeant at first and then promoted to lieutenant in the same company as Addison. Brunson was wounded at Middleburg, VA and died 19 June 1863. In doing genealogy research I found Addison and Brunson were cousins not uncle and nephew as I indicated in this story. (pg 453, Preston's regimental history)

Yes, there was a Frederick Beardslee in the Signal Corps, enlisting 19 November 1862. His father, George, invented the telegraph machine. You can do a *Google* search on Beardslee's Magneto-Electric Signal Telegraph and see what the machine looks like and how it works. One of the machines is on display at *Chatham Manor,* a museum near Fredericksburg, Virginia. Frederick Beardslee and Addison Beardsley are distant cousins.

According to Preston's regimental history...

Amos Arnold was 22 was born in Unadilla New York, was a farmer and had blue eyes, brown hair and a fair complexion and was 5'10. He enlisted as a private on 30 August 1862 and was wounded in Sulfur Spring, Virginia on 12 October 1863. I used Amos as the fictional tent mate and fellow scout for James. (pg 457 Preston's regimental as a private on 29 August 1862. He was discharged 1 February 1864 with a disability. He had blue eyes, brown hair, light complexion and was 5'8". His friendship with James is fiction. (pg 459 Preston's regimental history)

Harris P Moak was 18 when he enlisted on 29 September 1962 and was held as a prisoner of war in 1864. He had blue eyes, dark hair and dark complexion, and was 5'7" tall (pg 462 Preston's regimental history). This is fact. I created the friendship with James and his girlfriend.

William Padgett was 18 when he enlisted as a private on 31 August 1862. He was promoted to corporal in 1865. He had black eyes, brown hair and fair complexion and stood only 5'4 ½" (pg 463 Preston's regimental history). My account of his friendship with James is also fiction.

Civil War ID Tags were the predecessor of the military dog tags of today. At the beginning of the Civil War, men did not think of identification in the event of their deaths. Soldiers would mark their clothing or write their names on paper tags or cloth and pin them to their clothing. Others made these tags out of wood, which they strung around their necks. In other cases, sutlers sold these tags to the soldiers.

The rest of the story is fiction.

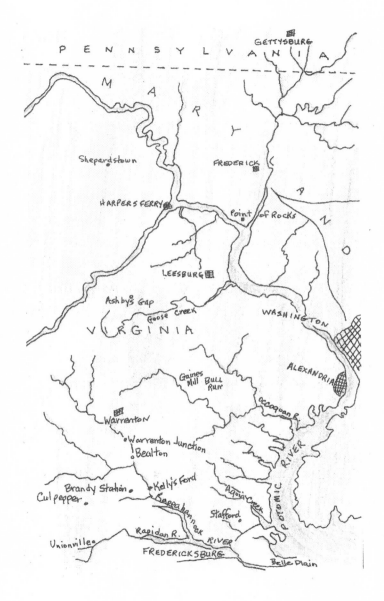

LIEUTENANT B. BEARDSLEE, Co. K
CORPORAL C. A. RAY, Co. K.   A. BEARDSLEE, Co. K.
                    B. HAXTON, Co. K.
S. A. BROOKS, Co. K.   WILLIAM A. MILES, Co. K.

Photo from Nobel Preston's *History of the Tenth Regiment of Cavalry New York State Volunteers*

Bibliography

The year 2011 begins the four year commemoration of the 150th anniversary of those dreadful years of the Civil War. If you are interested in knowing more you might want to read some of the following.

Alan Sessarego Collection. *Letters Home III Camp Life and Battles.* Gettysburg, PA.: Garden Spot Gifts, Inc. 2003.

Blue and Grey Press. *The Photographic History of the Civil War, Volume 4 – Soldier Life and Secret Service Prisons and Hospitals.* Secaucus, NJ: Blue and Grey Press a division of Book Sales, Inc., 1987.

Bolotin, Norman & Herb, Angel. *For Home and Country: A Civil War Scrapbook.* Lodestar Books/Dutton 1995.

Carson, Ray M. *The Civil War Soldier: A Photographic Journey.* Gramercy Books, 2007.

Chappell, Frank Anderson. *Dear Sister: Civil War Letters to a Sister in Alabama.* Huntsville, AL.: Branch Springs Publishing, 2002.

Conner, Jane Hollenbeck. *Lincoln in Stafford.* Stafford, VA: Parker Pub., 2006.

Denney, Robert E. *Civil War Prisons and Escapes: a day-by-day chronicle.* Sterling Pub. Co., 1993.

Denny, Robert E. *The Civil War Year: Day by Day Chronicle.*

Gone for Soldier: Memoir of Private Alfred Bellard. 1992.

Feis, William B. *Grant's Secret Service.* University of Nebraska Press, 2002.

Frank, Lisa Tendrich. *Women of the Civil War.* ABC-CLIO, 2007

Garrison, Webb B. *Civil War Curiosities: strange stories, oddities, events, and coincidences.* Rutledge Hill Press, 1994.

Goolrick, William K. *Rebels Resurgent: Fredericksburg to Chancellorsville .* Time Life Books, 1985.

Gragg, Rod., *From Fields of Fire and Glory: Letters of the Civil War.* San Francisco, CA.: Chronicle Books, LLC., 2002.

Harper, Judith E. *Women During the Civil War: an encyclopedia.* Routledge, 2004.

Hurst, Patricia. *Soldiers Stories, Sites and Fights,* from Orange VA Historical Museum.

James River Park System. An Interpretative Guide to Belle Isle. Department of Parks, Recreation and Community Resources.

Kostyal, K. M. *Field of Battle: Civil War Letters of Major Thomas Halsey:* National Geographic Society, 1996.

Lowry, Thomas P. *Love and Lust: Private and Amorous Letters of the Civil War.* Thomas P Lowry, 2009.

Marten, James A. *The Children's Civil War.* University of North Carolina Press, 1998.

Matteson, Ron. *Civil War Campaigns of the 10th New York Cavalry with one Soldier's Personal Correspondence.* Lulu.com, 2007.

McCutcheon, Marc. *Everyday Life in the 1800s: A Guide for Writers, Students & Historians.* Cincinnati, Ohio: Writer's Digest Books, 1993.

Parker, Sandra V. *Richmond's Civil War Prisons.* Lynchburg, VA. H. E. Howard, 1990.

Photographic History of the Civil War: Soldier Life and Secret Service, Prisons and Hospitals. Blue & Grey Press, 1911.

Porter, Burton B. *One of the People: His Own Story.* Burton. B. Porter, 1907.

Preston, N.D. *History of the Tenth Regiment of Cavalrry New York State Volunteers.* New York: D Appleton and Company, 1892. Reprinted by Higginson Book Company, Salem MA, 1998.

Rhodes, Robert Hunt. *All for the Union: The Civil War Diary and Letters of Elisha Hunt Rhodes.* New York: Vintage Civil War Library, Vintage Books, A division of Random House Inc., 1985.

Roberson, Elizabeth Whitley. *Weep Not for Me, Dear Mother.* Gretna, Louisiana: Pelican Publishing Co., Inc., 1991.

Robertson, Jr., James. *The Civil War: Tenting Tonight – a Soldier's Life.* Time Life Books, 1984.

Rummel III, George A., *72 Days at Gettysburg: Organization of the 10th Regiment, New York Volunteer Cavalry.* Shippensburg, PA.: Beidel Printing House, Inc., 1997.

Ryan, David D. *Cornbread and Maggots, Cloak and Dagger, Union Prisoners and Spies.* Dietz Press, 1994.

Salmon, John S. *The Official Virginia Civil War Battlefield Guide.* Stackpole Books, 2001.

Sneden, Private Robert Knox., *Eye of the Storm.* New York, NY: The Free Press, a division of Simon and Shuster, Inc., Virginia Historical Society, 2002.

Stern,PhilipVan Doren. *Soldier Life in the Union and Confederate Armies.* Bloomington, Indiana: Indiana University Press, 1961.

Stone, James Madison. *Personal Recollections of the Civil War, 1918 (21 Vol. Infantry, Mass), 1918*

US Gen Web: Chenango County
http://www.rootsweb.ancestry.com/~nychenan/

Varhola, Michael J. *Everyday Life During the Civil War: A Guide for Writers, Students and Historians.* 1999.

Wiley, Bell Irvine. *The Life of Billy Yank: The Common Soldier of the Union.* Indianapolis: Charter Books, 1952.

Whittaker, Frederick. *Volunteer Cavalry: The Lessons of the Decade.* New York, 1871.

Wittenberg, Eric F. *Protecting the Flank: The Battles for Brinkerhoff's Ridge and East Cavalry Field, Battle of Gettysburg, July 2-3, 1863.* Celina, Ohio: Ironclad Publishing, 2002.